Alexandra Heminsley is author of three books about women, bodies and sport, including bestselling memoir *Running Like a Girl*, and *Some Body to Love*. She is also an experienced co-writer, whose top ten *Sunday Times* bestsellers include Judy Murray's William Hill Sports Book of the Year nominated *Knowing the Score* and Sara Davies's *We Can All Make It*.

After working in publishing, she became a freelance journalist, broadcaster and author in 2004. She was the books editor at *Elle* for eight years, and spent ten years at BBC Radio 2's *Claudia Winkleman Arts Show*. She regularly appears at literary festivals as both co-host and guest, and was a judge for 2011's Costa Novel of the Year Award.

# UNDER
*the*
# SAME
# STARS

## ALEXANDRA
## HEMINSLEY

SPHERE

SPHERE

First published in Great Britain in 2022 by Sphere
This paperback edition published by Sphere in 2023

1 3 5 7 9 10 8 6 4 2

Copyright © Onion Publications Ltd 2022

The moral right of the author has been asserted.

A CIP catalogue record for this book
is available from the British Library.

ISBN 978-0-7515-7686-3

Typeset in Baskerville by M Rules
Printed and bound in Great Britain by Clays Ltd, Elcograf S.p.A.

Papers used by Sphere are from well-managed forests
and other responsible sources.

Sphere
An imprint of
Little, Brown Book Group
Carmelite House
50 Victoria Embankment
London EC4Y 0DZ

An Hachette UK Company
www.hachette.co.uk

www.littlebrown.co.uk

*For my mother: my first storyteller, and this novel's first reader.*

# PART ONE: SPRING

# Chapter 1

At last. A morning without reaching the station to flecks of London sludge kicked up the back of her tights, drying into muddy pennies as she waits for her train.

After months of grimy winter, and with it the endless sensation of being encased in a grubby Tupperware container, this morning felt as if the lid had been opened. The blue sky was back – perhaps it had even been there all along. Clara's tights were dry and her hair remained as smooth and untroubled by drizzle as it had been when she had slammed her front door. And now her train was pulling in, just on time.

The crowd parted as the train doors stopped directly opposite her, and she was able to swing straight into her favourite seat, which was empty for the first time in weeks. She rested her head on the glass and watched as the station faded from view and her train rattled towards Central London. For once, Monday morning was going her way. She checked her messages, replying to Nikita about dinner that night with a quick emoji, and put in her headphones in time to enjoy the view over the river. After months of the Thames looking like nothing more than dirty dishwater, today it sparkled. Boats glided serenely beneath the wrought ironwork of the bridge, leaving the water a wake of electric blue sequins. Clara whipped her phone up from her lap and managed to snap the view as the train dipped onto dry land.

Hiya Dad – You were right of course, spring is coming after all. The Thames is looking gorgeous this morning. Thank you so much for the chat yesterday. Hope you're feeling better. C xxx

She pressed send and waited for the comforting 'whoosh' in her headphones to tell her that the image had been delivered. This morning, life was almost as she had imagined it would be when she finally moved to London.

An hour later, Clara had shrugged off what remained of the cosiness of the weekend and stiffened herself into work mode. She was returning to her desk with a cup of coffee in each hand when she saw her mobile screen light up as a message arrived. She put the second cup on her boss's desk, then sat down at her own, took a sip of coffee, and reached for her phone. It wasn't a text that had arrived, but a voicemail.

'Could you give me a call back please? It's quite urgent, so as soon as you get this if possible.'

She rolled her eyes and wondered what in her mother's life could possibly be urgent. An emergency request for numbers at Easter lunch? A fervent reminder about SPF application? Some intel on Kate Middleton's hairdresser of choice? Either way, she slid her phone under her in-tray when she saw her boss approaching at speed, and accepted that the return call would have to wait.

'Good morning, Clara,' said Julia as she swept towards her glass-doored office. 'How are those contracts coming along?'

'In your inbox,' replied Clara. 'And your coffee's on your desk. Would you like a sparkling water?'

'Fabulous.'

Was that a yes or a no to the water? Clara had no idea, but she figured a wander back to the kitchen couldn't do any harm on a Monday morning. As she held a tall clean glass to the fridge door, waiting for the satisfying clunk of ice cubes emerging, then opened a fresh bottle of sparkling water, the metal seal of its lid crunching against the green glass, she daydreamed about what she might do on a day like this, if she weren't obliged to show several well-shod French families around some of Kensington's smartest properties in the hope that prestigious European law firms would pay for them to live there.

A meander through Brompton Cross, maybe; coffee at an outside table as the sun hit her ankles and she watched the wealthy of SW1 from behind her fake designer sunglasses. Lunch in St James's Park watching the ducks … Actually, no. They always got a little too close for comfort and made the water smell fetid. Lunch in Belgravia – moules frites – after a brisk walk through the park, and then some shopping. How lovely it would be to have a day to fritter away like that, she thought.

Sparkling water fizzed at the top of the glass and Clara abruptly stopped pouring, yanked from her fantasy life. She wiped the underside with a kitchen towel and took it through to Julia, who was on the phone and barely acknowledged her. She blew on her hand where the bubbles had popped up and out, and realised as Julia hung up that she would probably never find out if the drink had been wanted or not.

'Off to do a couple of viewings for Cornwall Gardens,' she called back as she reached her own desk and took her coat from the back of her chair. As she picked her phone up she saw another text from her mother, but ignored it, fumbling around in her bag for the keys she needed then heading out of the office.

As she began walking to the property, her imagination returned to her fantasy day of leisure. She even let herself wonder what it might feel like to live in one of these places that she let other people into all day, before she returned home to her un-chic corner of south London.

She stood on the red-brick steps outside the Cornwall Gardens flat and turned her face towards the sun, taking a deep breath and inhaling the scent of the lavender that bordered the black-and-white-chequered pathway leading to the smart red-brick apartment block. She felt her phone buzzing again in her pocket and sighed, her Kensington daydream interrupted.

'Hi, hi, I can't talk, Mum ... ' Her mother's persistence was not uncharacteristic. She had little patience with waiting for a digital reply, and Clara had long resigned herself to seeing texts as little more than warnings that a call was incoming.

'Clara darling, I really do need to speak to you.'

The 'darling' grated. The synthetic endearment a sure sign that something was to be required of Clara.

'Yes, but my clients are going to be here any minute, I just can't chat. I promise I will c—'

'Clara, it's your father.' Wearied by years of diplomatic conversation between her long-divorced parents, Clara became ever keener to end the call.

'What? Is he OK? I texted him about an hour ago.'

A sleek Audi turned in to the street, its driver checking building numbers as he went.

'No, Clara. I'm terribly sorry to have to say this, but he isn't. It sounds daft but ... he died in the night.'

The car door slammed and, startled, Clara dropped her phone. As she picked it up she saw that the call had not ended;

she stared at the screen, unable to absorb what she thought she had just heard. A pair of navy women's driving shoes stepped towards her and she shoved the phone into her pocket, ending the call.

'Mam'selle Seymour?'

'Yes!' Clara smiled cheerily, dusting off her skirt and holding out her hand to shake. 'That's me!'

The face in front of her had a startling brightness, all wide smile and clear skin – while the conversation she had just had seemed to be speeding away from her, words jumbling and focus fading. Had her mother really said that? And meant it? It didn't seem like something her father would do, simply dying on her like that. Making a drama out of a misunderstanding was her mother's style, though – perhaps that was it? Yes, Clara's mind seemed to have chosen a course. Go with that for now, it told her. *Just a misunderstanding. We can sort it out later.*

'Madame Jarry. Pleased to meet you!' Clara tried to match the glistening clarity of her smile, but felt like a painted clown.

There was a static buzz in the air as Clara shook her hand, then smiled at the two toddlers on the pavement beside her. Little girls, symmetrical hair slides in their side-parted hair, each holding a floppy toy rabbit. Behind them, their driver returned to his seat in the car and fiddled with something on the dashboard.

'So, 8 Cornwall Gardens. Shall we?'

Her hand was shaking as she opened the front door; the hum seemed to be getting louder. Could they hear it? It seemed not. The door was open now, light flooding the hallway. All this space, and in Central London. She wondered if Madame Jarry knew how lucky she was to have a husband whose job meant relocating here.

Clara showed the three around the apartment, room by room. First, the vast subterranean kitchen, leading out onto a garden at the back.

'And this is where you two can have a lot of fun ... ' she smiled at the girls, remembering the advice Julia had given her a year ago. *Paint a picture of the client living there.*

'Oh, Maman!' they exclaimed on seeing the children's play area off the main kitchen, complete with a built-in wooden play-house and matching miniature kitchen. Clara smiled at them as they scampered to sit on the wooden banquette, bunnies chattering to each other.

As they headed upstairs, Clara thought she might be floating rather than taking each step with her actual feet.

'The skylight adds so much sunshine to the hallway,' she heard herself say. ' ... plenty of space for toys in here ... and this is the master bedroom, en suite of course ... '

The babble continued to pour out of her as she demonstrated voice-activated lighting, how to disable it in the children's rooms, and the advantages to the underfloor heating. Her mouth just kept moving, and a semblance of sense kept coming. But behind it all, that sentence, running on a loop.

*It sounds daft, but he died in the night.*

The girls scampered from room to room, gabbling among themselves and testing various windowsills with their toys. Each seemed to know what the other would like about each room, calling across to one another, laughter bubbling with delight at various high-end features. How lovely to feel so known by someone, Clara thought, as the older girl took the younger by the hand while they walked back downstairs ahead of her.

'As you can see, we've an Easter tree here at the moment, but it's the perfect space for a fir at Christmas,' Clara continued, winking at the girls. One of them pinged an ornamental twig with a chubby finger, and her mother bent forward to still the small wooden eggs now bouncing on the branch.

'And this is very special,' Clara said as led them into the main living area, resplendent with its smooth marble edges and dipped modernist fireplace. 'Lovely and cool in summer, but so cosy during winter.'

*It sounds daft, but he died in the night.*

The younger of the two girls clipped her hip on the forbidding stone edge, letting out a little yelp. Her mother winced and reached to rub it better. Clara's gaze followed her, instinctively checking to see if it might have put her off the property, but found herself gazing at Madame Jarry's thumb, rubbing in a circular motion while the little girl reached up to be held. The girl leaned in to her mother, soothed by the attention, the moment's pause. Panic over, the girl tottered over to her sister and nestled into her. Clara felt a tug somewhere inside her.

'OK?' asked Clara. The sisters held hands.

'Yes, thank you,' replied Madame Jarry. 'It really is very beautiful. What do you think, girls?'

They looked up at the adults, smiling.

*It sounds daft but he died in the night.*

The sentence wouldn't go away, no matter how firmly she pushed. She swallowed hard and took a slow blink. Maybe she had misheard. Maybe this wasn't happening. *We'll sort it out later.*

'So, any questions while we're still here? Of course, you can get in touch with me on the number you have at any time, but is there anything else you need to know while we're *in situ*?'

'No, but thank you for your time.'

Clara locked the door behind the family as they left, turning in time to see the sisters scramble down the red steps and towards the waiting car. She shook Madame Jarry's hand and waved at the girls, before heading back towards the office.

By the time Clara was back at her desk, the sense of being a step behind reality was starker than ever. She had rushed back to the office and hadn't given herself the chance to steel herself as she usually did at the start of the day. Having a job at all, let alone this one, had always felt something like role play. She knew she didn't belong there. But unsure where she *did* fit, she went through a sort of shapeshifting each morning, trying to slither into the skin of an urban working woman, climbing the career ladder and enjoying her time in the big city. She often wondered if her colleagues knew that when she closed her eyes, she didn't see spreadsheets, but doodles.

Now, she was staring at her desk, not sure if she needed to take her coat off or not, an empty space where her to-do list for the day was meant to be. She blinked and gazed around.

'What did she think?' Julia leaned round from behind her screen.

'She thinks he died in the night,' muttered Clara.

'What?'

Clara slumped into her chair. There was something she needed to be doing, she was sure of it.

'Clara!' Julia was standing directly in front of her. The buzzing in her head faded, and she realised everyone in the office was staring her way.

'Clara, what did you say? Is Monsieur Jarry OK?'

'Yes, yes he's fine.'

'Then what is the problem?

'I'm so sorry, but I think my father's died.'

'Clara! Wait, you *think* he has?'

'Well, my mother rang me just as Mrs Jarry arrived and I dropped my phone.'

'And what happened when you called back?'

'I haven't. It's probably nothing. A misunderstanding.'

Julia dipped her head to try and catch Clara's dazed stare. Clara tried to wave her boss away, an act of impertinence she would never have dared under normal circumstances. Julia wasn't a bad boss, but she was an entirely self-possessed one, and that garnered respect. She had the steely confidence of someone who had grown up around money and felt completely at ease with how to acquire more of it. And this self-assuredness was intimidating to Clara, who still felt like a fraud.

'Listen, darling, you really need to find out what's going on. Use my office – call her back at once.'

Julia ushered her in, urging her to sit, before leaving and pulling the door closed behind her. Clara, still in her mac, was dwarfed by the ergonomic luxury of Julia's chair. The sparkling water she had brought in an hour earlier remained on the glass desk, untouched and surrounded by a pool of condensation.

Clara opened her phone, and scrolled to the last call, making sure that it had been from her mother, and not some horrible misunderstanding. She pressed 'return call' and slumped into the chair.

'Oh, thank heavens it's you. What happened?' Her mother's tone was abrupt.

'I'm so sorry, I dropped my phone just as some clients arrived.'

'I really do think you ought to have called me back.'

Was she ... being told off?

'I'm sorry, I just ... '

'Never mind, never mind, I just wanted you to *know*.'

'Know what?'

'About your father.'

11

'So it's true.'

'Yes, darling, of course it's true. I'm so sorry.'

'Oh.'

'Clara?'

'Yes, I'm here.' Clara felt unbearably heavy. It wasn't a mis-understanding. 'What happened?'

'Well the silly bugger still had me down as his next of kin, so despite everything it was me the paramedics called when they found him. Honestly it's been a hell of a morning and I was supposed to have been helping Ian with his—'

'No, Mum, not to you. What happened to Dad?'

'Oh, of course. He had a heart attack. Oh, Ben. Just like I always knew you would. Apparently the ambulance didn't make it in time and it all happened rather quickly.'

'Oh, Mum, I'm so sorry.' Clara could see her foot, resting on the ball of her big toe, shaking furiously as she sat slumped with her back to Julia's office door.

'Well, yes, it wasn't the Monday morning I had planned. Least said, soonest mended, sweetheart.'

'Shall I come over? Do you need me?' It seemed easier to tend to her mum than to pay any attention to that heaviness, which was now transforming into a sort of jittery panic as she realised that this really was happening to her. That it was just her and her mother now. That her father had died.

'No no, I'll be fine, Ian will be back soon. But there is the coroner to deal with and then obviously someone will have to make a start on a funeral but I'm afraid it simply can't be me. I'll pass details on to Auntie Liz and perhaps she can take up that baton – unless you want to. But it can't be me. Not any more. Those days are long gone.'

Indeed they were. Clara's parents had divorced a decade ago, leaving behind them a toxic trail of resentments and unspoken slights, which Clara had been delicately trying to step around ever since. Somewhere, deep in her subconscious, Clara knew that it should have been her mother consoling *her* in this moment, but yes, there was a certain comfort in everyone playing to type, knowing their roles. That the available cast was no longer big enough for all the required parts was something Clara was still struggling to grasp.

She was sure they made sense, but somehow her mother's words seemed to melt into each other before they reached her ears. What did a coroner actually do? How did you organise a funeral? What was Clara supposed to do? What was Clara supposed to *want* to do?

'So you don't need me?' she repeated.

'No sweetheart, I'll be in touch if I do. But you get on with things your end and I'll call later. You make that Simon take care of you, won't you. And I'll see you at Easter. Much love to you, Clara.'

'OK then, and I'm so sorr—'

Her mother had already hung up.

She ran her finger up the side of the glass of water. It was now almost entirely flat. How could pouring it have been part of today? How was this all happening on the same day? That text she had sent from the train – it was only a couple of hours ago.

He would never have seen it.

# Chapter 2

Grief? Is that what this was? Clara felt little more than dazed, suspended, waiting for the feelings to come. There was a sense she had been sent home so she could get on with the business of grieving in private. Did that mean crying? Should she be weeping? Uncontrollably? She felt sure Julia had intended her to head straight to her mother's arms, but that was clearly not going to happen. What she wanted to do was head to her dad's flat and put the kettle on. That's what she thought would be comforting right now. She wanted to be staring at the bird box in his garden from the kitchen window as the water boiled and she waited for him to enter the room.

But she didn't live there any more. She hadn't done for a while. And now he was gone.

Nevertheless, heading back over the river to sit in the small Tooting flat she shared with Simon, her college boyfriend, seemed ridiculously indulgent. It was still Monday morning. What would she even do when she got there? And what would she tell Simon?

So she walked straight past her bus stop and headed to Brompton Cross, where she turned into the French cafe she passed day after day without ever entering. A waiter in a long, crisp white apron gestured towards a prime table on the pavement under the canopy, and took her coffee order. Clara settled into her seat, ready to watch the passers-by, just as she had daydreamed she would do so many times.

White vans were parked up on the pavement, their drivers heaving boxes of vegetables or crates of milk into the nearby cafes. A woman walked by with the focus of someone who belonged here, her body encased in expensive-looking high-elastane gym wear, a tiny dog trotting out ahead of her. A smattering of continental businessmen strode past, their periwinkle collars glinting against luxurious navy-blue wool jackets, each on the phone.

Clara had longed to sit back and watch these glamorous creatures gliding through their enchanted lives as she had scurried in and out of work these last few months, hoping each morning that this would be the day she felt she felt like one of them, part of the team that Julia so often referred to. That moment had never come, no matter how often she had tried to slip on the effortless confidence of the west-London career girl her mother longed for her to be. And now that she had an excuse not to try, it felt as if this life she had longed to watch at leisure was out of focus, too remote to watch properly. Everything seemed to be going on behind a wall of Perspex, and her a metre behind it. A car horn beeped and she didn't flinch. It took a moment before she realised that the waiter was at her shoulder, coffee in hand.

'Madame,' he said as he leaned forward to put the cup and saucer on the small bistro table in front of her.

'Thank you,' she replied. But as she said it, her voice cracked at the sight of the small French biscuit on the saucer in front of her. All of a sudden she was a teenager, back in Paris with her dad, being taken for her first coffee. A treat to celebrate the end of her exams, on that magical trip to the city he loved so much.

They had arrived early, and he had whisked her fresh from the Eurostar to the Place des Vosges, a spot he had spent some time telling her about on the train. Clara was used to spending weekends away with him, and had even been on holidays with him since his marriage to her mother ended a couple of years before, but Paris had been the special one. She had nagged him about going since she found a copy of *Madeline* in his study as a child and immediately fallen in love with the idea of Paris.

Each time there had been talk of the two of them going away during the school holidays she hinted heavily about the city. But each time the hints were met with a no – and a vague explanation which never quite rang true.

'Not yet ... '

'It's not the best time of year to see the city ... '

'We should really save it until you're older ... '

So they took other trips instead, each one always shot through with a mixture of thrill and anxiety. After her parents separated when she was twelve, Clara had longed for those extended bouts of time with her father, rather than the regular-but-somewhat-rushed weekends and evenings that swiftly became the norm. She craved his relaxed company, that time once they had already been together a day or two and had stopped merely catching up and started to let conversations meander.

The first few hours of each weekend with him were always so busy, trying to fit in all the important stuff, the chats that had been taken care of effortlessly when they lived under the same roof and now seemed to mount up, gaining emotional intensity with every shared breakfast that they missed. Those were the times that she had missed the most since their separation – and now looked forward to most.

She even loved the planning for the trips. Her dad didn't have the money to impulsively book hotels, so they would buy guidebooks, scour the travel sections of the weekend papers for B&B advertisements and pore over recommendations on nascent travel blogs.

Once away, Clara could bask in the sunshine of her dad's attention, talking about what she was reading at school, sharing recipes she had tried out at home (and the ensuing kitchen chaos) and asking his opinion on anything from classic movies she had discovered to whether he had ever been to places she had been researching and longed to visit herself.

Only on these trips did she feel free to talk this way, taking her own time, without the pressure to get a check list of topics 'done' before she had to get back to her mum's, where such conversation was treated like an indulgence rather than an insight into who she was becoming, or might have the potential to be.

It seemed hard to believe that those trips had ever happened now. Clara pictured her dad's hands as he scooped the veg she had just chopped for him off a wooden board into the cast-iron casserole dish in a holiday villa. She saw them on the steering wheel of a continental hire car as the sun hit them through the windscreen; untangling a fishing line as she sat cross-legged next to him, excited about what they had caught that day and how he would barbecue it. He seemed to be able to focus harder while his hands were busy, his attention held by a practical task in hand, letting the conversation find its own path.

Excitement would mount before each trip, but alongside it the dread that it would all be over too quickly, leaving her mourning for their time together almost as soon as it began. She often ended up overwhelmed by how much she had to say and how much she wanted to hear.

They went to Amsterdam for her thirteenth birthday where

they cycled along the canals together on candy-coloured bikes, stopping for stroopwafels and spending hours in the Anne Frank House, indulging in Clara's recent fascination with the girl and her diary. She spent the trip home furious that she had wasted so much time in the museum when she could have just been talking to her father about the book.

They went to Berlin at Christmas that year, where they visited an advent market before concluding that it was far too touristy, and went for a posh, whipped-cream-topped hot chocolate which they declared exactly the right degree of touristy. The next year, a visit to Barcelona was tarnished by the encroaching panic she started to feel about a boy she had been flirting with not texting her back. She had sat over plates of bright meats and perfectly fried seafood, her stomach in knots, preoccupied by what she could possibly have done to make the replies dry up, before realising that she didn't have data roaming switched on on her phone. When she finally did hear back from him, she felt the tension almost physically draining from her body.

A fug of shame crept over her as she realised how little attention she had been paying to such precious time with her dad. How could she have known how few of these trips they would have?

The next summer they had been to the north coast of France for a holiday of such emotional intensity that Clara slept for almost two days on her return. Torrential rain for most of the week meant that she and her dad were cooped up in a small gîte for the first half of the trip, while she became increasingly melancholy about everything her dad tried to chat about or distract her with. The boy who had so dominated the Barcelona trip had faded from importance months before, but stresses about both exams and the complicated dynamics of her friendship group were bearing down, leaving her stooped with anxiety, completely unable to inhabit the self she had imagined she would be on this trip – on the beach, chatting about *Orange is the New Black* with her dad, perhaps having a small glass of wine if they went out for dinner. On the evening of the fourth day she – entirely unexpectedly – began only her second ever period, and had to ask him to drive her to the nearby pharmacy before it closed.

His gentle patience on realising why she had been such doom-laden company had made her flush with self-consciousness – even more than the moment she had dithered in front of the display of chic French moisturisers, holding only a box of tampons. She slept for most of the next day, before re-emerging a different person, just as the sun came out. Those final few days were a blissful mix of beach walks, seafood lunches on sunny terraces and the sense of closeness she had been craving for months – all of which served to make heading home more bittersweet.

It wasn't until the summer Clara took her GCSEs that her dad had finally relented and took her on her dream trip to Paris. At last, she was going to visit the city she had spent so long dreaming about. Since finding that book in the study, she had held the city as a sort of dreamland in her imagination. Grey-roofed houses covered in vines, glass-topped boats gliding serenely down the Seine, the Eiffel Tower twinkling at dusk: these images had tantalised Clara for years in books, Instagram posts and movies. And it wasn't just the physical beauty of the city but the characters who peopled it. Open-minded, urbane, devastatingly cool.

*Madeline* itself was now largely forgotten, but it had inspired a fantasy Paris that only grew more vivid as every year passed and Clara discovered more about it. Old French movies, trashy modern movies starring Selena Gomez, even images of Beyoncé visiting the Louvre. In Paris, you could be your ultimate you.

And her enthusiasm only grew stronger the more her mother dismissed talk of the city as daftness. Because, of course, the dismissal was part of the attraction. Clara knew that her father loved the place, no matter how much he tried to play that down. And she suspected that her mother knew too. And, just as she longed to escape the suburban concerns that preoccupied her mother – how much a neighbour's new car cost, how much a friend from the gym had slimmed down since Christmas, how much a perceived rival at her book club had got in the divorce – she longed to see what she imagined was the metropolitan version of her father. She wanted to access that part of him, the academic who loved long walks not just around Bristol Harbourside but along the Seine. The man who was more than dad jokes or sad smiles on a Friday-evening pickup, but enjoyed art, and style, and long evenings sitting on pavements talking about *ideas*, rather than obligations. Would seeing *this* Ben help her to access a freer, more self-assured Clara too? Or would simply being in Paris itself be enough? Either way, her teenage years had done nothing to convince her that Paris wasn't the answer.

When, at last, she was going to be able to visit for herself, free from squinting at Instagram's squares or the juddering path of Google Street View, she could hardly believe it. She had spent a week listing pastry shops she wanted to visit, specific walks she wanted to take, and of course planning her wardrobe, discussing 'looks' online with her friends late into the night – much to her mother's apparent disdain.

'Why do you have to be so sour about it?' Clara had snapped at her mother. 'It's not as if you have to come with us.'

'Oh, *I've* never been invited to Paris by your father, that's for sure,' she had snapped back, lacing up her tennis shoes with a vigour that would surely mean restricted blood flow to her toes within a couple of sets. 'I just don't want you building it up too much. I know how these trips can unmoor you a little.'

But Clara scoffed at her.

'They don't unmoor me! They are actually very inspiring. We go to places a hell of a lot more interesting than the bloody tennis club.' She all but gasped at the boldness of swearing at her own mother, a woman for whom the word 'ruddy' could render a sentence scandalous – even if it was a sentence dripping with casual prejudice.

Jackie looked up, knees together, her hands sitting neatly in her lap, a pristine tennis skirt above her slim, tanned calves. She took a breath. Her voice was softer now. She was holding Clara's reluctant gaze.

'Of course you do. And of course you treasure time with your father. That is as it should be. But, well ... ' Another sigh. 'I just don't want you to build Paris up too much. It's not ... it's not healthy to adore a city the way that you two do Paris.'

Clara didn't bite back, perplexed at the idea that her father – whose arm she had had to twist to take her there – really was such a fan of the city too. He had seemed to be avoiding it for as long as she could remember, and she was flattered to have persuaded him at last. Now he *adored* it? It didn't make sense, but then again so much of what Jackie said about her ex-husband merely skirted around what Clara saw as the truth. So Clara didn't dwell on it; within moments she was back in her bedroom, lying prone across her eiderdown and scrolling through her phone once again.

But as she sat there on that Monday morning, in Kensington's finest French cafe, she remembered that her mother's observations had not been misguided: Ben's delight at being back in Paris was obvious from the moment they arrived. They had hopped straight out of the cab, their bags still at their side, and taken a pavement table in one of the cloistered arcades edging Place des Vosges. The weather was warmer than England already, the air a little hazy. Her dad arranged the chairs so that they both had a view of the square, before looking up with a grin that in those days she very rarely saw.

'Coffee?' he asked her, as if it were the most natural thing in the world.

'Sure,' she said, not wanting to blow her cover. A coffee! At last!

Had he forgotten that she had never been allowed to drink coffee before, or did he leave home before she'd asked? In the few years since they split up, it had become increasingly difficult for Clara to remember how either of her parents had truly behaved back when the three of them lived together. Had her mother's laser focus on behaviour, nutrition and even friends, who could somehow bring shame on Clara (and thereby herself), been as sharp back then? Or was it simply a recent manifestation of the status anxiety that seemed to have run riot since she was free of her marriage to Ben, in all his crumpled corduroy glory. And had he really smiled and laughed more back then, or was it just that she worried about him so much, living alone in his slightly chaotic basement flat? Yes, there was a delicious freedom in the way that he let stacks of papers, books and newspapers teeter around his desk, the kitchen table and even at the feet of his most comfortable armchair. But he did often seem to have forgotten to buy them any sensible groceries, and almost as soon as it stopped making Clara feel uncomfortable for herself, it made her feel anxious for him.

So could he really not have known that Jackie had long

forbidden coffee from the house as if it were an opiate? 'So acidic! So dehydrating for young skin!' Or was it just that when she was younger, more exhausted by life as a nurse on a busy ward and all that she saw there, Jackie had not taken such a hard line on it? Ben, on the other hand, had never seemed to care about any of its health implications, preferring to regale Clara with tales about the birth of London's coffee houses and how they had changed the marketplace of ideas for centuries to come.

When the waiter arrived ten minutes later with their drinks, each white cup had an identical complimentary biscuit on its saucer and a perfect crown of froth on top. The air smelled of hyacinths, fresh coffee and freshly baked pastries. Clara had never felt so free. As soon as the waiter left, her dad had lobbed his biscuit straight into his mouth with a grin, letting go of it an inch before his lips. He moved it, whole, to one of his cheeks and nodded at her cup, saying as he turned to survey the square. 'You don't have to finish it if you don't like it. But isn't today a great day to try one?'

She thought she saw a wink as he smiled back at her over his sunglasses. She hadn't been sure at the time. But now, as she sat all alone in the Kensington sunshine, holding an identical small biscuit between finger and thumb, the damp of a first sip of coffee on her lips, she realised that of course he had known. And he'd wanted her to have a proper cup of coffee because he wanted her to be happy, to experience life, to taste it all.

A fat tear landed on top of her cup, leaving a dent in today's milky foam. How could it possibly be true that they would never share another coffee? How could it have been *yesterday morning* when they had sat at the kitchen table together, hands echoing each other, clamped around mugs, chatting about how he was longing for spring? None of it made sense. Clara drew a finger along her eye to stem any further tears and took a sip. Today, there was none of the delicious warmth of a flavour shared. Today it tasted like ash.

She took a few pound coins from her wallet and left them on the table, grabbed her bag and headed down Brompton Road before any further tears came. Despite the sunshine, a shiver went down her back, and she realised that she didn't really know where she was heading next. She might as well walk home, something she had been promising her boyfriend Simon that she would start doing for months. *Make the most of an unexpected day off*, she told herself, *it'll clear your head.*

But the walk didn't clear her head. Despite the sun there was a spiteful breeze, the traffic continued to roar past at an exhausting volume, and she couldn't get a decent pace up because of the sheer number of people staring at their phones as they meandered in front of her. It was only when she reached the river that she felt any sense of relief. Cars and buses continued to rumble past her even as she paused to look over into the water; boats buzzed beneath her, a seagull pecked malevolently at some litter on the roof of a houseboat, and the steady movement of the water provided a moment's peaceful distraction.

The sky was clouding over though, and after ten minutes of watching the river Clara felt too chilly to stay static. She tugged her bag over her shoulder and headed further south. At last her feet found something of a rhythm, her soles pushing the pavement away with every passing step, her heart rate picking up as she headed down and over Queenstown Road and into Clapham. If she could keep moving, perhaps she could stop any more upsetting memories from catching up with her. She could deal with this encroaching swarm of thoughts and feelings later.

'Clara, you're a doer,' she remembered her dad telling her only yesterday as she had told him about her anxieties about work, about how she never felt part of the team, how she wasn't sure whether to leave in search of a job that felt right for her, or to stay and save, as she seemed to have agreed with Simon to do.

'You'll get where you need to go,' her dad had said. If only she knew where that was.

But yes, she was a doer. She wouldn't mull. She wouldn't waste today. She would go home and get something useful done.

True to her word, the minute she got home and into the tiny flat, she was a whirlwind of cleaning and tidying. Everything she had meant to do the previous evening when she had got back too late from her dad's was going to get done today.

Shoes were dug out from under the bed; fresh linen was found in the storage box under the bed, shaken out in the afternoon sunshine and put on. She scrubbed the bath, and even the tiles surrounding it. Then she rearranged her and Simon's toiletries so that they were symmetrical, taking up perfectly equal space on each side of the basin, and in the basket to the side of the bath. Any overspill of her own, she shoved into the mirrored cabinet, hoping that Simon wouldn't look in there for a while yet. She vacuumed each of the small three rooms before wiping down the kitchen surfaces and drying up the crockery that she would usually leave airing to the right of the sink, but which she knew irritated Simon when left out overnight. He would come home to a sparkling palace, she told herself. Then he'd be so much more relaxed when she told him her news. And that would make it easier for him.

All the while, as she wiped, polished and folded, the flickering reel of memories continued to scroll across the back of her mind. She tried to move faster, as if she could outwit it, to find a way to move forward, think of something to do next. But it kept scrolling. Eventually, as she waited for the kettle to boil, staring out of the window on the gardens below, she felt a sort of thud of defeat. This was happening. Her father was dead. She made her tea, walked to the sofa and felt her breathing judder as the tears started to surface.

But just as she sat back, her phone pinged.

> Hello Clara, I am so sorry about your dad. Silly thing, leaving us like this. Call me if you can. I have something for you. Auntie Liz xoxo

# Chapter 3

Clara stared at her phone, feeling like nothing less than calling her aunt. Her dad's older sister by five years, Liz could be a brittle woman. Clara's finger hovered over the button to call her back, when another message disrupted her train of thought.

> Hola! All ok for tonight? Coming straight from work
> obvs, so I'll be 7ish unless I hear otherwise. xx

Nikita. She had forgotten. It was still Monday, the day they so often tried to spend together, despite now living at opposite ends of the city. An old friend, and someone with whose family she sometimes felt more at home with than her own, Nikita was a whirlwind of positive energy. But also scatty. Really scatty. But today was so upside down that it was Clara who had forgotten she was hosting and it was Nikita who was on the ball.

> Of course. Weirdly am home already so come round
> whenever suits xx

The thought of company and the distraction it would provide lightened Clara's heart a little. She had meant to buy them some dinner at the fancy deli near the office and now realised she had entirely forgotten. What could she give Nikita now? She couldn't even remember what she had in. Her cup of tea went cold as she rifled through cupboards, trying to scrabble together a meal, that incessant flickering reel still running.

It felt as if the next thing Clara knew, the doorbell was ringing and her phone was vibrating on the sofa. She looked at the screen: Nikita. She checked the time: 7 p.m. Could she really have been tidying and daydreaming that long? Apparently so. It was only once she was halfway to the intercom that she remembered why she was at home early anyway, and had to swallow hard not to let emotions come rushing at her while she buzzed Nikita in. She threw on some clean-ish jeans and a sweatshirt from the chair in her bedroom, ran her hands through her hair and was shoving on a second sock by the time Nikita had made it up the internal stairs to her flat's door. She took a deep breath and opened it with a smile.

'Hello friend!' Nikita reached her arms out to Clara. Clara collapsed into the hug and braced herself to tell Nikita her news.

'Hello friend,' she said quietly into the warmth of Nikita's shoulder.

'I was just starting to worry about you up here! Thought the buzzer was bust again or something.'

'No, I was just—'

'Well no worries, I'm here now. And guess what?'

'What?'

'We're CELEBRATING!' Nikita walked past Clara, giving her a squeeze on the shoulder, and headed into the flat, yanking a bottle of Prosecco out of the bag schlumped over her shoulder.

She shoved it in the door of Clara's fridge and turned to give her another hug.

'I did it! I really did! And you're the first person I've told! I know we're not meant to drink on Mondays, BUT ... '

Nikita had a fledgeling career as a documentary maker, thus far funded by her temp work around the city. Now it seemed she had finally won her first grant to make a passion project she had been working on for months. Her visible joy was so cheering that for a fleeing moment Clara felt the heaviness in her chest ease up a bit.

'Oh, that is *fantastic*! I can't believe it! How did you find out?'

And as Nikita started to regale her with a story of missed phone calls and good news received over WhatsApp, Clara felt her desire to talk about her dad slip away a little. As Nikita leaned on the kitchen door frame, chatting away, Clara crouched into the cupboard of less used and more dusty kitchen kit and found two champagne flutes. An image of her and Simon clinking them on New Year's Eve, just the two of them, just how he liked it, flashed to mind, but as she ran them under a tap she pushed the thought away, wiping them with a cloth before taking the Prosecco from the fridge and opening it. When the cork popped she gave her friend a wide, sincere smile, but found a quiet voice inside saying that she could just hang on to this life a couple of hours longer. She could be the happy, smiling friend, not the grieving lonely one. Just for tonight. Until everything inevitably changed.

Clara had long been welcomed into Nikita's family with a warmth she had not always experienced in her own, particularly the years she had spent living with her mother alone. The two had been friends since their late teens, having met while doing temp work in a particularly austere architect's practice near – although not as near as it clearly would have liked to have been – to the Barbican. Nikita had been a ray of sunshine in the largely silent eggshell white office and Clara had warmed to her immediately.

It had only taken a couple of days of them sharing a reception desk and plentiful typing duties before they started buying each other lunch and eventually hanging out after work. When they were no longer required at the practice, they stayed firm friends, comparing notes about their mutual temping agency and eventually meshing their respective groups of friends as they each headed to college, returning to take on more temp work during the holidays. She adored her friend's relaxed manner and indulged her hippyish attitude in a way that she wouldn't with anyone else because Nikita had a dry sense of humour – particularly about herself – and an open heart. Where Clara could be impulsive, and sometimes closed, Nikita had the confidence to wait things out, to see the bigger picture – and to encourage her friend to do the same. Where Clara had rushed into a job she had no real passion for, keen for the security of a salary and the perception of a career, Nikita had been content to carry on temping, ever sure that someone soon would see her artistic potential. Today, she had been proved right. In some of her lower moments, Clara thought that she might just have taken her own job in order to please her mother and her boyfriend, while Nikita seemed to face no such compromise: following her passion was what would please those around her. So Nikita had temped, squirrelling away at scripts in the evenings, and Clara had taken up the nine-to-five in earnest, quietly shelving dreams of art school and life as an illustrator.

But Nikita's family had had a big impact on Clara too. She had an older brother, Jay, and a younger sister, Vee, as well as parents who were still together and seemed to actually enjoy each other's company. Her dad had grown up in India while her mum had always lived in north London. Together, they had created the sort of home where ideas and emotions could be discussed and frequently were. Mealtimes were for family and chatting, rather than a fresh opportunity to 'slip up' on one's diet – which was so often how Clara's own mother approached eating – albeit under the guise of a nurse's watchful advice. With just the two of them in the house, meals were rarely relished, but it felt very different sitting around the old wooden kitchen tables at Nikita's: chopping herbs, discussing film or politics and bathing in the atmosphere as the family listened, laughed and teased each other. It was the sort of family experience that Clara craved, and she cherished the times she was invited to join in.

It seemed so obvious that once she mentioned Ben's death, the dynamic between the two women would shift even further. She wouldn't just be the one with divorced parents, longing for a big family, she would now be the one with even less family. She could deal with the shards of loneliness she felt when she said goodbye to the family on a Sunday evening or when she overheard Nikita chatting to her mum on the phone. But she wasn't sure she was ready to deal with pity. Not just yet.

Just an hour or two more.

So Clara sat, cross-legged, on the living room floor and ate prawn curry. She sipped the celebratory Prosecco, raising a glass to her friend and relishing this break from the inside of her own head. Chat bounced around from topic to topic, pausing to focus on what seemed like frivolities in a way that only good mates with years of context can. Once they had dissected plans for the documentary, Nikita made a swift change of topic and confessed that she was trying to work out whether she was ready to go back to spinning classes.

'I have a confession,' she said as she put her bowl down with solemnity. 'I miss those stupid stationary bikes. I know it's terrible, but I do! The music, the sweat, the whole de-stress. Even though I *always* hated it there.'

'But you swore less than a month ago that you'd never go back! You said that a bike that took you nowhere was offensive to you!'

'I know. I *know*!'

'What happened to "you're literally using up energy in order to use up energy"?' laughed Clara.

'Look, I *have* enjoyed my walks. And I *do* want a real bike. But that after-class burrrrn. I miss it. And the music!'

'Oh GOD, now you want a real bike too. Why don't you just come round when Simon's here and you can talk about it all night?'

'Well I think we both know the answer—'

'Anyway.' Clara cut her short, wanting to keep the chat aloft, breezy, up in the air and far from conflict. 'At least you are experiencing some positive thoughts about exercise. I mean, we all know how bloody rare that is.'

'I know, right? Maybe I really *will* become a proper biker. After a few more spins? I wanted to hate it so much but the night they did a Prince ride was the best! Even you would have enjoyed ...'

'Ha! Well I *seriously* doubt that!' laughed Clara. 'You know full well I haven't done any exercise since school.'

It was true. Despite Nikita's attempts to get her to various classes from Zumba to spin over the years, Clara had given them all a swerve, much to Simon's increasing judgement.

'You're right. Maybe we should both just ... I dunno, spend some time outside?'

'Well, I walked home from work this afternoon,' admitted

Clara before realising that she had opened the door to discussing why she had left work so early.

'I don't even know if I *know* you any more.' Nikita reached for the Prosecco to top them both up.

'Yeah, it was a weird one. I didn't ... not enjoy it though.'

'How did you have the time?'

'Yeah, um, long story ... ' Clara looked into her lap, feeling the conversation sag as she failed to keep that breeze in her voice.

'Clara, is everything OK?'

'Yeah ... '

'Is it Simon? What has he done?'

That this was Nikita's assumption on seeing Clara downcast was mortifying. Clara knew she had been no fan of his for years, but there was genuine concern in her voice now. Her cheeks flushed and she blinked, trying to keep her breath steady.

'No, no, it's nothing like that,' said Clara, caught. Turning the conversation one way meant defending Simon, when – even though there wasn't anything new to report – she still didn't really have the energy. But turning the other way meant telling Nikita about her dad, and stepping out into the reality of this new future.

'Babe, I don't believe you.'

'Why? Because you don't like him? So he must be somehow bullying me or *controlling* me? Just because you think he's boring? Or because I don't meet your impossibly high standards of artistic endeavour, or boss-girl feminism, or dream-couple relationships?'

Nikita reared back startled and raised a hand in protest. Clara caught her own breath, shocked at the strength of her response.

'Excuse me?' said Nikita. Her voice was quiet, calm, only serving to accentuate the lashing Clara had just given her.

'Oh, come on.' Clara's voice cracked. 'It's not as if you're not constantly trying to get me to leave him.'

'Only because you always seem miserable with him. You do have choices, you know.'

'Sure.' A strange, bitter laugh left Clara. The sticky sweetness of the Prosecco was starting to taste acidic in the back of her throat. She pushed her glass away.

'Clara, I have no idea what has happened here. Yes, Simon is not my favourite person. But only because of what he seems to do to you. But there's no need to be so—'

But as Nikita spoke, Clara's phone pinged. Another text. She looked down at her phone and frowned.

> Dear Clara, Do get in touch, I so hope you are okay. And I have some bits I have to send your way. Sending much love, Auntie Liz.

'Sorry, am I boring you?' asked Nikita as she leaned forward to take the two glasses from the coffee table next to Clara. 'Or is it He Who Must Come First?'

'No, it's my aunt, just wanting me to call her back. No biggie.' Clara's voice had steadied, and she brushed her hair off her face. And yet as Clara paused, staring at the screen and trying to find a way to start what she needed to say, a further thread seemed to snap between her and the world she was trying to cling on to.

'OK ....,' said Nikita, brushing down her trousers and looking to the corner of the room for her bag. 'I'll leave you to your phone then.'

'It's not like that, Nikita. I'm sorry. I know you're just trying to be kind but honestly, you have no idea.'

'I have no idea because you won't tell me.' Nikita's bag was now slung over her shoulder. 'It's difficult enough to get to see you alone, and honestly I just want you to be happy. But I can't come round here and be reprimanded for giving a shit about you.'

Clara got up and followed Nikita as she moved into the kitchen and put their glasses on the countertop. Out of the window she could see Simon arriving outside the building in his cycling gear, pausing to fiddle with his enormous sports watch. She felt as if she was stepping out onto a bottom stair that wasn't there as she looked at Nikita pleadingly.

'It's my dad. He died this morning. It's just ... it's just really heavy, OK?'

'Oh my god, Clara, why didn't you say?'

'I don't know, I didn't want to ruin the evening I guess.'

'But of *course* you should have said ... '

The tears were coming now. Now just for her dad, but for her frustration at this dynamic and how it was now changed for ever.

'Well, I guess I'm sorry I'm not doing bad news correctly.'

'Don't be daft! I just meant you should have been *able* to tell me!'

Clara was sobbing as the reality of her new situation cascaded towards her. Her dad was gone, her best friend seemed inexplicably furious with her, and her boyfriend was back. And this time there was no dad to send a cheering text to, no one to discuss how she was feeling with, no planned walk at the weekend to look forward to. She was alone, and this time she was truly alone rather than just feeling lonely.

'*Should should should*,' she said. 'I'm clearly such a relentless let-down to you. I'm sorry. I forgot you were coming. I didn't know what to say. And I felt like ... I don't know ... I felt like I should tell Simon first.' Tears were meeting snot down

Clara's face as she tugged at the kitchen roll, trying to wipe her face dry.

'Oh my god, I'm not trying to tell you off, I'm trying to tell you I'm here for you. It's not an unusual thing to want to do for a friend.' Nikita was backing out of the kitchen, heading towards the door.

'Well, contrary to what you think, you're not the most important person in my life. You weren't my first port of call.'

As if summoned by a reference to him, Simon slammed the front door to the building two flights below. A sense of urgency came over the women, as they realised this moment was about to be interrupted.

'Are you going to be OK?' Nikita mouthed at her. Clara meekly nodded, shoulders slumped, the last ten minutes having been more tiring than her whole walk home. She felt shame blossoming at the fact that Nikita was asking her this at the mere sound of Simon returning.

'Call me later,' Nikita said, before pulling Clara's soggy face into her chest in an embrace that left her feeling as sad as she ever had.

'I will, I'm sorry.'

'Stop saying that.'

As the insistent clack of Simon's cycling shoes on the stairs grew louder, Nikita blew Clara a kiss and turned out of the flat.

'Hey Simon,' Clara heard her say as she passed him.

The front door was nudged open by a bicycle wheel which was soon followed by a sweating Simon, who said hello as he turned to hang the bike on its stand on the hallway wall.

'Hey there,' said Clara, trying to stifle her sobs. 'Good ride?'

'Yep,' he said briskly, giving her a kiss on the top of her hair without making eye contact. 'Need a shower now.'

*

Clara stood at her kitchen window and watched Nikita walk out of the building two floors below. She felt the stickiness of the Prosecco, and blinked slowly, her eyes now burning with dehydration. Her feet were throbbing from her walk. A blister had formed on her heel from wearing her work shoes all the way home. She could feel blood pumping through her body as if it were too thick for her. She washed up the two bowls, forks and Prosecco glasses in cool water, enjoying the soothing effect it had on her clammy hands. She stacked everything neatly on the drying rack, wiped around the sink and then reached for a bottle of Scotch she had on the side and poured a slug of it into her water tumbler.

She wasn't sure if it was too late to text her aunt back but started composing a message anyway, only to send it in error before she had finished writing.

Hi Auntie Liz, sorry not to have got back to
you sooner—

Her aunt called straight back. Clara answered, shaking.
'Hello Clara?'
'Hi there, Auntie Liz.'
'How are you doing? I am so sorry about your father.'
'Oh, you know. I—' Clara broke off. 'Anyway, how are you?'
'I'm fine, my dear. Sad, of course. Silly Ben, he was no age at all. I was always so worried about him by himself.'
'I know. Me too.'
Clara was having to swallow even harder now. She was pressing her fingers into the side of her glass, watching the pads of flesh going white, flush with pink, then white again.
'Now listen. I've got something for you from your dad. It's a letter. I have had it a couple of years, but he made me promise he wouldn't give it to you until ... ' Her voice faded. 'Well,

in the event of his death. That's what they say isn't it? "The event of".'

Clara took a huge gulp of whisky.

'Yes, I think that's what they say,' she replied quietly.

'It's just ...' Auntie Liz's voice was breaking now 'It's just the first time I have said it. *Death.*'

'I'm sorry.' Clara's voice was even softer now, and while she felt bad for having been annoyed by Liz's rambling, she desperately wanted her to get to the point.

'Oh, I'm just being silly. Such a silly woman!'

The shrillness Clara was used to hearing in her aunt's voice was creeping back. She edged away from the handset, not ready to engage with the emotional shrapnel her aunt seemed to be giving off. She stayed silent.

'Clara?'

'Yes ... '

Clara heard the water running in the shower across the hallway stop, and the soft slam of the glass door.

'This letter ... Are you able to meet and collect it?'

Her Aunt lived up in north-west London. It would take forever to get there; she'd have to take time out of the office. But then again, Julia could hardly refuse her.

'Um, yes I think I probably could.'

'Oh, wonderful. It will be such a weight off.'

As Auntie Liz said this, Clara could almost feel that weight being lifted directly onto her. She wanted to end the call and go to bed.

'OK. Shall I come up to your house tomorrow morning?'

'Yes please, that would be wonderful. Perhaps we should have a conversation about the funeral too? I am not even sure I know what he wanted.'

This was too much. Clara had enjoyed her evening of

pretending she could avoid these feelings, but now they were rushing at her too fast.

'Yes, um, yes well I don't really think I will have much that is useful to say but yes, yes ... '

Her words faded away before a final, 'Anyway, tomorrow, it will be lovely to see you!' flourish, which she meant precisely none of. And then she hung up.

While Simon shuffled around in the bedroom, Clara wrote a quick email to Julia, explaining that she had some bits of personal admin to sort out and would it be OK if she was back in the office on Thursday, before scrolling aimlessly around the internet for ten minutes. The world seemed to be carrying on with its chatter, its memes, its updates. The temptation to just keep clicking, following link after link, as the whisky dulled her resistance, was enormous. Only once she realised she was sitting in the dark, her head starting to nod, did she persuade herself to get up, wash her face and teeth and head to bed. Simon was already asleep, his hair smelling fresh from the shower, and his forearm smooth and tanned where it lay over the top of the duvet.

She tried to slide in beside him silently, anxious not to provoke him by disturbing his sleep. It had been a long time since she had learned how important it was to him. Nevertheless, she risked rolling to kiss the back of his head before returning to lie on her back and stare at the ceiling in the dark. When she closed her eyes, she felt queasy. The seasickness of an evening's drinking when she had least expected it. The fact that she still hadn't told Simon. And the jitters after such a disastrous attempt at telling Nikita. Her heart was hammering in her chest at the thought of this letter. She had always known her dad had things he didn't talk to her about, but what could he possibly have had to say that had to wait until after *death*?

# Chapter 4

In months to come, Clara would probably have described herself as 'waking with a start' that morning, but in truth she hadn't really slept enough to have woken up at all. Her mind skimmed consciousness for six or seven hours, taking small dips before wild, jumbled dreams yanked her back into the present, her mother's words echoing in her mind again and again.

*It sounds so daft, but he died in the night.*

Her breathing had been shallow, her hair too hot, and sweat gathered in the small of her back no matter what position she arranged herself or the duvet into. The pint of water she had drunk before bed had done little more than leave her stumbling to the bathroom for a wee every couple of hours. At 6.15 a.m. she decided to give up, and swung her legs groggily out of bed. Her throat was dry, her hands felt shaky and her eyes were stinging.

She boiled the kettle, poured hot water over a teabag and poked at it with a spoon from the draining board while staring blearily at her phone. She was dreading facing an aunt she barely knew, who was sure to expect some degree of cheering up rather than offering any sort of consolation herself.

She carried her tea into the living room and sat cross-legged on the floor in the spot where sunlight was pouring into the south-facing window. It was the sort of morning where Clara felt she might just slide off a chair if she tried to sit on one, so the carpet seemed safer. She pulled her phone from her dressing gown pocket and went to call her aunt back. She was about to press dial when she changed her mind and sent a text instead.

> Hey N. I am sorry about yesterday. All of it. I was a mess, and you were only trying to be kind. And to CELEBRATE! Hopefully see you soon? I'm so proud of you my friend, xxx

Hopefully this would repair things with Nikita, she thought, as she lay flat in the quad of sunlight on the carpet and pulled up her aunt's number. This time, they were both a little more coherent, Clara agreeing to head up to north London to collect the mystery letter, and to discuss 'arrangements'. The vulnerability in her aunt's voice now seemed to have gone, replaced with the more familiar briskness that Clara associated with her. She was more than happy to take the trip up, now convinced in the cold light of day that this letter was going to be a note written years ago – perhaps it would be something cute like her dad wishing her luck with her exams, or to do with taking care of her mum. If Auntie Liz had had it for so long, then it would surely not be relevant any more.

It took most of Clara's concentration to get herself together and up to Kilburn for 10.30, when they had arranged to meet. While she was in the shower, she rehearsed how she was going to tell Simon about her dad, but she was still rinsing her hair when he put his head round the door and told her he was heading out for an early meeting. Making toast, having a proper shower, trying to find her keys: all of these tasks seemed to require the utmost attention, perhaps because of her mild hangover or perhaps because she was focusing intently on life's mundanities to try and stop the strangeness of the day from creeping any closer. Either way, with the house to herself she got ready with a slow deliberateness that suggested she was being marked by an unseen expert. *She seems to have it all under control.* Clara swung her bag over her shoulder, checked that her favourite podcast had downloaded, and headed out to the bus stop.

Her aunt's house was on the sort of ordinary red-brick road that must have been deeply unfashionable when she moved there in the late nineties, but was now dotted with the tell-tale charcoal grey painted front doors, wide white plantation blinds and peeking monsteras within that suggested an area well and truly gentrified. Clara hadn't been here since she was a teenager, and she remembered Auntie Liz's house as faintly hippyish rather than part of this newly chic neighbourhood.

Liz had been drinking herbal teas since you needed to go to a health shop to buy them, was a vegetarian a good decade before it became stylish and had long believed in a homeopathic remedy for everything. None of these things seemed to make her markedly more relaxed or healthy than any other women Clara had known her age. But her kitchen, full of Kilner jars, herbs propagating on windowsills and an almost admirable amount of ignored cat hair had seemed positively exotic to fifteen-year-old Clara, who was at that point only used to the chilly grey quartz surfaces of the Teflon-pristine kitchen of what had until recently been her family home.

Clara had last visited the house with her dad, when Liz had insisted that they come round to dinner together to celebrate his birthday, not long after he and her mum had separated. Smiles were forced and dinner was heavily garnished. Liz made a vegetarian lasagne thick with slightly undercooked slipper-soles of aubergine, clearly hoping to hide any flaws with an extra flourish of parmesan, fresh from a visibly rusting grater. Halfway through dinner Clara realised that she had been brought along by Ben as a benign human shield, someone with whom to try and deflect Liz's less than subtle interrogation about 'how he *really* was', 'when he was planning to *get back out there*', and 'what *Madam* was doing with herself these days'. The trouble was, Clara had done a terrible job – largely because she too wanted to know the answer to many of Liz's questions. She saw the sadness in her dad's face when he got out of the car and walked up to his old front door to collect her for their weekends together. She saw his new flat, with its solitary peace lily on the bookcase, and wondered if he felt as lonely as he sometimes looked. And she was itching to know if he was indeed getting back out there. But she could barely articulate these questions to herself, let alone ask him.

So as she walked up the black-and-white tile squares of Auntie Liz's front path that morning, the idea that she would not sit around a dinner table with her dad ever again seemed nonsensical. It was only as she pressed the buzzer and heard the scrape of a wooden kitchen chair on chipped floor tiles that she began to realise that it really might be true.

Liz opened the door, her hair as long and frizzy as Clara had remembered, but her eyes now red-rimmed from either sleeplessness or tears. She extended her arms to give Clara a hug, but as Clara leaned in, the hug never quite materialised. Instead, Liz gripped the sides of her upper arms so their upper chests and cheeks brushed each other, keeping her niece at a slight distance. To a passer-by it might have looked

43

like an embrace, but to Clara, who was suddenly feeling less than sure about this visit, it was nothing like the warmth that she needed.

'Clara my dear, it's so good of you to come,' said Liz, as she extended her arms, now holding Clara back from her so she could look her up and down. 'My god you look like Ben,' she muttered. She was of course right; Clara did indeed have Ben's sandy colouring, fair hair and freckles.

'That's OK,' replied Clara, suddenly the eager-to-please teenager she had been when she was last at this house.

'Come in, come in,' said Liz, ushering her in and directing her into the kitchen. 'Can I get you a tea?'

'Oh, I'd love one,' said Clara, thinking that she'd actually rather have a coffee.

'I've got nettle, fennel and some sort of gingery manuka thing,' said Liz, opening a cupboard drawer as Clara's heart sank. No caffeine at all in this house then.

Liz pulled out a chair for Clara, who sat down at the table only to feel her stomach lurch as she caught sight of the manila envelope on the table, her name in her dad's scrawl across the front. She pretended not to see the chair that Liz had readied for her and sat at the other end of the table from it, too scared to even acknowledge its existence, while Liz poured hot water over two herbal teabags into two thick-rimmed ceramic mugs and brought them to the table.

'There,' she said, placing a mug in front of Clara. 'A nice cup of tea makes everything a bit better, doesn't it?'

*This isn't the sort of tea they're usually talking about*, thought Clara with a pale smile.

'So, here's the letter,' said Liz, sliding it across the kitchen table, catching a smear of jam and a few toast crumbs as it made its journey. 'I'm sure you don't want to read it now.'

Clara realised that she was not being invited to. Liz carried on talking.

'So much admin, and it all seems to have fallen on my shoulders! As I'm sure your mum's told you, your dad had left her as his next of kin on some of the ID in his wallet, and that's what the ambulance crew found ... '

Clara had not yet considered that strangers had had to go through her father's wallet to work out who he was. The thought made her shiver. She stared down at the table, blinking fast.

' ... but I had a chat with her yesterday and I've taken over now. Several years ago, Ben asked me to arrange a cremation for him should the situation arise, and your mother says that I should go ahead with that. So if it's OK with you I'll get cracking with things. I have no idea how these things work, but he did leave me a letter saying it's what he wanted. To this day I'm still not sure what prompted it – he never said he was ill. More a fit of melancholy I suppose – it hit him hard when your mum wanted him out, didn't it? Anyway, look at me, I'm babbling like a brook with the upset of it all. What I'm trying to say is that when he gave me that letter with his wishes, he also gave me this one for you ... ' The briskness faltered again, and she brushed her frizzy hair away from her face. Or was it a tear, wondered Clara.

'How long ago did he give them to you?' Clara asked.

'Oh, um, it's hard to remember. It was a while after the divorce, maybe even five years. So why he still had his next of kin in a muddle is anybody's guess, the daft bugger. A good five years ago, I'd say.'

'Oh, so it might be irrelevant now? Like, "good luck in your exams" or something?'

'It might be. I really don't know. He did ask me every once in a while if I still had it kept safe though. All I know is that he didn't want you reading it before he was gone. There were years when we weren't close, so I sort of forgot about it.'

'Oh, oh I see. I didn't know that.'

'There's no reason why you would, darling. It was a while before you came along.'

Clara stared at the letter, unsure what to do with this new information.

'He was a very private man,' she ventured.

'Yes, he was. And you know what men are like!' Liz's forefinger was picking at the skin around her thumbnail as she grinned at Clara, the smile a little too wide.

Clara was uncomfortable with her aunt talking like this, but it was hard to disagree that her dad had been the sort of man who thought being emotional was being indulgent. It was, however, a rule he had applied to himself rather than her. So she smiled at her aunt and reached for her bag, which was hanging on the back of her chair.

'Well, I suppose I had better get going. Thank you so much for updating me about the cremation and stuff. Please let me know if there is anything else you need me to do. But I'll head home now; I have taken up enough of your time already!' She tried to sound nonchalant as she picked the envelope up off the table and slid it into her bag.

'Alrighty then, lovely girl.'

'And thank you for letting me know about the letter.'

'Oh, not at all, I'm just glad I managed to keep it safe all this time!' Her forefinger dug deeper into her thumb.

Clara walked to the front door, and Liz rubbed her on the back gently.

'You take care of yourself,' she said as she opened the door. 'We'll be in touch soon.'

'Yes,' said Clara. 'And thank you again, Auntie Liz.' She

waved awkwardly, unsure if to lean in for another hug. But Liz's hands were firmly on her hips, so Clara once again understood that an invitation for intimacy was not being extended. She turned and walked back down the tiled path, gripping her bag and its contents to her side.

# Chapter 5

Clara turned onto the pavement the way she had come, and realised within a few steps that there was nowhere she needed to be. She just wanted to find somewhere quiet to sit and read the letter, so she headed down to West Hampstead, where her dad had taken her for ice cream once after Sunday lunch with Liz.

She was glad to leave Kilburn and its newfound gentrification behind. Traffic still roared down the High Road towards Maida Vale and Edgware Road, but the Irish pubs of her teenage years had all gone. She crossed the main road at the lights, left the traffic behind her and wound her way towards West End Lane. To her surprise, the old-fashioned little cafe was still there, so she wandered in, smiled at the proprietor, ordered a coffee and took a seat facing the hustle and bustle of the road outside.

She sat, staring into space, wondering what to make of her aunt's paper-thin cheeriness. She stroked her name on the front of the envelope, brushed the crumbs and a smear of butter off it, then picked at the seal, her foot jiggling against the table leg as she waited for her coffee. When it had arrived – in a very dated bistro-style glass on a white ceramic saucer – she took the end of her teaspoon to the letter and opened it. She spread the clean white sheet of A4 out on the table in front of her, thinking about how the last hands who had touched it had been her father's. She stroked the page, pressing her fingers into the indentations that the ballpoint pen had made. Seeing those familiar loops and curls took her back to opening birthday cards, seeing notes left on the kitchen counter for her and, more recently, shopping lists and bits and pieces of admin pinned to the fridge door in his new apartment with a variety of cheerful coloured magnets. The whole letter looked very neat, as if it had taken a couple of attempts to get quite right, but even touching it, before she read a word, Clara felt as if she could reach through time and hear her father.

*My sweet Clara,*

    *Whenever and wherever you are reading this letter, I do hope that you know I love you. And I hope that you are well, and are happy, and that you know that wherever I am, I am already missing you. As such, I have asked Auntie Liz to only give this letter to you in the event of my death, so first of all I would like to tell you that I am terribly proud of you, and how much faith I have in you. You have brought immeasurable joy into my life, more than you could ever imagine.*

    *But there are some other matters I must tell you about, things that have not been appropriate before now. Some things about me, and my life before I was lucky enough to have you, that we have never discussed. And while I have not felt ready to talk to you about them up until now, I do not think it is fair that you never know about them.*

    *We never talked about it, but I think you are already aware that before I met your mother I had a previous marriage. My first wife was a lady called Stéphanie. But what you don't know is that we had a daughter. Her name is Marguerite, or Maggie. She was born in 1984, and she is your sister. She is a wonderful woman, as are you. But we are, to my huge regret, currently estranged.*

*I have never discussed her with you – not because I didn't want to, but because she left the UK a few years ago and elected not to keep in touch with me. This is – as I hope you can imagine – a great source of pain to me, but I have tried to respect her desire to start a new life. To the best of my knowledge she now lives in Northern Norway, up in the Arctic, where she has very limited means of being in touch. I can only assume that this is the truth, although perhaps this inaccessibility has been exaggerated on her part in order to keep my attempts at contact to a minimum.*

*But now, assuming that you are reading this as a consequence of my death, and in the absence of her feeling obliged to have any further contact with me, I feel that it is only fair that you know about your sister. In fact, I would very much like you to meet her. I am sure that you would get along very well, and I am equally sure that if anyone can impress upon her how much I love and miss her, then it is you, sweet Clara.*

*As such, I have named you and Maggie the two primary beneficiaries of my will. There are a few others I have named – I have of course put aside some bits from our childhood for your Auntie Liz, and made provision for a couple of charity donations. But my home, and any remaining savings, are for you and Marguerite to share.*

*In addition to this, I have a folder of photographs, documents and so on which rightfully belong with Maggie now. And I would be hugely grateful if you could return them to her. They are her history, and she deserves at least to have the chance to own them, even if it is not a chance she leaps at. This, and all of the other details regarding my will, are with my lawyer, Bill Tandy, at the below address. (You have met him, at my fiftieth birthday party – he is a dear friend from my Bristol childhood days, and he was the one you thought was called Mandy!)*

*The one address I am not sure of is Maggie's. I have put the* details that I do have below. I know that the area is remote, and that mail there is erratic as the journey there is not straightforward. But if you manage to make contact and return what is hers, I would be filled with eternal gratitude. And in leaving you these details, I am holding out the hope that perhaps someday, even if not in my lifetime, you young women will meet and find comfort in each other. You are the two real successes of my life, and that you may yet spend time together is my greatest hope.

My darling Clara, as I write this it seems clear to me that you are not as happy as you have it in you to be. Regardless of whether I am still here to see it, please keep trying, aim higher – for yourself and no one else – and know that you have it in you to truly shine, and far brighter than you believe. You owe no one your happiness, but you must also know that that happiness is your responsibility to seek out.

Thank you, my sweet daughter, for all of the love and kindness you have shown me over our time together. I cherish the memories of every trip we have taken, and every meal we have shared. Please think of me when you stare at the sea on the bad days and when you look up at the stars on the good days. And here's hoping that one day you will find a place that makes you happy somewhere between the two.

With all love, Dad xxx

Bill Tandy

Tandy, Nitt & Co

9 Wilbury Mews

SW18 4DP

Marguerite (Maggie) Seymour (I am not 100 per cent sure that she has kept my name)

Bakkegata

Måsholmen

8383 0113

Norway

Clara looked down at her hands, resting on top of the piece of paper, flat on the table. They were still, but her heart was hammering and her breathing was shallow. She had a sister. She had *always* had a sister. But to find out, she had had to lose her father.

# Chapter 6

Clara left the cafe with no idea where she was heading, but for the second time in two days she felt an unusual compulsion to walk. She set off along West End Lane, following the road as it wound uphill, curving around the red-brick houses and shops. She didn't really know where the road led, but she was aiming for the scrap of green she had spotted higher up the hill. She wasn't sure what it was, or even if it was public, but she was aiming for it. Just a bit of green space. Somewhere to pace, to breathe, to think, away from all the cars, the buggies, the endless rushing. A couple of minutes later she reached it: Hampstead Cemetery. She turned off the main road and towards the grassy calm, leaving the roar of traffic and hustle of the pavement behind her, when she saw to her relief that it was a larger space than she had imagined.

The pedestrianised path led her to a dramatic entrance: an ornate arch with a huge grey stone spire supported on either side by a forbidding gothic style chapel. The buildings were dark, cold and damp-looking in comparison to the cheery red brick of the surrounding roads. But once Clara had passed underneath the arch, the path widened and the cemetery spread out before her. The atmosphere changed the minute she reached the cemetery proper.

It wasn't just the quiet she sensed, but that distinct sense of stillness that a graveyard manifests within its boundaries. Like a child up after bedtime, tiptoeing into an adult space, Clara instinctively understood that to be allowed here, she had to play her part, to be quiet, respectful. And that suited her fine. Her pace quickened, finding a rhythm, but her breath slowed as her adrenaline started to subside, working its way from her hammering heartbeat and jittery stomach to her toes and fingertips. She held a hand out in front of her, wiggling her fingers a little. Her legs felt like jelly; it was only keeping them moving that reassured her that they were still there.

*Am I actually alive? Am I me? Or have I imagined the last twenty-four hours?*

She clenched and released her fist. Yes, she could definitely feel the blood in her veins as it pumped back down through her hand. This must be real. She was here. It was happening.

She carried on walking, down paths that wove their way through endless ancient headstones. Most were well over a hundred years old, mossy and forbidding in their Victorian splendour. Huge angels looked down from pedestals, an entire upright organ stood carved over the details of one long-dead inhabitant, the occasional grey carved dog or cat watched over almost illegible slabs. Many graves were almost hidden by the grass sprouting up around them, and at the further edges of the green Clara spotted clusters of spring's first bluebells. The mood shifted slightly as she reached more recent, more modern shapes, with bouquets beside them which seemed to have been left in the last month or so. But the same consistent calmness held as Clara passed between them, her mind churning with every step.

She had been ready for some sort of 'I'll miss you' note from her dad. Perhaps something thoughtful to read at her wedding, or even to any future grandchildren. She had read about families where an ill parent bought Christmas presents for years in advance for their young offspring, and had half consoled herself with something like that. An adorably out-of-date good luck note for some exams, a bit of career advice she'd never take. But she hadn't been prepared for a revelation like this.

Clara turned away from the wider paths and towards the edges of the cemetery where the spring grass was wilder, making its way from the gravestones and edging over the path to scratch at her ankles. She loved the increasing sense of wildness in the middle of the city. She rummaged in her bag for her phone, her instinct being to take a photo of this wilderness and post it with some sort of 'Wherever can I be?' caption.

First, she checked that Simon had not been trying to get hold of her, then she fiddled around with her phone camera, trying to get a shot of the sunlight peeking around a particularly lichen-splattered gravestone. She spotted a small snail clinging to a leaf next to it and took a hasty snap of that too, making note to maybe try and draw it later. Crouched in the stillness of the cemetery she felt momentarily safe from the intrusions of the outside world. No one knew where she was, no one at all. But just as she was going to slide her phone into her back pocket, she felt the ping of a breaking news alert.

The resignation of a minor minister prompted her to unlock the screen again, and before she knew it she was checking her email, making sure that Julia was ok with her absence, then, in the familiar autopilot mode that characterised so much of her day, she did a loop of the usual social media, gossip and news sites, the sticky methadone of the internet slyly distracting her from the emotional shrapnel that the last twenty-four hours had flung at her.

What was she looking for? Something diverting? Something uplifting? Something dramatic? She no longer remembered, when The Scroll began. Her thumb barely seemed to know it was moving, as tiny darts of anxiety, envy, curiosity gently needled her. The quiet of the graveyard faded away as the mental buzz grew. She could have been anywhere, but wherever she was she'd rather be responding to the screen than sitting in the company of her own emotions. A photograph of two sisters spending 'one of our special days together' yanked her back to the present.

For years Clara had yearned for a sibling. Over endless, dreary summer holidays while her dad had worked long hours and her mum had spent her days 'making things happen' at the local tennis club. During lonely Sunday evenings watching costume dramas while her parents bickered in the background. And more recently, when she had moved further into London after years spent in the suburbs. Surely an older sibling would have known where to get the best bao, how to find the cheapest flat, what to take to get across the city fastest. And a sister! Someone to stand before and see a shared childhood reflected back at her.

But she had never had these things. She had texted her mates on Sunday evenings, posted her freckles on Instagram (#frecklesfordays) to compare and be compared by others, and she had never seen a shared childhood reflected back at her. The closest she had ever had to a shared childhood was Simon, who had become her boyfriend while she was still a teenager, patiently waited for her while she was at university and had the flat ready for her by the time she graduated. She had seen other friends making their way in careers, finding the London that felt most *them*, or even returning to their home towns, now with renewed vigour after having seen more of the world. Clara had stepped straight into a sort of ready-made wifedom, a situation she was both supposed to be grateful for and seemed to have had very little active choice in.

Now, a door had been opened and a world of sisterly joy was flooding her imagination. The two of them trying on each other's clothes before an evening out, the two of them having cocktails, leaning in to each other across a small circular table. The two of them in pyjamas with hot chocolate, wearing matching fluffy slippers. Discussing men, discussing bodies, discussing confidences that she had so long felt uncomfortable sharing with others. 'One of our special days together.'

Clara started to get cramp, having forgotten where she was, crouched for so long in the same position. It was futile trying to pretend to herself that she was still taking photos, gathering inspiration for her illustrations. She stood up, shook out her legs and got walking, as she let her thumb have 'one final swipe', only to stumble immediately, her toe catching a raised piece of pavement distorted by the tree roots beneath. She reached out as she tripped, hurling her phone a few feet in front of her before righting herself then bending to pick it up. The abrupt break in the rhythm of her feet and her breath left her momentarily dazed. As she stood there, pausing to catch her breath, she realised that she might never share any of these imagined scenarios with a sister. Because this woman, Maggie, seemed to want nothing to do with her. Or at least her father.

'Excuse me dear,' said a quiet voice behind her. She turned, and saw a small, white-haired woman in a neat coat with a stiff patent leather handbag clamped to her side. 'May I get by?'

'I'm so sorry,' replied Clara. 'I was somewhere else.' It was true, and she hadn't realised how much the path had narrowed, leaving the woman no way to pass her without wading through the long grass and over the graves. Clara stepped aside to let her pass, and as she waited, she felt the tiredness wallop her like an incoming wave. The late night, the whisky, all this new information. Suddenly it rushed over her, leaving her reeling as the small, quiet women ahead turned off the path and went to kneel quietly at a graveside.

Clara's chest started to heave. She was taking in great gulps of air, swallowing sobs down hard. Why had this hit her now, so far from home? She walked along the edge of the cemetery – slowly now, trying to regulate her pace and her breath – until she came to a small bench beneath a magnolia tree, where she plonked herself down, shoulders slumped, and at last began to cry.

The strange thing about crying alone is that there is no one to explain yourself to. If your voice cracks while speaking in public, what you were saying will indicate to your audience what has prompted your tears. Eyes dabbed discreetly in the dark of the cinema are a shared acknowledgement that the film has succeeded in moving you. But to weep openly in public with no one to either listen or demand an explanation is a reminder both that no one cares, but that also ... no one *cares*. Clara only stayed there sobbing for a few minutes, but it used her whole body: her shoulders rising and falling, her throat aching and her nose streaming. Here, where no one was asking her why, she embraced the fact that there was no simple answer, and let herself go.

A few minutes later the gulpy sobs were slowly giving way to little whimpers as Clara's breath juddered and her shoulders started to steady themselves. The sun had reached over the trees around the cemetery and her back was dappled with its warmth as it crept through the large, still-tight buds of the magnolia, stiff cream candles ready to explode. She held her dad's letter in her hands and sighed. He had left her a lot to do. Why so much? Why hadn't he told her more when he was alive, and he could have been some help to her? Why had he felt the need to keep any of this secret at all? The only thing that seemed to quell the waves of sadness was a sharp fury that she had been left like this: so tired, so alone, so let down. But as her shoulders stilled and the fury seemed to calcify a little inside, she saw that it was time to get on with it. She reached into her bag, took out her mobile and called the solicitor whose number her dad had put at the bottom of his letter. A couple of minutes later she had made an appointment for the following morning.

Next, she pulled up her mother's number and waited for the dial tone. The sun was even warmer on her back now and her whole body better able to deal with these first few steps as she sat here alone, in a neutral space, with only some passing wildlife as witnesses to this maelstrom.

'Clara darling ... '

'Hi Mum.'

'So how are you?'

'Um, OK, I guess.'

'Good ... good. Have you been to—'

'Yeah, I heard from Auntie Liz and I went to visit her this morning.' Were the contents of her dad's letter as much of a mystery to her mum as they had been to her?

'Oh!' Hmm. Perhaps.

'There didn't seem to be much point in hanging around, and she was quite insistent ... '

'Yes I remember, she can be very clear about her intentions, can't she?' Her mother's voice was wary.

'Yeah, she can. But this time with good reason.'

'What do you mean?'

'Well, she had important information for me. She gave me a letter from Dad.'

'Oh, darling.'

Her mother's voice was now unmistakably worried. Clara felt a familiar irritation. She had been here before: her mother somehow trying to 'protect' her from the one person she wished she could see more of, share more with, be closer to: her dad. Well, now he was gone and she couldn't do it any more.

'Why didn't you tell me?' Clara asked, feeling the smouldering irritation spark.

'Tell you what, darling?' Still, that wariness. Oh, give me a break, she thought.

'You know.'

'Clara, where your father is concerned I most certainly do not.'

'Maggie.'

Silence.

'Yeah, Maggie,' Clara repeated. 'My sister. The sister you neglected to tell me about these last twenty years or so.'

'Now Clara, that is hardly—'

'Hardly WHAT?' The embers had caught. So she *had* known all along. And she had chosen not to tell her. Every day, every month, every year. She had let Clara carry on, never knowing about her sister.

'Har—'

'Go on, what possible excuse can you have for never telling me that I had a sister?'

'Clara.' Her mother's voice was sharp now. She had caught up. 'This is hardly fair. It never was.'

'Fair to who?'

'To me, well, and you. Both of us.'

'Oh, sure, it must have been agony.'

'Clara, this was your father's doing.'

'Don't blame him just because he's not here any more to explain things. Can you even hear yourself?' Clara's voice caught in her throat as she stated his absence out loud for the first time.

'I'm not blaming him ... '

'Mum, you just *did*.'

'WAIT.' Shouting now. She knows she's in the wrong, thought Clara. She said nothing. 'Clara, I am not trying to *blame* your father, I'm just trying to explain my position. The position I've been in.'

'I really don't get what can have been so complicated about it.'

'Trust me, I believed it was for the best.'

'Did you? So you let me blunder on through life not knowing about my own sister because it was for the best?'

'If you would just let me finish ... '

Clara waited.

'Thank you. Decisions were made about this Maggie which I had nothing to do with – and frankly nor should I have.'

'*This Maggie*?' Clara seethed.

'This Maggie *situation*,' corrected her mother. 'Your father had to make his own choices; she was never *my* daughter.'

'No, but I was!'

'Clara, what could I have told a baby? That she had a sister somewhere? Somewhere that I was not privy to? And once your dad and I were separated it was not my place.'

'I don't get it Mum, wasn't it your place to tell *me*? Didn't you think *I* would want to know.'

'Well, hindsight is all very well once you're there, but at the time—'

'You have still had over a decade to tell me.'

'I can see that. But it was not so much a decision as—'

'As what?' Clara could feel her heart hammering against her chest. The sun was bright overhead now and starting to make her skull feel too tight. She reached for her water bottle. Empty. Her breathing was shallow as she tried to fathom what her mother might say next.

'It was less a decision than, well, than an absence of one. There just never seemed to be a good day to talk to you about it. To betray those confidences. I had already overstepped the mark—'

'So you didn't bother.'

'Again. I really would ask you to respect the fact that it has not been easy for me either. I did what I could—'

'Yeah. I'm sure it's been dreadful knowing more about my family, my *actual life*, than I do.'

'Clara. Sometimes things are better left unsaid.'

'Which suits you just fine, doesn't it?'

'If you will just let me speak.'

'Oh, *now* you want to speak!' She knew she was making things worse, that she was stoking an argument that she didn't even really want to be in, but she couldn't stop.

'Perhaps this is best discussed another time. It is far more complicated that you seem to think. It's very clear that your emotions are running high, and I completely understand that.'

'No! Just tell me!'

'Clara, perhaps call Mr Tandy and we can discuss things after that. Would you like me to come with you to see him?'

'No, it's fine. I've made the appointment already. I'll go by myself. After all, it's increasingly obvious that *by myself* is exactly what I've been all along anyway.'

And with that, she ended the call.

# Chapter 7

Clara had never visited a lawyer before, and the prospect had instinctively made her reach for work clothes: a dark dress, flats instead of trainers, and even a pair of tights for the March chill. Clean hair, which she had tied back into a neat ponytail and brushed through at the nape of her neck. She'd had a cup of coffee and a slice of toast at home, and had bought herself a green juice on the way to her train. None of it was quite quelling the nagging anxiety she had felt for forty-eight hours now. Like a wave that had splashed over the side of a boat and continued to slosh around the hull unbidden, her disquiet continued to lurch in the pit of her stomach.

As the train chugged towards Central London, Clara reached for her phone to text her dad for reassurance. It was only once the screen lit up that she remembered it was the very fact he had gone that had prompted this meeting. She let the phone drop, ran a hand over her hair, smoothing imperceptible frizz, and bit her bottom lip.

The lawyer's offices were neither as chic nor as intimidating as she had imagined. No deep leather sofas. No smug receptionists. No language she couldn't keep up with. It was a modern office block just off Shepherd's Bush Green, where she was buzzed into the second floor then welcomed by a softly spoken middle-aged lady wearing bright spectacle frames and a surprisingly cool pair of trainers. Clara waited, nursing an ashy-tasting Nespresso, in an unprepossessing hallway on a bog-standard office chair while absent-mindedly staring out of the window. A couple of minutes later, a crinkly eyed man with a smooth, babyish face popped his head around the door and smiled.

'Clara?'

'Yes.'

'Lovely to meet you again. Has Audrey got you everything you need? Come on in.'

Clara mumbled about how happy she was to have a coffee and followed him into his office. It was more of the same sort of basic office design, but with a huge photograph of Clevedon Pier on one wall. Mr Tandy showed her to a seat before settling behind his desk and fiddling with his mouse a bit. Once he seemed content with what he had brought up on his screen, he looked up to smile at her. His face really was unnervingly smooth for someone at least two decades older than her.

'First of all, let me say how sorry I was to hear of your father's passing.'

Clara nodded and looked into her lap. Was she supposed to look sad, to share her emotions with this stranger, or to keep up the sense of a brisk business meeting in full swing?

'He was a lovely chap, a long-term client of mine, and some-one whose advice I valued as much as he did mine. He is a great loss.'

'Yes,' she said quietly.

'Now then, with this in mind, to business.'

Clara had no idea what 'business' was at hand, but she smiled in what she hoped looked like a helpful way.

'I understand that there was a little bit of a muddle regarding next of kin, which must have been uncomfortable for your poor mother, but that your Aunt Elizabeth is on top of things regarding a memorial service now?'

'Yes, so she tells me.'

'And as far as the administrative side of things goes, I am taking care of that. She and I were your father's named executors, with me looking after the paperwork, so I will be dealing with things such as the sale of his property, and putting funds aside for those named in the will.'

'Right.' It had never really occurred to Clara that her dad might have had any money. He never really had fancy things or went to chic restaurants – much to her mother's frustration during her childhood. As far as she knew, the only time he really went abroad was with her.

'And I hope that you will be pleased to know that you are one of the beneficiaries of the will.'

'Oh, OK. Thank you.'

'And besides the will itself, I understand that your father left a letter for you with your Aunt Elizabeth?'

'Yes, she gave it to me yesterday.'

'Splendid. So you have had a chance to read that letter?'

'Yes, I have.'

'Excellent. Your father was anxious that you should receive the news about your sister while in the presence of a family member, rather than from me. So you do understand that it is you and your sister, Marguerite, who are the two main beneficiaries of the will?'

'I see.'

65

'As I understand it, there is still some question over the best contact details for Marguerite.'

'Yes, I don't know if the details he gave me are up to date.'

'I understand. Nevertheless, there was no small anxiety about your aunt losing the letter with the details, so I have had a spare copy here with me.'

Clara smiled. Classic Dad.

'Would you like that second copy for your records?'

She went to say *no thank you*, but stopped herself at the last minute. The thought of another piece of paper in her father's handwriting, something else he had touched, taken time over, was too much to resist.

'Yes, please,' she said, trying to sound professional rather than like a silly grieving daughter who just wanted to see more of her dad's writing.

'No problem. All the material is with Audrey on the front desk. On to the matter of Marguerite. Your father told me that he was planning to leave it to you to get in touch with ... ' his eyes flicked back to his screen to double check ' ... your sister. Is that something that you are happy to undertake?'

'Yes, well, I think so. He said I had to return something to her?'

'Yes, I have that here. Well, with Audrey.'

'Do you know what it is? Is it, like, a precious artefact or something?'

She had never used the word 'artefact' before, and felt sure that Mr Tandy could tell. Her facade was slipping. But he smiled reassuringly.

'Oh no, it's nothing like that. I think it's documentation, mostly: her birth certificate, old photographs, a bit of what I suppose we'd call memorabilia. Nothing heavy or awkward. No heirloom cello or anything like that.'

'OK. Phew, I guess.'

'We can give you those bits when you leave today, if that suits you. Or we can hold them here if you think you might want a little bit longer to, well, to find Marguerite.'

Clara had a sudden image of her dad tapping into an old iPhone, the font enormous, his fingers moving at a pace somewhere between slow and disinterested.

'I'll take them today,' she said. 'How hard can it be to find someone? She's probably on Facebook.'

As she heard her voice say this out loud, Clara marvelled at how she had not thought of this last night. Now though, her voice sounded clear and confident. Mr Tandy however, looked a little apprehensive.

'OK, I shall leave it to you. But if you need my assistance at any point, I am happy to try to help.'

'I am sure it will be fine. It might even be fun!'

'Well, yes. I feel it is part of my professional responsibility to gently warn you that it might also be costly. As such, your father authorised me to pay you an advance on your inheritance, should you need expenses.'

'It doesn't cost much to send someone a Facebook message.' A rush of warm excitement was soaring through Clara at the thought that she could be chatting to her sister within a couple of hours. That secret door to a whole new relationship, gently being nudged open.

'There is also the return of the documents, Clara.'

'Of course. But, it's not anything heavy though, you said?'

'Clara. I think your father was rather hoping you would return them in person.'

'Oh, oh I see.'

Clara had really not understood this. Her dad had wanted her to go to meet Maggie.

'Yes, so if you need funds for flights, accommodation or any other expenses, you are to let me know, as these costs will be coming from the estate, prior to and separate from your inheritance.'

The thought of her dad planning all of this made Clara's heart feel full. A balloon was being filled in her chest.

'This is a lot to take in.'

'I can imagine, especially after yesterday's news.' Clara could see rain starting to fall outside of the window behind Mr Tandy's head. 'What I suggest is that you take a some time to get in touch with Marguerite—'

'Maggie.'

'Yes, OK. Maggie. Take some time, get in touch, and then drop me a line when you are ready to plan your trip.' He pushed a business card across the desk towards her. 'Should I be unavailable, Audrey will be fully apprised of the situation and be able to help you out with funds. And as I said, do let us know if you need any further assistance getting in touch with Marguer— Maggie.'

'I will do.'

'And when you have a chance, let me know how you have got on. If you have made touch, met her and so on? She is of course the other beneficiary – but your father was always very clear that it wasn't me who should break the news to her in the event of his death.'

'Yes, and thank you.'

Mr Tandy walked Clara to the door and showed her out. At reception, she smiled at Audrey, who was standing at her desk, smiling widely.

'It was a pleasure to meet you, Clara,' she said. Her bright, Perspex earrings danced as she looked up.

'Thank you – and you.'

'I understand you'll be taking some documents home with you today?'

'Yes, if that's OK.'

'Of course, they are for you. Now then, do you need a separate bag, or ... I might have some plastic carriers in a drawer somewhere?'

'Don't worry, I can just take them in this.' Clara opened her large tote bag. Normally it would be rammed with paperwork for the office, or her Kindle, or even a magazine. But today it had sagged limply under her arm all the way to Shepherd's Bush.

'Wonderful!' Audrey really did seem to have an extraordinary level of job satisfaction for someone who must deal so often with the recently bereaved. 'You clever thing.'

Clara leaned over, squashy leather bag opening towards Audrey, who popped some manila envelopes inside and grinned again. Clara smiled back, not wanting to let her down. But her face sagged as she headed through the fire doors and down the echoey staircase to the main entrance. She had never imagined that dealing with a death would involve so much forced politeness. It was like chewing dried biscuits when all you really wanted to do was sip a cold Coke and forget about it. Or at least lose yourself in the sting of a shot of vodka. She longed for home. Once again, she found herself walking there.

# Chapter 8

As Clara turned her key in the door, she pushed away the sense of relief at having the place to herself, a sense she knew wasn't really healthy to feel each and every time she hung her coat on the rack. She paid so much less rent than Simon, she had significantly less say in how the flat was run, and she hadn't even chosen the property – all of which meant she rarely felt a sense of belonging there unless she was alone. There was always a small voice in the back of her mind reminding her that she was lucky to be there, that she had a lot more stability than some of her other graduate friends who were still slumming it in huge house shares or living with parents outside of London. And yet. Increasingly that had stopped feeling like compensation enough. She just hadn't found the space to allow that damp, cloudy emotion somewhere in the pit of her stomach to become words. She had tried with Nikita a few times. She had even written emails in the drafts section of her phone. Most recently, she had hoped that some way of starting the conversation would present itself on that last Sunday lunch she had spent with her dad. But rather than facing the worries that gnawed deep at the wordless parts of her, she had enjoyed an afternoon not thinking about them instead.

Now, as she scanned the few small rooms of their flat that afternoon, she couldn't help but wish there was someone there to ask her how the meeting had gone, to offer her a cup of tea, or at least to have put her whisky glass from the night before beside the kitchen sink. Just not the person she shared it with. Still, at least she now had a few undisturbed hours to begin her exciting sister-mission.

She slung her bag off her shoulder, dumped it by the coffee table, and gave the cushions a brief slap where she had been sitting the night before while Simon worked late. Somehow, they hadn't seen each other face to face for nearly two days now, so she was still nursing her news, almost protectively. For once, she was the one that something important, something dramatic, was happening to. Yes, it had turned all of the certainties she thought she had inside out, and no, she had no idea how she was going to handle any of it, but for once she was playing the lead in the story of her life, instead of being swept along by his confidence, his decisions, his somehow bigger and bolder life.

She went next door, made the bed, took off and hung up her dress, then shoved on a pair of trackies and a T-shirt. She looked around the kitchen, realised she still hadn't done the grocery shopping she had been promising herself she would all week, and put the kettle on instead. For a second, the memory of the last time they had run out of almond milk flashed across her mind. Simon's face, an inch from hers, spittle hitting her upper lip, but her not daring to swipe it away for fear of provoking him more. She had tried, but the shop had been out it, she had wanted to explain. She wanted to get it, but she had calculated that not getting home in time to get dinner on would be worse. She had known how hungry he'd be after training, she really had done her best. But she had also known that to defend herself would only make things worse. This time, a second thought overwhelmed that memory. She had a secret now, a potential way out. A reasonable excuse to get away for a bit.

Minutes later, less than twelve hours after she had left it – but with her world feeling very different – she was curled up on the sofa again. Her laptop was back on one armrest, phone on the table in front of her and, she realised as she unravelled and shook out her ponytail, it was time to reach for her chance to change things.

But first she decided to take a quick look at that second copy of the letter from her dad.

Reaching forward, she rammed a hand into the depths of her handbag and pulled out the A4 manila envelope that Audrey the Cheerful had popped in there earlier. In the bottom-right-hand corner there was a small printer label, with her surname, her father's initial, and what looked like a reference number. In the centre of the envelope was her name, handwritten in pencil. She smoothed its surface with two flat palms across her knees. She felt bumps beneath the paper: clearly there was more in there than Mr Tandy had told her.

She slid off the sofa and sat cross-legged at the coffee table, moved a scented candle to one side and gently shook the contents of the envelope out onto the cheap wooden tabletop. There was no letter from her father here. She scrabbled in her bag for the other envelope, saw that it had a similar label system on it, and pulled out a second version of her dad's letter. Nothing else. She put it carefully behind her on the sofa and returned to the tabletop. None of this was for her.

She had opened Maggie's envelope.

Documents in paper sizes she had never seen before, whisper thin and almost transparent, were mixed in with old photographs and even a small album from what looked like a print shop. Cellophane pockets held images of people she didn't recognise. An old beer mat with a French brand on it tumbled out from beneath the pages of a French passport. Notes written on the back of small paper napkins from Parisian bars, a small plastic wrist band from what looked like a hospital admission. A swatch of fabric that looked like it might have been a handkerchief before it had become so threadbare. None of this was hers. But here it was, in front of her, evidence of a life truly lived. And each item seemed like a clue to understanding something about the person she had long thought she knew best in the whole world. Only now was it dawning on her that perhaps she had known nothing at all.

She turned some of the bits and pieces over in her hands, flipping through the photographs, trying to make out who was in them, and why her dad had kept them all of this time. There were doctors' notes, seemingly between English and French hospitals. And the passport belonged to a Stéphanie Ganteaume. Date of birth, 1960. She flicked to the photograph page and saw a solemn-looking, pale-eyed woman wearing a round-necked white T-shirt with a dark-brown spaghetti-strapped dress over the top. Her hair was glossy, shoulder length, and parted in the middle. Blue eyes looked back at the camera with unnerving intensity. Clara's instinct was to look away briefly, as if she were being stared at by a painting. Caught rifling through someone else's belongings.

1960. So this woman was over sixty now. Nearly her dad's age. Place of birth, Paris.

Paris.

The penny dropped. She heard her mother's voice, intonation rising urgently as she tried to persuade Clara against visiting the city with Ben.

*Don't think it will make you happy.*

*Paris isn't all pastries and black polo necks, you know.*

*You'll realise the French don't care about your dreams when you get there.*

Stéphanie. This was Maggie's envelope, from her father. These were Maggie's things. And yes, this must be Maggie's mum.

Clara stood up and stepped away from the table. She knew she was snooping. This was not her past to be snooping in. But then again, *wasn't it*? These were things that Ben had kept from her, his own daughter. Didn't she have a right to know about his past, what had made him *him*? After all, hadn't he basically said in the letter that he would have told her about all this if he could? So yes, they might be Maggie's things, but they were her past too. And the only way to really understand what they all were and why they were so important was to get in touch with Maggie herself.

Clara reached for her mug, but the tea she thought she had made only five minutes ago was already cold. She took it to the kitchen and put it in the microwave for twenty seconds while she stood, her fingers drumming on the kitchen counter as she stared out at the street, wondering what this Stéphanie was like. Where was she? Did her mum know her? Was she still in Paris?

The minute her tea was hot again she took a gulp, wincing at the burn as it hit the back of her throat, and sat back at the coffee table. This time she opened her laptop and brought up Facebook. She rarely used the site, but she knew that someone Maggie's age, late thirties, surely would. Unexpectedly confronted with a recent design update, she took a minute to find her bearings on the page. Then she was distracted by an update from someone she had once endured a deeply tedious summer tennis camp with, before finding the search bar and typing in *M A G G—*

She deleted and started again.

*MARGUERITESEYMOUR*

The search came back with nothing. Surely she wouldn't ...
not be there? Everyone was, weren't they? She came out of
Facebook and tried the same name in the Google search bar.
Nothing. Plenty of references to people who had one or other of
the names, and neither together. She tried the search combined
with some keywords such as Norway, or Paris, but again – nothing. She stared into space, chewing her lip. She took another
sip of tea. And as she did, the French passport caught her eye
again. Of course.

Facebook again.

*MARGUERITEGANTEAUME*

And there she was. The name came straight up, but the
profile was locked, security settings as high as they could be,
and her avatar was what looked like a sunset shot. She was a
member of no groups, she came up under no other pages, and
had only seven friends. And her messages were set to private.
But still, there she was.

She tried Google again, but the only result was the same
Facebook profile. But still ... there she was. Her sister. Her
big sister.

Clara paced the small sitting room, trying to work out what
to put in a message to Maggie, in the vague hope that she had
Message Requests still available.

*Surprise! I'm your sister! Let's chat?*

*Hi! I guess you don't know me but I have some of your mum's stuff.
Turns out we share a dad!*

*Dear Ms Ganteaume, please get in touch as a matter of some urgency.*

It was impossible to know whether informality would be
more disarming and provoke a response out of curiosity, or
whether a professional tone implying a degree of obligation
might be better. She thought of Nikita, who seemed to find these

things effortless. What might she do? Clara took a deep breath and typed. And retyped. And retyped.

Dear Maggie, or Marguerite if you prefer

Dear Maggie, or Marguerite if you prefer,

Dear Marguerite,

I am writing on behalf of Mr Ben Seymour, who I understand was your father. I am sorry to say that he has recently passed away. He has asked me to get in touch as he has some personal effects that I understand should be returned to you. Please contact me here, at Clara.Seymour99@gmail.com, or on 07959 219968 if you prefer.

Best wishes, Clara Seymour.

And as she pressed send, she realised that by disclosing her surname, she had potentially revealed her own relationship to Ben. But the message was off into the ether now, and with it her contact details. She wasn't sure if it would work, but suddenly she was sure she was exhausted. She clambered up onto the sofa and pulled her knees in to her chest, eyes closed, thinking of what her sister might reply. She dozed for twenty minutes, but woke with her mind fizzing with ideas.

Next, she had to try and work out if the partial address in her dad's letter was somewhere that Maggie could conceivably still be living. At first she zoomed in and out on Google Street View, following rural Norwegian roads around the perimeter of various islands, trying to spin the camera as far as it would go in order to get a view across the ocean. Infuriatingly, the island Maggie seemed to be on had not been covered by the roaming cameras, so she had to resort to zooming in on images from adjacent land masses, trying to work out if skylines matched those she could see on various tourist websites.

She managed to work out that there was a lighthouse, and it was on the island in the address given to her by her father. But there was no evidence of any other dwellings on the island. Maggie's address came up in no searches: whatever permutations of the address she tried, they all brought her back to the same lighthouse. She grew weary of scrolling down lists of Google search results, and ended up clicking on a travel blog belonging to what seemed to be a retired couple who had stayed at the lighthouse on Måsholmen.

As she felt the laptop start to heat up and its fan come on, struggling with the number of website tabs she had open, she read about the warm-hearted couple's trip to the island. They were Dutch, and had gone to celebrate their fortieth wedding anniversary. They had both longed to see the Northern Lights for years, and promised themselves they would find them one day. While there, they had enjoyed kayaking in the Baltic Sea, catching fish and watching sunset 'at the edge of the world'. And they had photographed it all. The blog was cute, but the photos interminable. Clara scrolled, one ear out for the door, half a mind on giving up on this search: view after view, each one as beautiful as the one before, but almost all of them obscured by one of the bloggers in fleece and walking boots, giving a grinning thumbs up to the camera or with one hand extended as if to say, 'Look! These views we found!'

And then she saw it. The small cornflower-blue house, barely bigger than the cursor, in the very bottom on the image. The couple talked about having taken a big walk 'to the other side of the island' because they had wanted to look for some plant or other. And the weather seemed to have changed on them at the furthest part of the trek. Peering out from beneath the hood of a sturdy-looking waterproof, the wife was giving a theatrical shrug, eyes rolled heavenwards. And down there beyond her left shoulder was a small house, in what seemed to be a bay looking out to sea.

Someone else was there. Someone else was on the island. Maggie.

The late spring sunshine was casting a shadow of the window frame across the coffee table by the time Clara stirred. Confusion – which room was she in? Was Simon back? Had he realised she wasn't at work? – was quickly followed by a smack of sadness as she remembered why she was on the sofa in the middle of the day and why she might have drifted off. She sighed, knowing she could spend half an hour crying if she let herself.

But clean, icy clarity crept up on her once she properly woke from her dreamless nap. That shard of glassy terror at the prospect of being caught idling at home by Simon had been so automatic, such a reflex to momentary disorientation. It clarified a truth she had been avoiding for too long: it was no longer a dream to get away, she *had* to get away. The worst of the arguments had been infrequent, but they had left a footprint. Not a literal one, of course, it not yet come to that. But she was no longer sure that it never would. The iPhone, thrown in the kitchen bin when 'she wouldn't get off the fucking thing' while they were watching a documentary Simon was enjoying. The trainers he had bought her 'to encourage her to take proper care of herself', only to disappear, taken to the charity shop 'for someone who might actually use them' when she hadn't taken up running within the week. And the matches in the sink, sitting amid a pile of ashes. Ashes that it had taken her a while to realise were some of her illustrations, little ink line

78

drawings of some feathers she had done one evening when she had no idea where he was. Destroyed within forty-eight hours when she had had the temerity to question him on where he might have been.

Escape was too strong a term, she was still telling herself. It was more that she needed a bit of a change of scene to help her deal with her grief. She tried to keep this reasonable train of thought going as she ran her fingers through her hair and opened the laptop again, deleting her cookies as she did it, as had become her habit. Because beyond the reasonable part of her was a less verbal, more animalistic self, who saw that this journey was more than just a trip to the Artic. It was an excuse to reach beyond what she had for so long expected of herself, to defy Simon at last, and to reach for someone who might show her the sort of connection and sense of belonging that she now realised she could never find here. Her fingers tingled with fear as she started to type. But eventually her mind felt less muggy, shaking off the layers of doubt, the endless, fear-driven excuses. It was reaching for clearer skies: she had a sense of purpose.

Now that the path ahead was widening, she knew that she had to follow it. She checked Facebook, just in case Maggie was one of those fastidious types who checked their folders for messages from strangers. As she had suspected, her note remained unread. Plan B it was then. She opened her inbox and started typing.

Dear Mr Tandy,

Thank you so much for your time, and your kindness today. I have been in touch with ... –

she hesitated and took a deep breath –

my sister this afternoon, and I have started to make arrangements to go and see her as soon as possible. I am planning to fly to the island mentioned in my father's letter later this month in the hope that this approximate address will get me close enough to find her. So if you could clarify the financial situation regarding the trip at your earliest convenience, I would be hugely grateful.

Best wishes, Clara Seymour

A deep breath. Another email.

Dear Julia,

I am very sorry not to be able to do this in person, but my circumstances have changed since the death of my father and I now have to take a trip abroad at very short notice. As such, I am resigning from my position at Lambert & Tarritt and will not be returning to the office. I do not think I am owed any further days' holiday but please contact me immediately if there is any information that HR needs.

Please send my best wishes to the rest of the team.

Yours sincerely, Clara Seymour

And now the hardest.

Mum,

I'm really sorry about how we left things yesterday. I was a bit of a bitch. It has just been a lot to take in.

I had a meeting with Mr Tandy today and I have learned a little more about Maggie. I have also learned that Dad had put aside some money for me to go and visit her. There are some documents and things he wanted me to return personally. So I have decided to go as soon as possible, to Norway, where she lives. Time for a bit of an adventure!

Don't try to stop me. I have handed in my notice at work already.

Auntie Liz has told me that Dad is going to be cremated, and I would like to be a part of scattering his ashes, but I would like to do it with Maggie too, if that is possible. So please don't make any decisions, or let her make any decisions, without me.

I will let you know as soon as I have an address for where I am staying, but at the moment that slightly depends on how things go once I get there.

Lots of love, Clarrie xx

She thought the next one, to Nikita, might have been easier. But there was so much she didn't feel able to say yet, so much that wasn't right for an email, and yet so much that she knew she would now reveal, that this one seemed hardest of all.

Hey hey hey,

Listen, I am so sorry about the vibes between us recently. I have so much to tell you, but it just kept coming out wrong. I am so stoked for you and your grant – you are going to do amazing work.

I have news too – surprise! I have a sister! No shit. It turns out that my dad had a daughter, Maggie, before he met my mum, and she lives up in the Arctic and wasn't speaking to him when

81

he died. So guess who is heading noooooorth to go and find her. Yup, your girl Clara.

And before you get all 'have you thought it through?', the answer is no. I haven't really. Because all the stuff I have ever tried to think about carefully and all the times I have tried to do the right thing have got me absolutely freakin' nowhere. Seriously – you're chasing your dream, and it made me so envious to see the other night. Maybe that's why I behaved like such a freak. I am in a job I know my dad thought was a fool's game and deep down I always knew it too. I don't want to live the life my mum wants for me either, so I'm going to go and see this Maggie, find out what her story is, just ... see some different horizons, you know.

Also – I have turned notifications off on my phone for a while, as I don't want Simon knowing what I'm up to. So keep in touch, but forgive me if I don't see stuff straight away. I guess I'll have to pick my moments to check messages etc. till I leave. But if you can meet me next Sunday, in Balham, and maybe look after a suitcase of my stuff for me while I'm gone, I'd be really grateful. No need to let me know straight away. I'm sure my mum will understand if I want to dump stuff at my dad's place for a bit. Will explore more when I see you.

I'll message as soon as I can. Don't worry about me, babe. You're an inspiration, remember that.

Love you, C xxx

PART TWO: SUMMER

# Chapter 9

Clara pressed her feet to the plane floor as it started to pick up speed. The wheels left the runway and she felt the small of her back pushed into her seat. She exhaled slowly, her lips pursed as if to whistle. She had made it. And Simon still had no idea.

She knew she should have told Simon she was leaving, just as she should have worked out a proper plan for her return. But she had felt so intoxicated by the trip, the freedom, the promise of a new life that it offered. At least, that is what she had told herself, avoiding the small voice that knew she had been terrified of having the conversation for as long as she had been preparing the trip.

Her imagination had sparked in all sorts of directions, worrying that Simon would hide her passport, would stop her from getting to the airport, or, likeliest of all, would just chip chip chip away at her with details of how treacherous the trip might be, how unlikely it was that she would survive, and how unlikelier still that Maggie would want anything to do with her. It was just too easy to visualise him reminding her how difficult she could be to love, how much it would be for Maggie to accept someone like her, how the best thing would probably be if she didn't go at all.

So she hadn't told him. Not even that final morning, when he seemed to take forever to leave for the meeting she knew he had that day.

Through her fast-evolving cloak-and-dagger system of messages sent and deleted when she knew that Simon was nowhere near his phone, Clara had asked Nikita to collect her once Simon had headed out. She had left her larger suitcase with Nikita days before, but hadn't dared to pack a smaller bag or hand luggage until Simon was out of the house on the actual morning of her departure. Instead, she had kept a list of what she'd need, low down in the Notes section of her phone, headed *FITNESS GOALS*.

The minute Simon had slammed the door behind him, she had sprung into action, gathering her headphones, passport, water bottle and everything else on the list, knowing she didn't have all too long until Nikita pulled up outside. So when she heard the keys in the lock five minutes later, her mouth went dry in a second. She was damp with sweat, and only just managed to scoop her bag and packing up and under the duvet in time.

'Fucking headphones,' Simon had said, his eyes making a sweep of the room before grabbing his AirPods from his side of the bed and walking out again, with barely a backwards glance. But there had been something about his eyes as they'd scanned the scene that Clara was still thinking about now, even as the plane drew up its wheels. She knew she had looked guilty as he'd walked in the room. She knew he knew something, and was determined not to show it either. It hadn't been until she heard her flight called and saw that he wasn't in the departure lounge that she had truly let herself believe that he wasn't somehow following her.

In the end, packing had been surprisingly easy. Clara had known she couldn't take too much, but she had also figured out that the last week of April was a time of year when Arctic weather could head in pretty much any direction. Once she had got hold of all the items she had decided were essential, there wasn't much room left for reserve shoe choices or just-in-case holiday reads. She had a coat for warmth, a coat for rain, and a scarf to wear with both. She had walking boots, cosy boots and Birkenstocks for indoors, chunky jumpers, some waterproof trousers, and four floaty folded dresses which were the sort of thing fashion bloggers called 'capsule'. And then she had a hat to keep the wind off her face, a hat to keep the sun off her face, and the bobble hat she had got in the Lake District with her dad a few years ago. She had moaned at least every twenty minutes for that entire drizzly weekend, only really cheering up when they discovered that the Grasmere gingerbread shop she remembered from her childhood was still there.

Why had she been so grumpy? Sure, the endless grey skies hadn't helped anyone's mood, but all her dad had wanted was to spend some time with her, taking her somewhere he had remembered her having fun as a small child. That lunchtime in Grasmere, as she treasured her gingerbread, carefully wrapped in stiff opaque paper, had been the highlight. They had sat in the pub together, waiting for their scampi and chips, giggling at the toddler causing merry mayhem with the salt and pepper pots just out of his parents' view. Once they finished eating, her dad ordered them coffees then said he needed to pop out to make a call. When he reappeared ten minutes later, he thrust a thick-ribbed bobble hat into Clara's hands. He must have spotted her admiring the hand-knitted goods in the gift shop, and had nipped out to get her one as soon as he could.

'Something to keep that Cumbrian chill at bay,' he'd said

into her ear as he hugged her. 'Thank you for indulging an old man with some long walks.'

She felt safer knowing the hat was safe in her suitcase, somewhere deep in the plane's hold. He had touched that hat. It was one of the few threads linking her current reality to times spent with him. As she had folded it and slid it into the side of her bag, she had stroked its grey pompom, remembering her dad ruffling it as they left the pub. Moments like that had made time melt at least once a day since his death. They still left her reeling, desperate for the world to stop spinning quite this fast, so she could stop and spend a little longer with each memory, taking time over each one as if she were turning a smooth gold coin in her hand. But there hadn't been time. There had been too much to do, and the images just didn't seem to want to stay still.

The last few weeks she spent in England had left her feeling suffocated by her present and terrified for her future. She did not work out the fortnight's notice at Lambert & Tarritt that she should have done. To her surprise, Julia had been very accommodating when she had simply announced that she couldn't return. Instead, Clara had got up and dressed for work each morning and left the flat on time, before taking the escalators down to the Northern line and heading to corners of London where she was sure that Simon would never find her.

She had written to the lighthouse on Måsholmen from a seat in the British Library's extortionately priced but conveniently busy cafe in an attempt to book a stay. She researched the weather in Norway at this time of year in a greasy spoon on Finchley Road which she had once admired on the bus. She had sorted out some Norwegian cash in a Post Office in Chiswick, on the way back from a long walk along the river to try out her new hiking boots – boots she had ordered on eBay on her phone while sitting at the top of Parliament Hill, trying to imagine how the view might compare to the Arctic mountainscape that they were intended for. And she had arranged the transfer of some money via Audrey at Mr Tandy's office while sitting in a small tea shop in Walthamstow. When she bought things online, she had them delivered to Mr Tandy's office. 'So you can see what I'm doing with the money,' she had told Audrey. But the truth was that she did it to avoid Simon either laughing at her sturdy new hiking kit or questioning her need for it.

At first, she had only intended to keep her plans discreet. Not a secret, so much as just not making a fuss about the changes in her life. Time had taught her that Simon was not a fan of sudden changes, unless they were ones instigated by him. He might panic if he realised she was planning to go away, she thought at first. Then, one night at 3 a.m. as she lay staring at the ceiling listening to the rumble of his PlayStation from next door, she realised that of course he would panic. And with panic so often came broken plates. And – only the once! – broken skin. But still, better not to upset him, she whispered to herself as she tried to steady her heart rate, which was suddenly galloping at the memory.

So discretion had slowly crystallised into secrecy. And with secrecy came greater risk. Despite that, there was a part of Clara that had started to enjoy the secret. At last, something just for her. A project *she* had to take care of, all alone. For so long Simon had been the guiding hand, advising her on what to study, where to work and how to cook. What had looked like lambent kindness when she was seventeen – and a path out of her mother's house while her dad had been lecturing abroad for a year – had calcified into a something closer to control by the time she was twenty.

It was only when Clara had started work that she had realised how few friends she had, how hard she found it to just ... hang out. She'd frequently walk into the kitchen at the office and find three colleagues her age chatting excitedly about last night's reality TV, some influencer's latest scandal, or planning where to meet at the weekend. She tried to smile, to join in, to laugh along. And sometimes she was invited to the pub with them, or whatever they were doing, and had been thrilled. But – just like during her later years at college – she ended up having to cancel because Simon had made plans with *his* friends. A dinner party: chats about childcare, house prices, cancel culture. The flightiness she had felt as a teenager who would lie in the park until 10 p.m. drinking cider and talking about boys seemed to have faded like a book jacket left exposed to the sun.

Once her father had left the family home, persuaded by her mother that Clara would be happier, healthier, living with her, Clara had swung between a sort of sullen obedience, learning quickly how to keep the peace at home, and a party spirit who could persuade schoolfriends to spend the evening drinking and gossiping as easily as she could make a teacher laugh. Shapeshifting according to what room she was in had become second nature. It was only with her dad that she still felt herself. And when she had met Simon, at her first proper job at an upmarket kitchenware shop and cookery school, he had somehow outshone those simpler pleasures. But he had also tested her ability to transform into what the room needed her to be with greater force than anyone else in her life.

An up-and-coming food reviewer with a fast-increasing following on social media and a passion for what he called 'the art of cooking meat', his confidence about the best way of doing things was intoxicating at first, before it became something dangerously close to addictive. He was only ten years older than her but his life already seemed so adult, so glamorous, so out of reach. So when he appeared in the store, asking about the prestige knives they sold but always with time to spare for chatting, she had quickly felt dazzled by his dimpled smile and dark curls.

Perhaps she should have stopped it all the day she told him he had an 'umami sense of humour'. It was a quiet Sunday following a big Saturday night and her nerves were jittery after too many coffees from the in-store barista, but she had wanted to punch the air when he roared with laughter at her comment, still chuckling as he turned to leave the store and shoved his wallet into the back pocket of his jeans, nice and snug next to his undeniably cute bum.

But they hadn't stopped. He asked her out within a week of her finishing her exams. It had only taken a handful of dates for Clara to be smitten. He didn't take her anywhere showy, just for a nice night in the pub, and then to the launch of a street-food place in Streatham. Then he had invited her over to his, and made them steak before kissing her in a way that Clara had never dared to imagine was possible.

And so began the slow process of everything Clara had ever thought about herself or what she could be being slowly enveloped into Simon's life, Simon's goals, Simon's personality. At first it had felt warm, gentle even, to be so entirely absorbed into someone else's existence, like a sprinkle of flour into a softly folding sourdough mix. And her mother had loved him, of course. As Clara had looked at him under the expensively flattering lighting of her mother's kitchen, every detail of him had seemed perfect, put together like the sort of man she had never dared dream of landing. It was at least six months before she started to realise how much effort went into that casual perfection.

These days Simon rarely saw her mother, but in those early

months while Clara was still living at home, she would regularly come downstairs for a date to find him at the gleaming kitchen island with a chilled glass of wine, telling an indiscreet anecdote about some chef whose latest book might be doing well but who was otherwise an absolute scoundrel. Her mother lapped it up, head thrown back, laughing throatily and begging him to stay. But somehow he managed never to make it over for a Sunday lunch, and once Clara was safely installed at his place in Tooting, he no longer went there at all. They rarely saw either of her parents, and as his mother was dead, Clara had no corresponding responsibilities. His father lived in Wiltshire, and was rarely mentioned, much less seen.

By the time Clara had had that phone call about her own father's death, having a long-term boyfriend 'for security' no longer felt like she had thought it would. There was no glamour in waiting for Simon to come home drunk – maybe even high – from another hipster pop-up opening. It had stopped feeling grown-up to spend another evening watching what he wanted on Netflix while he raged at a stranger who had disagreed with his opinion of a chicken-heart kebab on the internet. And the security of a boyfriend with a nice flat for the two of them now felt suffocating, as if she were flour trying to extricate itself from a loaf.

The isolation had intensified imperceptibly, particularly when Simon started to become more successful, going out more often, and staying out later. He was often asleep when she left for work, or in a hungover daze in the shower. She stopped knowing what mood he might be in when she came home – cock-a-hoop because of a viral review, sullen with booze or some other point between the two. So the path of least resistance seemed to be agreeing with him wherever possible, which in turn meant that each time he had told her she made terrible Bolognese, didn't understand a meme he was laughing at or could never have kept up on a bike ride with him, she let these insights seep under her skin, until they had become just as much a part of her as any other.

So when she had the chance to spend hours at a time quietly scouring eBay for a bargain on hiking books, reading up about trekking gear or quietly checking out Instagram accounts to see what the weather was looking like in Northern Norway at this time of year, she leapt at the chance.

Clara had not seen much of her remaining friends in the run up to her trip. She'd had messages of support and condolence from a few mates she shared with Nikita, but the first hints of spring were peeking through after a long grey winter, and most people seemed to have forgotten about her. Weekends away, exercise classes in the evenings, dates in the park. Lots to do, it seemed. She tried to look the other way, to face forward, planning her trip – or at least the journey there. And every night before bed she would check her Facebook inbox: no reply. Her message remained marked *unread*.

This was why, after having to be practical about so much else, she was allowing herself a moment of sentimentality about the hat. After all, she had managed to talk herself out of putting together a 'reconciliation outfit' for when she met Maggie, despite daydreaming for hours about what colour skirt might be appropriate. This in turn had led to a couple of hours of idly wondering whether this meeting would really count as a reconciliation if she had never met her before – particularly as she had yet to make contact with her.

She was too nervous to read anything of any substance on the flight. She wanted to flit through her social media on her mobile but the budget airline had no Wi-Fi, leaving her with nothing more than photos to look at. She scrolled through her favourites folder, a finger gently stroking an image of her and her dad hugging on the South Bank, a dreamy London sunset melting away behind them. An image Nikita had sent her last night, fingers crossed, tongue sticking out. Her mum, smiling at the dinner table last Christmas Day, Ian's hands on her shoulders as he stood behind her.

Her eyes were burning from the early start and the harsh air conditioning in the airport and then the plane itself. She blinked slowly, turning her head to look out of the window as the plane nuzzled through the cloud above the North Sea then emerged above it, as if floating on a second white-crested ocean.

Trondheim airport was not the hub of Scandinavian chic that Clara had been hoping for. She arrived discombobulated by the flight and anxious about the next leg of her journey, an overnight train further north to Bodø. She had expected something a little more mid-century, perhaps a little more 'fika', but this was just a standard modern airport, lined with the usual advertisements for financial companies and nearby tourist spots. Nevertheless, as she blinked her tired eyes, trying to get some moisture back into them, she felt very far from home.

She had hours before her train, even after wheeling her case from the airport to Trondheim's main rail hub, so she ventured into the bowels of the station, found a locker to stash the bag, and decided to take a walk through Trondheim and find something to eat. Once she had wiggled through the fishing area around the station and found her way to the older parts of town, she found the hit of Nordic beauty she had been waiting for: the riverfront, its glacier-still water reflecting the autumnal reds, oranges and yellows of the vast wharf buildings along its banks, was stunning. The traditional warehouse buildings were now stylish restaurants offering meals that described themselves as 'authentic' and even 'foraged'. There were adorable wooden-fronted coffee shops with great sacks full of delicious smelling beans lined up in the entranceways. Each place seemed to be filled with urbane older customers with clear-framed glasses and neat monochrome gilets, and slim, stylish younger folk who looked like they worked for social media companies or microbreweries. There was more blonde hair than she had seen for years, and a general sense of Scandinavian contentment that she would have been prepared to believe had been invented by bored marketeers in Swindon if it weren't so visible on every street.

She stopped to take photos on the traditional wooden bridge, and then some more as she passed the imposing cathedral. Eventually, the sky threatening rain, she found somewhere that looked akin to myriad east London pizza places she had been to with Simon and ordered herself something to eat. The prices were – as Mr Tandy had warned her – breathtaking. But so was the thrill of sitting there alone, pulling slice after slice from her bresaola and parmesan pizza, wallowing in the solitude without fear of being discovered. No need to have an opinion, to listen to an opinion, to chat to a foodie PR she had no interest in and slightly suspected Simon would like to sleep with. If he hadn't already. And no need to look over her shoulder in case Simon appeared, unexpectedly, in the corner of London she had chosen to hide in that day. This stillness, this sense of just being able to sit and watch the world go by. Was this what her father had wanted for her from this trip? She sipped an organic beer and tried to just enjoy the moment, to arrange her face like that of someone who was entirely at ease with who they were.

The shimmering uneasiness about what she was heading towards never quite left her though. Ripples of curiosity, wondering what would happen when she met Maggie, never eased.

What would be the skeleton key to unlock their relationship? Would they stand before a mirror and realise how similar they looked at a certain angle, that they had the same Orion's Belt of freckles across one cheek, how they were so obviously sisters? Before hugging in recognition of a closeness they had never known was coming? Would it be a turn of phrase, or a tone they both adopted while chatting? Or a TV show they had both adored as children, a book they had both been bewitched by? Or maybe it would be something more recent: a moisturiser they had both realised they couldn't live without, a lipstick shade that they were both devoted to.

Clara stopped herself. Would Maggie even wear lipstick? Could she even get hold of it? She lived on a very remote island, who might she be wearing lipstick for? But was it patronising to wonder about this? Maybe she was a thoroughly modern woman who wore it day in, day out, for herself. With each memory from her past, Clara's mind now seemed to be producing idealised situations from her future. Mini memories-to-be, a new relationship with someone that would tether her to her past and yank her into her future like one of the tug boats she had seen as she left the station, engine working hard, dragging its cargo behind it.

An indecently good-looking waiter appeared at her elbow, asking if she needed anything else. She decided not to have pudding but to buy a bag of the own-brand coffee beans that they had stacked by the till. A gift for Maggie. It was Norway, after all; there was no way she wouldn't be drinking coffee.

On her return from the bathroom she lifted the bill from the saucer on her table and went straight to the till to pay. She actually felt excited at the prospect of whipping out her card and paying for herself – no expectation to be grateful to Simon. She waited a moment as a family in front of her settled up, and as she did, she rummaged in her handbag for her wallet. Her hand reached it immediately, but as she pulled it out, she realised what she *hadn't* felt in the bag. She pulled the strap off her shoulder and opened it up in front of her, spreading one hand to keep it open and using the other to scrabble around, feeling through glasses case, keys, guidebook. She shoved fingers into the side pocket and unzipped the credit card pouch. She kept searching, desperate, but while she did she saw herself, three hours ago, fiddling with the zip on her handbag as she walked off the plane, her coat falling on the floor, sending her phone scattering. She had been so anxious about the phone that she had never gone back to check whether her bag was closed.

Her passport was gone.

She felt a chill run down her back, sweat prickling at her hairline as she realised what she had done. She checked her jacket pocket for her phone and touched her wallet on the counter in front her, making sure that everything else was safe. She paid for her dinner, shoved the bag of coffee beans into her handbag and hurried back to the station at a breathless trot. The cyclists who had seemed so charmingly, confidently continental now seemed lethal. There were cycle paths everywhere, and she kept forgetting to look out for them as she darted across roads, trying to get to her suitcase as fast as she could.

There was still a small chance she had slid the passport into a side pocket on her bag. Maybe, she told herself, she had done that and forgotten all about it. She had a clear visual memory of putting the passport in the aeroplane seat pocket, of it getting caught on her earphones as she went to listen to a podcast, and then pushing the magazine in. But she had no recollection of taking it out again before leaving the plane. It had been busy though; hers had been a window seat, but she had been sitting quite far towards the front, conscious of the queue forming behind her as she reached for her hand luggage in the rack above. Maybe the pressure to move fast had made her forget pulling it out of that pocket. Maybe she had slipped it straight into the side pocket of her suitcase, and that's why she didn't drop it as she left the plane. *Maybe*, she kept repeating to herself as she punched the numbers into the keypad on the station luggage holder. Maybe.

But as she pulled her bag out of the huge locker, and crouched beside it on the tacky laminate of the station floor, the icy jitters, the jumpy hope that it might yet be there, slowly turned to a sinking despair as she realised what she already knew was true. It was gone. It really was gone.

For the first time in weeks she wanted to cry. She was desperate for someone to see her weeping and rush to help. But no tears came. All she could summon was a gulpy gasp, fluttering hands and fresh clamminess across her back and neck.

She was the other end of the country from the embassy or any official sort of help. Could she sort something out online while she still had easy internet access? Did she even need her passport for the rest of the journey?

She had no idea where to start, but found the information point in the station where a calm, shiny-haired official explained to her that she would not be asked for her passport on the sleeper nor on the short final flight to Hestøy.

And, above all, there was no way that she could turn back.

'So I should keep going?' she asked the woman.

'I don't know where you are heading.' came the reply.

'To Måsholmen, to find my sister.'

'Måsholmen? I didn't know anyone still lived there. I remember reading about that place when I was at school. Famous lighthouse.'

'Yes, yes there is. Well, I think there is; my sister is supposed to be there.'

'Listen, you can get there without a passport, but ... can you *get there*?'

'What do you mean?'

'I don't know if there is even a way to get to that island any more, unless you have a boat yourself.'

'I spoke to the lighthouse.'

'OK, I see. But make sure you've got some supplies before you fly to Hestøy. You can't always make the crossing, it's ... well, it's very remote.'

'Thank you, thank you for your help. I understand it's very remote. It's why I have to go there, I have some things to deliver to my sister and, well, it's just not the sort of stuff you can leave up to the postman.'

The woman smiled warmly, but her head was tilted just slightly. Was that sympathy, thought Clara. For my passport, or for the expedition itself? Do I look like I need help? Like I might not make it?

'Well, good luck!' said the woman. 'And here, take these numbers just in case.' She passed over a credit-card sized piece of laminated cardboard with a few basic touristy numbers on it. Arctic Tours, NordAir and others.

Clara smiled back, then wheeled her bag across the station to the waiting area. She plugged her phone into one of the immaculate charging points, sat on the leatherette stool next to it and googled *lost passport abroad uk*.

# Chapter 10

The train slid away from the station softly, a gentle sway as it left the city and followed the curve of the fjord, which began directly as the suburbs ended. Clara had booked a sleeper cabin, and she sat on her bunk as the scenery unfolded.

She was glad to have left Trondheim station behind. As clean and safe as it had been, she was quite sure she'd never hold fond memories of it. When she had been finishing her dinner, she had wondered how she would fill the remaining couple of hours before the train's departure, but as it turned out, the time had easily been occupied by completing emergency travel document forms, flight details spread in front of her, flicking back and forth on her screen between the UK government website and the photographs of her passport that Nikita had thankfully reminded her to take just a couple of days before.

'Take photos of everything, they'll ping straight to the cloud!' she messaged her, with the emoji of a nerdy face with buck teeth and glasses, then a fluffy white cloud.

It was still light, despite being mid-evening, and the view from her window was one she had never imagined might actually exist beyond screensavers or jigsaw puzzles. Her guidebook told her that the fjord was 130 kilometres long – the water stretched as far as the eye could see. The train followed its curve tightly; the edge of the track itself was invisible, so she could only see the sharp drop down to the endless water. And it really did seem endless. A vast expanse, reaching out ahead of the train, despite its constant forward movement. She felt herself gently untethering from the world she had left behind her, and wondered how long it would last. It was bedtime in London. Would Simon have spotted the missing toothbrush – or anything beyond it – yet?

They were travelling quickly now, the repetitive chug chug of the engine and the train's sway as it hugged the edges of the lake lulling Clara into a relaxed sleepiness that she hadn't felt for weeks. It was as if, now that her eyes were more relaxed, and the view to the horizon expanded, her mind could follow. Instead of having to tick endless items off her to-do list before leaving, it was now all done. She had researched her journey, packed her stuff and said her goodbyes. Well, most of them. She couldn't hide behind planning any more, couldn't imagine the journey a second longer. She simply had to live it.

The physical sensation of the train was relaxing, but the state of hyper-alertness she had been living in for so long seemed impossible to shake off. The relief of not wondering what mood Simon might be in had been replaced too quickly by panic of travelling without her passport, leaving her whiplashed by the speed of switching from over-monitored to ... completely unverifiable? It wasn't just the lack of documentation that had left her with a sense of suspension, but the total solitude.

Instead of relaxing as the scenery floated by, her subconscious unwound in ways that seemed to trick and deceive. Those spaces that had been wedged full of admin, packing lists and eBay bids for hiking kit now seemed to go slack, allowing bigger, more complicated thoughts to sneak in like smoke under a doorway. Childhood memories played over and again, as if screened through different filters, each one asking nagging questions about who her dad really was. Why had her parents split up? Clara had always assumed it was, in short, because her mum could be insufferable and her dad had simply suffered enough. But now, from this distance, as air started to circulate around the remains of her own stifling relationship, she realised that her father had never really carried himself like someone hugely relieved to have been out of that second marriage. He was always kind about her mum – to a fault, especially when Clara had been younger and longed for an ally in discussing how awful, how unreasonable, how *unbearable* her mother was. And he had never found anyone else, nor seemed inclined to.

Then more recent events muscled forward, colours still garish in her mind. She thought back to her father's memorial, only ten days ago. The minute she had returned home that night – the flat empty as Simon was on a convenient work jolly to Berlin – she had buried any further thoughts about it under a duvet of so-called life planning. Busy-ness. Details. Urgent items. But now, like a long-forgotten potato sprouting at the back of a cupboard, visions of it were spreading in her mind.

It had been a grubby day. Clouds that never quite lifted and a breeze that whipped out of nowhere before vanishing just as shoulders were braced and hair tied back. London's concrete was barely distinguishable from the sky, high rises looming over Clara, closer than ever, yet outlines ill defined. Auntie Liz had organised the event: a small humanist ceremony at the West London Crematorium in Kensal Green, then a gathering of some of her dad's mates in the function room of a pub after-wards. Clara had been asked by Auntie Liz to do a reading, but even she knew that the same old W.H. Auden poem from *Four*

*Weddings* showed a spectacular lack of both imagination and genuine understanding of her dad. Was it the only one Auntie Liz knew? Clara had read it obligingly though, reluctant not to let anyone down and keen to get the whole day over and done with as soon as possible.

Her mother had collected her from the flat an hour before the service, ringing the doorbell bang on time, apparently irritated that Clara wasn't ready and waiting by the kerb. By the time Clara had made it down to the main door her mum was sitting in the passenger seat of Ian's smart black car while he drummed his hands on the steering wheel. He smiled impassively as Clara got into the back seat. Her mother stretched around to smile tightly at her, checking she had done up her seatbelt, no doubt, and Clara noticed the skin of her neck, stretched and papery as it folded over the neat black peter pan collar of her dress. Her hair was up in a perfect blonde French twist, stiff with hairspray, and her eyelashes were spidery with mascara. She could see the swirl of her blusher, not quite properly blended, smeared a little beneath one eye. As she reached round, trying to give her a reassuring smile, Clara thought that her mum looked older, less imposing than she had ever noticed before. There was a fragility to her as she asked Clara if she was OK, if she was prepared for the service, her words asking one thing but her tone begging to be asked the question back.

'Yes, I'm fine, Mum,' she had replied. And she did feel fine. If fine was a blanket of nothingness.

Her mother turned back to face the front of the car, putting on a huge pair of sunglasses despite the dreariness of the day, and offering no further signs of vulnerability. Once parked up, Ian extended her an arm as they entered the crematorium, but she didn't take it. Clara walked slowly behind them until they took up their seats in the second row.

As the ceremony progressed, Clara noticed her mother's head dip until she was looking directly down to her lap. She removed her sunglasses to reveal eyes glistening with tears. Ian discreetly passed her a hanky and she dabbed as Clara watched with a detached curiosity.

Rather than feeling frustrated or even a little fearful of her mother, on that day Clara found herself feeling unusually protective of her. The normal digs and quips had been replaced with what certainly felt like a sincere concern for her daughter since they had fallen out on the day she had discovered her sister's existence. It was as if a window had swung open in the breeze and let in a little fresh air, the atmosphere between the two of them fonder than it had been for many years.

For so long Clara had felt as if she were just a couple of sentences from getting an answer wrong with her mum. As she later got used to with Simon, there had long been a sense with her mum that she might set things off, start a catastrophic argument without realising, or create the petri dish for further bad feeling a few weeks down the line. There was always evidence of a rule book at play, but the rule book itself never seemed to make itself known.

For as long as she could remember, this sense of anxiety had consumed her relationship with her mother, while she consistently found her dad easy to chat to. He made it seem breezy, both the art of chatting and of letting her feel heard. He understood when she was down and when her mind was fizzing with ideas that she wanted to discuss. There was never a 'Not now ...', a 'You shouldn't worry about that stuff at your age', or a 'What will people think?' He spoke to her like an equal, and listened just as intently.

But sitting on the hard wooden bench of the crematorium, she saw the quivering of her mum's hand fiddling with the hem of her jacket, and realised that the ease of her relationship with her dad might have been as frustrating for her mum as it had been reassuring for Clara. Her only daughter, always so excited to see her dad, so much to say to him about a film, a book, a plan. But so taciturn once home, just the two of them. Now that Clara had been given a peek at her dad's previous life, and glimpsed his ability to keep lifelong secrets, she wondered if he might not have been as easy-going a husband as he was a father. In fact, as she pushed the front door open on her return home, knowing she had only a couple of hours to herself before Simon's return, she wondered if perhaps he had been rather a lot like her boyfriend.

As she rattled further north and away from that home she had longed to escape, she realised that perhaps all those invisible rules her mum seemed to have in place had been there to protect her, rather than to catch her out. All her mum really wanted for her was a nice life – it was just that *her* idea of a nice life, with its moneyed security and socially acceptable accoutrements, had turned out to be so very far from Clara's own. Because as Simon's grip on her had started to tighten until it felt like something closer to pain than security, Clara had longed for freedom, for open spaces, for horizons beyond herself. All the things her mother feared.

Clara wished she could rewind time and do a better job of the last few weeks. She wished she could have been a bit kinder to her mum in the run-up to the trip, instead of being so obviously desperate to get away. And she wished she hadn't acquiesced to reading that stupid poem, that she had written something herself, or at least come up with a few silly words that her dad might have appreciated. In truth, she wished the memorial hadn't had to happen at all, that she could be on the train with her dad right now, chatting about some obscure sea bird he was excited about seeing, or what he had thought about the quality of the airport food, or the nifty little electronic lockers at the luggage hold in Trondheim station.

All alone, the consequences of her decisions now seemed to be bearing down on her, suffocatingly, as if she were unable to grasp who she might actually be without the twin mirrors of her father and her boyfriend to remind her how she emoted, where she belonged, who she was. She gave herself a shake and decided to head to the buffet car for a drink. She grabbed her phone, locked her cabin and walked through a few carriages, pressing her hands to the windows to steady herself as she passed. A middle-aged couple sat chatting to their next-door cabin-neighbours, discussing plans for their trip. Their easy manner – the women were in brushed-cotton pyjamas, their husbands in the comfortable slacks of a pair approaching retirement – made Clara yearn for her father's company yet again.

She was still thinking of him as she slid into a seat, pouring her small Scotch into the glass she had placed on the table in front. It was fast approaching midnight but the sky showed no sign of darkening in any meaningful way. How would she ever sleep, she wondered, realising that the onboard Wi-Fi was infuriatingly slow.

'Do you mind if I join you?' said a voice bearing the slight American twang that she had discovered so many in Norway spoke with. She looked up to see a man perhaps five years older than her, smiling as he stood at the edge of her table. The buffet car had filled up while she had been fiddling with her phone, and here he was, asking to share a booth.

'Of course,' she said, wondering how he had known she was English. A flicker of electricity seemed to run up her spine.

'Thank you so much, it has become a little busy,' he said,

as he slid into the banquette opposite her, his knees brushing hers. His blond hair was a little longer at the front, a few curls springing up as he ran his hand through them. He was wearing a neat shirt, the collar tucked into a dark-green sweatshirt. On someone walking along Fulham Road it might have looked like exactly the sort of retro-Sloane that Clara usually sought to avoid. But on him there was more of a continental preppy vibe. She wished she had had the chance to see his shoes, and just as she had that thought she wondered why she cared.

But as he opened his bag of cashews and pushed them across the laminate of the table towards her, she realised why.

'Are you going all the way?' he asked.

'I'm sorry?' Clara blushed. His eyes were very blue.

'To Narvik?'

'Oh no, I'm getting out at Bodø, taking the plane to Hestøy.'

'Ah. Shame. What are you doing there?'

'I'm going to visit my sister.' He leaned in closer. Clara felt his eyes scanning hers.

'Wow, where does she live?' He lifted his can and took a swig of what looked to be a local beer. She watched his throat as he swallowed, and took a sip of her Scotch.

'Måsholmen.'

'Oh, fantastic, what a place.' He was leaning back now, one arm draped across the back of the seats. She felt his knee shift, his legs splaying. It was the closest she had been to anyone but Simon for a very long time.

'Mmm.' Clara's instinct was for him not to find out that that she had never been to Måsholmen, but she couldn't put her finger on why. Simon would never know what she was up to now. Or was it that she wanted this man to think she was more familiar with the country that she was. Before she had a chance to quiz herself any further, he offered her a glug from the half bottle of red wine he had nudging out of the top of his rucksack. To her surprise, she realised her whisky was already gone.

'Thank you,' she said, her face flushing.

'So have you been there before?'

'No, never,' she found herself blurting in response.

'Wow, you sure have a treat in store.'

Clara smiled and looked down at the table. A muscle some-where in her was being asked to flex, but seemed not to be working like it used to.

'Are you having dinner?' he went on.

'I wasn't going to ... ' she said, aware of the pizza she had eaten only a few hours ago.

'It's OK, I have food, let's share.' He looked up at her, trying to lift her gaze from the tabletop. And before she really had the chance to answer properly, he whipped out an aluminium tin from the bag next to him. From it he produced some sliced rye bread, then some cheese which he started to layer onto the bread. He began chopping a small gherkin between his thumb and forefinger with a folding travel knife. It had been years since Clara had eaten a gherkin – Simon had long sworn he was allergic to them and consequently wouldn't have them in the house. She had never really been sure if he did have an allergy, or if it was just another of his little quirks, a way to just keep an eye on her diet.

The man was now sprinkling the sandwiches with seeds, and pushed one towards her on the lid of the tin.

'Bon appetit. My name's Erik, by the way.'

'Thank you.' Her voice was barely more than a whisper. 'And hi. I'm Clara.'

'So Clara, tell me about your trip.'

Just as she realised the alcohol was hitting her system she found a sudden flush of confidence.

'Tell me about yours first! You're the local.'

'Well, OK then.' He smiled broadly at her, a dimple on his left cheek appearing. She lifted the bread to her mouth, hoping she wasn't going to make too much of a mess of eating it.

Erik was a marine researcher, based in a government research facility in Oslo, but he travelled up and down the country. This time he was going as far as Tromsø, further north than even she was going. 'Last stop before Svalbard,' he explained. Sometimes he even went that far, to the global seed vault.

Clara kept asking questions in the hope that the focus never switched back to her. She listened to him describe his love of this journey, how work would pay for him to fly north but he preferred to take the more environmentally sound route and enjoy the views. As he said this, he went to gesture at the window, his hand brushing against hers. It was as if an invisible thread had been tugged, deep inside her.

'Maybe you'll even meet a handsome Scandinavian. You know, someone to keep your mind off things,' Nikita had told her in a hastily deleted voice note before she left. Clara had not even acknowledged the suggestion at the time, it had seemed so outlandish. And now it seemed to be happening, without her making any actual effort at all.

She didn't make an active decision to sit and chat with Erik until the bottle was gone, and she didn't remember suggesting she buy him a beer to say thank you for his 'hospitality'. And she certainly hadn't planned to start talking about her fantasy career as if it actually *was* her career.

But now, an hour later they were sitting, knees touching with increasing frequency as she described her job as an illustrator. She was explaining with confidence that sometimes her work was found in nature books, little line drawings of acorns, feathers, birds at play, dancing along the margins of bestsellers and sometimes even on greetings cards. She told him she had got into the art school she had ended up not applying to, and that she had been very happy there.

'There will be lots for you to draw on the island,' Erik told her approvingly.

'Yes, it's part of why I'm going,' she replied.

The image of a softly uncurling fern sat right at the front of her mind, her hand itching to draw it.

Erik yawned and stretched his arms up above his head. Clara tried not to watch as his sweatshirt rose with the stretch, revealing a couple of inches of skin above the edge of the table between them.

'It's past midnight. How did that happen?'

'It's so confusing,' said Clara. 'It's not even really dark.'

'I know right? It can send you slightly mad if you don't stay aware.'

'I can imagine.'

'There's still going to be enough light for some of the best views. Do you have a cabin at the rear of the train or ahead of this carriage?'

'It's ahead, I think.' Clara had to pause to remember which direction she had come from.

'The views are so much better in the rear carriages – do you want to come and see from my cabin?'

Clara glanced out of the window, wondering how much better a view could be than this one from the buffet car. As her eyes flicked back to Erik, she let herself wonder if she was really being asked to look at anything at all. The corner of his mouth, curling up as he slowly but unmistakably placed his knee next to hers, confirmed her suspicion.

The train seemed to be moving faster now. Clara

remembered that she was very far from home, without any ID, and heading to see someone who might not even know she existed. But instead of putting her off, this filled her with a sort of terrible liberty, a prod that this might be her chance to do all the things she had felt for so long that she never would.

'Sure,' she said. 'It's not as if I'm going to sleep anyway.'

Erik smiled, slid out of the booth, and held out a hand to direct her to the opposite end of the train from where she had come.

As soon as she started to walk, Clara realised that it hadn't been her imagination – the train really was going a lot faster. Erik, walking ahead, his bag slung over his shoulder, reached out a hand behind him. Clara watched as her own hand took his, as if someone else entirely had decided on the action. Erik's hand was broad and warm, but with each of them reaching like this, they weren't actually any steadier in the narrow train corridor. They reached a set of doors, and just as Erik slowed for them to open, the train lurched around a corner, slamming Clara into him. There was a muddle as the doors opened then started to close again, while Erik frantically put out a hand to protect her from them sliding into her. She was pressed against his chest, and almost felt her legs buckle beneath her: a combination of alcohol, tiredness, and motion sickness. Slowly, she looked up, and as she did, she saw Erik quizzically looking down at her. He was smiling, and his head was slightly tilted, as if he was asking permission to kiss her. She wanted him to, far more than she wanted to admit, but instead of the honey warmth of desire, she suddenly felt a chill of terror.

What was she doing? She had no idea who this man was. Hadn't he told her he took this route the whole time? He was probably some sort of locomotive predator, picking off young tourists like they were fools.

Clara reared back, moving away from the door's path and grabbing the side of the train.

'I'm so sorry, I can't ... I just ... I'm just so tired ... I'm sure you're very nice, and thank you for telling me all about your country ... ' As ever, she was trying, pre-emptively, to keep the peace.

'It's fine, I'm so sorry too ... ' Erik now looked genuinely shocked. 'Are you OK? Do you need a hand getting back to your cabin?' He raised his palms to indicate that he didn't mean *like that*.

'No no, I'll be fine, thank you though. For everything, and for being so sweet.' Clara was now confused by how sincerely kind he seemed to be. 'And I'm sorry.'

'You don't need to be sorry, I have had a lovely evening talking to you. Are you sure you're going to be OK?'

'Yes, honestly, and thank you.' Shame was now bubbling over the panic that had initially been behind her actions. Still, she wanted to get away, to be alone. She turned and headed back through the buffet car and towards her cabin, where she plonked herself on her bunk and sat, sipping water, until her heart rate fell a little.

Darkness fell at last while she sat there, watching mountains studded with crops of pine trees pass at speed while her mind hummed like a laptop with too many tabs open. Her bones ached from the long day's travelling, followed by the aimless walking around Trondheim and then the huge spikes of adrenaline that she had experienced since.

She shook herself, loosening her joints, and washed her face and teeth in the dinky basin only inches from the side of the now-made bed. She pulled the crisp white sheets and quilt up over her. She still couldn't quite believe that her dad had been so organised as to put aside money for the trip; she had been stunned when Mr Tandy had replied to her email with details of the funding – which would easily cover the flights, transfers and accommodation for a couple of weeks. Then, just as she snuggled down into the bed, the train swaying beneath her, she remembered the small packet that had arrived from his office a few days ago.

Packed neatly in a padded envelope, addressed with what she now recognised as cheery Audrey's looping handwriting, it arrived at the flat the day before departure, just as she was doing her own packing, clammy with panic that Simon might turn up at any point. Inside was a *Tandy, Nitt & Co* embossed compliments slip with the carefully written words 'For your journey' on it, alongside what felt like a hardback, wrapped in brown parcel paper. She had assumed it would be an out-of-date guidebook, something to do with Norway perhaps. Or maybe it was a secret diary, the key that would unlock all of the mysteries of her dad's past? She had popped it in her suitcase just as she was distracted by the ping of her phone, heart jumping at the prospect of discovery, and she only remembered it was there while in mid-air. She could have screamed with frustration when she realised the packet was unreachable, far away in the hold. Now, however, it was right there, shoved into the side pocket of her open case.

She reached down for it, sat up in her bed, and ripped open the brown paper. Her initials were embossed in gold on the navy-blue jacket. She opened the smart hardback cover and saw that it was a lined notebook. On that first page she recognised her dad's handwriting.

To my adventurer, enjoy your journey, With all my love, Dad xxx

She clasped the notebook to her chest, hugging this extra scrap of encouragement from him, wiped a tear from her eye with the sleeve of her pyjama top and smiled to herself.

Clara let out a heavy sigh, then opened the notebook again, just to run her fingers over his writing. This time, she noticed that behind the crisp white paper there was something written on the second page too. It was a short poem, entitled 'The Peace of Wild Things', which contained a line about 'the day-blind stars waiting with their light'.

This is one of my very favourite poems. I do hope that when you meet Maggie you can remind her of it, and of how I used to read it to her. D xxx

Clara read the poem again. It was beautiful, although not something she would have imagined might capture her dad's attention. But as she turned the notebook over she felt a bubble of petulance, a little irritation that he hadn't written the poem there for her, but for Maggie.

Did he want her to enjoy this journey, or was she just being a glorified courier for him? What had he done to make Maggie go so bloody far that even normal transport couldn't reach her? And why did he have to send one daughter cryptic poem-messages via the other? And why couldn't he have told her that he loved this poem so bloody much instead of leaving her reading something she *knew* wasn't right at his own fucking memorial?

She dropped the book onto the quilt on her lap. Suddenly it didn't feel much like a surprise extra present, but more like an obligation from beyond the grave. Is this what her childhood had been then? An attempt to right the wrongs that her dad had done Maggie? A rerun at parenting after a disastrous first attempt? Had he even seen her as *her*, rather than a second shot? No wonder he had always seemed so easy-going about everything: Clara had never fallen out with him and moved to the other side of the world.

A queasiness that was about more than the train rocking crept over her. It had never been just her and her dad at their grown-up lunches in Paris, or Berlin, or even at bloody home. There had been a ghost at the table: the daughter who had upped and left. But why? And why had it been left up to her to find out?

She flicked the light off and curled up under the duvet, pulling it over her head, her arms hugging herself beneath it. In the distance, she heard a bell ringing – the train conductor letting passengers know that they were now crossing into the Arctic Circle.

# Chapter 11

Clara nearly gasped in shock as she opened the blind to her cabin. It was 6.30 a.m. and she had decided to give up on any hope of further sleep. But the view! It made having her eyes closed a second longer seem criminal: a bright blue sky, the shimmering fjord in the foreground, and even more mountains behind it than there had been when darkness had fallen the night before.

Everything sparkled, each colour seemingly picked in order to contrast perfectly with the next. She had seen breathtaking views before – summer holidays to the Alps, the vista down over Montmartre, even the Thames on a sunny summer's evening. But this seemed infinite. It was already the longest train journey she had ever taken, and still the scenery kept coming.

And whenever she seemed to be lulled by the still water passing by the window, the endless clear sky above it, they would pass a small detail. A cabin nestled in amongst some trees, its warm red roof peeking from between branches. A small cove, complete with sandy beach, where the curve of the fjord leaned a little more smoothly, creating space between the rocky edges. A wooden sailing boat pulled up onto one of the beaches, tucked into a battered shed for protection, the tip of its blue and white stripes giving it away against the pale sand. These tiny variations broke up the larger vista, stopping her from becoming complacent about the almost relentless beauty. She wondered what other beauty she had missed while she had tried to rest.

She was jittery though, shaky from lack of sleep, with the tackiness to her skin that only a restless night could create. She had tossed and turned for hours, unnerved by the fact that she had lost signal and Wi-Fi on her phone entirely not long after midnight, when she realised they were going through frequent tunnels under the mountains. She had felt relieved not to be keeping half an eye out for messages from Simon, but also profoundly alone, overwhelmed by the landscape she found herself in, and afraid of what she had let herself in for. No passport, no phone contact, no idea what potential welcome was waiting for her. Yes, she had wanted freedom. But this much? After all, despite her daily checking, the last time she had looked – at Trondheim Station – the Facebook message was still unopened.

She had managed to establish that the address her dad had given her for Maggie did exist. It turned out that it *was* an old lighthouse, now converted to a sometime guesthouse for travellers. They had a very rudimentary website, and after trying to call several times, Clara had eventually got hold of someone there. She had asked if she could speak to Maggie, but the voice on the end of the phone had said that yes, they knew Maggie, but that no, she didn't live there.

'She lives on the other side of the island,' said the crisp Scandinavian accent. 'We receive mail for her from time to time though.'

'So she is there then?' checked Clara, shivering with excitement that she had finally made contact.

'Yes, she lives on the island. But the other side. The side without the boat.'

'So I can't get the boat to reach her?'

'No, not often,' came the reply. 'The maelstrom is in between. If you need to get to the other side of the island you have to come to our cove and then hike. Unless you bring a kayak.'

It had never occurred to Clara that a maelstrom was anything other than a mood, but a brief online search had explained that it was a sort of whirlpool. A very slim body of water between two landmasses, where the tide going in and going out in short succession in a small space created multiple whirls and gullies. Fair enough, she thought, that sounded terrifying. No wonder Maggie used the boat to arrive at the far side of the island.

The island itself did not look that large – not more than a few square kilometres. It was one of a series dotted north of mainland Norway, an archipelago of islands, some of which were better known than others. A few of them seemed to receive warm attention on Pinterest and Instagram: small bright-red fisherman's huts now converted into luxury accommodation for bloggers and bankers, glowing travel influencers photographed against candy-pink skies, rare birds shot in flight with expensive lenses. But the further reaches of the archipelago seemed wilder, dependent on cod fishing rather than tourism, some spots populated by cold-water surfers who seemed to live out of adapted vans, cooking on photogenic campfires while looking like wild-haired lighthouse keepers who had been forgotten by the rest of society. These islands were clearly much harder to get to, particularly without a well-equipped van. And it was on one of these that Maggie lived.

Clara had looked at what seemed like infinite ways to reach Måsholmen. The better populated, more glamorous spots had small airports, connecting them to Trondheim or Narvik. But reaching Måsholmen required a train all the way up the Trondheim Fjord, along the spine of Norway, and then a small connecting flight. Finally, it seemed that the lighthouse itself had a small boat which ran across from one of the larger islands every week or two, depending on the weather and number of guests.

Clara figured that if she could get to Hestøy, she could persuade the boat to take her sooner than it might otherwise be going. After all, she had some spare cash. And if not, she would have to stay on Hestøy and wait a while until she could get across. She had nowhere else to be, and she had waited this long to meet her sister. And once she had made it to Måsholmen, it would not be too hard to find Maggie. There were after all only a handful of people on the island, and presumably very few places to hide.

The plan had seemed so simple while curled up on her sofa at home, a glass of red wine in one hand and the TV remote in the other. At 3 a.m., on a sleeper train rattling through the mountainside, her passport who-knows-where, it all felt somewhat different. But she was here now, and there was only an hour or so left of the train journey. Then it would be time for the next leg of the trip. Whether she was an adventurer, a glorified courier or a sister, she had come too far to turn back.

119

# Chapter 12

The station was a huge, post-war block of concrete. It had a strange Soviet glamour to it, the sort of location she had seen in the classic spy films she used to watch with her dad. She half expected to see a man in a fur coat meeting a chisel-cheeked blonde in an enormous hat, speaking cryptically while smoking seductively. But she didn't. She merely saw what seemed like a couple of hardened travellers and some even hardier looking men from the port. There was a buffet breakfast available in the station, so she dragged her luggage up to the counter and paid for a coffee and the meal: a plate of smoked salmon, beetroot and slices of pale cheese with some thick chunks of white bread. She poured herself coffee from a large canteen into a huge tin mug, and orange juice into a tiny, worn- almost-to-opaque glass. As she sat, eating, her stomach fought a battle between being tight with nerves and angry with hunger after her sleepless night. Hunger won, and she devoured it all with relish, even the reassuringly authentic beetroot, nothing like the plastic supermarket packets she remembered her mother opening while extolling the virtues of superfoods. This beetroot did taste like a superfood, smooth and rich, leaving inky fingertips as she picked up a piece she had dropped from the tablecloth. She had time to kill, so she went back for seconds of coffee, sipping it slowly, looking out to the docks beyond the station and the North Sea and mountains beyond that. She had left the metropolitan world of Instagrammable coffee shops behind her. It was her and the fishermen now, she thought as she put her chin in her hand. The oily salmon had left its scent on her fingers, and the coffee was making her eyeballs sting.

Her whole body felt taut, as if she had been hunched for months. She wanted to lie prone on the floor and let a toddler walk up and down her back to flatten it. She longed to stretch like a cat, as she used to when she got up from watching too many hours of TV as a teenager. But she did not dare do either, and slowly wheeled her bags out of the cafe, nodding at the woman in a floral apron behind the till, and headed down to take a taxi to the airstrip.

When she reached the taxi queue outside the station she leaned her head into the first car and asked for the airstrip with a smile. The taxi driver, his arm languidly draped over the side of his car door, smiled back.

'I can't take you there.'

'Right, um, OK. How do you mean?'

'It's right there – just down there by the side of the boat. Right there!' He laughed, a rasping laugh which Clara was not sure was entirely kind. His hand slapped the side of the car, knuckles raw with cracked skin.

She could see where he was pointing and she understood his point. They were in a vast, wide-laned area where the docks, the railway station – and clearly the airstrip – all met; it was a drive that would probably take a matter of seconds. But Clara had heavy bags, she had had a bad night's sleep, and she would be traipsing down past the roar of freight lorries heading towards the docks for nearly a kilometre.

'Yes, I can see it,' she said.

'Right there!' More laughter.

'Yes, I understand, it's just … ' She gestured at her bags.

'Listen. Madam. I am not allowed to take you even if you want. Regulations say I cannot drive so short a journey. It's a small walk, you're a young strong woman. You just head down there.'

Clara's shoulders sagged. Why couldn't he just help her? It would probably only be a ninety-second round trip. But there was a couple behind her now, fresh off a more recent train. A smart-looking businessman had arrived from the airport and was leaning in, trying to hurry her interaction along. The taxi driver looked past her and smiled at him. He said something briefly in Norwegian. Clara sighed and turned away, wishing Erik had been getting off at the same stop.

She hoicked her handbag higher onto her shoulder and adjusted her backpack, before wiggling her fingers to refresh her grip on the suitcase. She braced herself. Erik wasn't coming to save her. No one was. So it was going to be a walk. The wind was whistling into the harbour, blowing hair into her face and mouth, covering her eyes just as she was trying to cross the road. Articulated lorries were whooshing past, and there was the noise of a plane landing overhead. The walk wasn't *that* far, but with the bag sliding off her shoulder, displaced by the rucksack, and the case getting its wheels caught in pavement slabs, it seemed to take forever. Her hand was rigid with cold by the time she reached the small airfield, her knuckles having been exposed to the wind for the twenty-five minutes it had taken her to walk there. She wiggled her fingers again as she stood at the kiosk waiting for the receptionist to scan the code on her phone. The underside of her hand was white where the pressure of the bag had stopped the blood flow to her fingers. She smiled hopefully at the receptionist, longing to sit down. Apart from her socks and pants, she was in the same clothes as yesterday, and it seemed like she had sweated through them all more than a few times.

'Yes, your flight will be departing in forty minutes. As long as the wind drops.'

'Thank you. Do you think the wind will drop?'

'It is forecast to. But the weather here ... ' she shrugged.

'I see. Is it a very small plane?'

'There are twenty passengers. So not the smallest.'

Clara blinked, realising how very much she wanted the wind to drop. The thought of flying in anything like this weather made her stomach lurch with terror. But the reality was that she was too tired to mind a delay. She wheeled her bags over to one of the plastic chairs in the waiting area. There was a small woman in a pair of sheepskin-lined rubber boots sitting opposite her. She looked as if she might be in her early seventies, her hair in a sharp grey bob, her hands showing early signs of arthritic knuckles. She gave Clara a friendly nod. Clara returned it, tucking a stray hair back into her ponytail.

She sat and stared out of the window at the water and beyond. It felt as if she were at the edge of the world, that the person creating it had run out of ideas and thrown a few rocks across their desk and left the sea and sky to do the rest of the heavy lifting. The sun was now out and the remaining clouds were just white wisps, blowing across her view at quite a disarming speed.

The thought of Maggie doing this trip for the first time, her motivation in reverse, preoccupied Clara. Travelling all this way, not *to* something but *from* it. Or perhaps not to *someone*, but from them. What could drive you this far? *Who* could? In that moment, as the embers of fury she had felt with her father for sending her on this wild goose chase still glowed inside of her, she felt for the first time that she could imagine what Maggie's frame of mind might have been. This sister she had never known existed had taken this journey, presumably all alone. What had Clara been doing that day, she wondered. How old had she been? Had she even been born? The thought struck her like a slap: perhaps Maggie had no idea Clara even existed.

It wasn't long before the woman behind the check-in desk announced that the flight would be departing in twenty minutes, and it was time to start loading and then boarding. Clara had never been on a plane this small, and even the wobble of the steps as she walked up to the vehicle felt unnervingly flimsy. She felt squeamish as she put her hand on the side of the plane and dipped her head to enter the doorway. Barely thick enough to keep the wind out, let alone keep them all steady against it.

She saw the neat curve of the bob belonging to the woman from the waiting area, and aimed to sit next to her. Again, they exchanged polite smiles, only this time, as Clara took off her coat and folded it ready to position under the seat, the woman said, 'Nervous?'

'Yes,' said Clara. 'I am a little. I have never been on one of these planes, and it's a bit ... '

'Blowy?'

'Yes, exactly.'

'Don't worry. I have taken this flight in worse conditions than today.'

'OK, thank you. I think!' Clara laughed, but the woman merely gave her an inscrutable smile and looked out of the window.

As her second flight in two days took off, Clara pushed her feet into the base of her boots, as if feeling rooted to the plane's floor might somehow help her stay safe. She felt where the seam of her thick hiking sock met the edge of her small toe, rubbing against the side of her boot. Everything had felt so fresh and exciting when she had packed it a couple of days ago. It had given her hope – a new start! – to have all this unfamiliar stuff. New kit for a new chapter, she had told herself. Now she felt like something closer to a fraud, hands gripping the edges of her seat while the elderly lady looked placidly into the distance, apparently unperturbed by the feeling that one hearty sneeze could knock the whole flight off course. Oh, for this woman's sense of self, instead of being someone people still referred to as a 'girl', someone whose sense of self was dependent on her ricocheting between the affection a boyfriend, a father, a stranger might feel like offering her.

Her stomach lurched as they ascended up and above the port. The container ships which had been so overwhelming as she had struggled past them with her luggage now looked dinky, little Brio toys ready to be pushed along a strip of blue carpet by a chubby infant hand. Even the mountains, so imposing while she had been sitting in the station cafe, were now beginning to resemble skimming stones leaping across the water. She saw her dad's hand, the confident flick of the wrist as a pebble exactly the right size and shape hopped in and out of the water on its way out to sea.

The captain – an immaculate blonde woman who looked as if she had stepped off the side of a shampoo bottle – read out some reassuring words, in Norwegian and then in English.

'The flight will be eighteen minutes ... please bear with us as it might take a little longer with the breeze.'

As she said the word 'breeze' the plane lurched, and Clara's stomach with it. The mountains looked far away, but not so far that falling and hitting them didn't seem like a realistic possibility. The sense of being emotionally unmoored, which had dogged her for so long, now seemed to be a literal one. Tethered to nothing, she might, at any second, simply blow away. As if she had never existed. Then, just as the plane had stopped ascending, it seemed to begin its descent. They passed more small islands, most of which looked uninhabited until they got a little closer and Clara spotted paths that were actually small roads, tiny houses dotted beside them from time to time.

Her stomach felt as if it were floating up and out of her as the plane dropped more suddenly. Her travelling companion's hand flinched, gripping the arm rest as her gaze remained steadfastly forward. Slowly, Clara realised that the wide road in the distance was a small airstrip and that they were going to be landing on the island ahead. As they approached it, she saw a few houses, fresh white-painted fronts and cheerful red roofs. Despite each house being at least a kilometre from its neighbour, most of them had white picket fences around a square patch of grass at the front. Almost American, Clara thought, before realising that traditional American homes were more likely to have been modelled on these than vice versa.

Finally, just as Clara thought they may have been heading straight for the snow-dusted mountain ahead, they reached the airstrip and landed. The wheels hit the tarmac with a thwack, Clara gasping and inadvertently grabbing the arm of the woman next to her.

'I'm so sorry!'

'It's OK. We are here now,' replied the woman. She lifted her arm away from the seat rest – and Clara's hand – and gave her a reassuring pat on the side of her leg.

'I hope you enjoy your visit to our beautiful island. May you find what you are looking for.'

'Who,' mouthed Clara silently as the woman bent forwards to pick up her handbag. 'Who.'

# Chapter 13

This time, Clara was braced for the fact that there would be a walk to get the boat, and that it probably wouldn't be fun. She had seen the small jetty from the plane, and was ready for the effort of getting there. She yanked the backpack on again, took a swig of water from the bottle she had refilled back at the station cafe, and began the walk from the airstrip to the harbourside.

There was a small building by the side of the jetty, with some laminated timetables and advertisements for a couple of cafes posted outside. She knocked on a stable door, and a moment later a man opened the top half and poked out his head and chest. He was smiling from behind an enormous moustache. Dense salt-and-pepper hair sat across his top lip, which looked like a brush that had been searching for a dustpan and had found a mouth instead. He was wearing a thick, chunky-knit jumper of the sort that Clara remembered her mum adoring about a decade before, when Scandinavian dramas had been all the rage and Ian had been yet to appear on the scene, calming some of her more forthright opinions on what made a 'Real Man'.

'Hello,' said Clara with another hopeful smile. 'I was wondering if this is the place to get the boat across to the lighthouse.'

'Yes, I go there. No boat today though,' he said, shaking his head.

'But I called the lighthouse – they know I'm coming today.'

'To the lighthouse on Måsholmen?'

'Yes!'

'No, they have no guests at the moment.'

'I know, I know, I am not an actual guest. It's ... I'm going to the other side of the island – to see my sister. I am going to see Maggie. She is my sister.'

'Maggie?'

'Yes, the lady who lives on the other side of the island. Not the lighthouse.'

'The lady with the dark hair? She is still there?'

'Yes! That's her.' Clara had no idea if Maggie had dark hair or not. Or, she realised, whether she was still there. But that small photo in Stéphanie's passport felt like enough. After all, there couldn't be any other women with dark hair around here, could there?

'Wait, let me make a phone call.'

'OK, yes – please. And I can pay, I have a card and cash.' Clara was starting to babble.

The man tucked his head away from the open top half of the door, and she heard him pick up the receiver and make a call in Norwegian. There was a fair number of 'OK's and 'tak tak's so she let her hopes up a little. A minute later, the moustache was back.

'So, I can take you when the gas arrives.'

'OK.' Clara looked at him imploringly. Would there be any further explanation? 'When is ... the gas coming?'

'Gas, Calor gas, it comes on the next boat. The boss says I

can bring you when I bring it. Wait here an hour or so, you can come on the boat with gas, mail, other items I have for them.'

'Oh, thank you, that's amazing,' Clara beamed.

'You're lucky,' he said with a smile, his top lip curling as if someone was bending the brush.

'I really am. Is it OK if I just sit here and wait in the sun?'

'Sure – you want coffee?'

'That would be even more amazing.'

'What can I say, I'm amazing.' Clara grinned as the man reached for a tin mug with a black rim and poured coffee into it from the Thermos in front of him. 'Take it, enjoy it in the sun. Welcome to Nordland.'

'Thank you so much. I'm Clara. What's your name?'

'Arve,' he replied, his eyes creasing almost to nothing as he smiled and handed over the coffee.

Clara left her bags by the wooden steps up to his hut, and took her coffee and sat on the rocks by the edge of the harbour. She cupped both hands around the tin mug and sipped slowly, feeling the sun hit her face as some of the wisps of cloud gently blew away. There were birds – she had no idea what kind – circling the rocky edges behind her, squawking at each other before heading back out to the water, looking intently at it as the lapping stopped almost entirely, the area clear of incoming boats and planes, at rest.

While she was drinking, she remembered a packet of nuts she had bought in the station at Trondheim, and found it in the pocket of her jacket. The sun was out but the air was still quite cold, so her new socks and warm waterproof jacket didn't seem as much like fancy dress as they had felt earlier in the day. She had her snack and let her eyes close as she sat, feeling something close to peace for the first time in weeks.

The water started to lap faster against the edge of the

harbour, and then came the distant buzzing of an approaching vehicle. Clara snapped her eyes open, momentarily dazzled by the sun, and saw a white boat heading towards them, a small triangular Norwegian flag fluttering on the mast. She turned and waved up at Arve, who was now standing at the door of his hut. To her surprise she realised he was wearing an enormous pair of yellow waterproof trousers with matching boots, held up by braces strapped over his shoulders. He pointed at a small RIB boat and grinned. Clara grinned back, partly because his smile was so infectious, but also with sheer relief at a man showing her kindness without any apparent agenda.

Clara dragged her stuff round to the jetty where Arve's boat was, and waited while the larger boat docked on the other side of the bay. Wordless bearded men hauled postal sacks, some crates of fruit and veg, and a few canisters of Calor gas from the boat, while a second man appeared, clipboard in hand, from another small hut. Things were briefly checked, the man's pen making quick flicks as he marked what looked like ticks on his spreadsheet. The boat men handed over a digital handset for him to sign, hands were raised and then they headed back to their boat or office respectively.

Arve immediately busied himself dragging a tarpaulin from under the seats on his boat and laying it out flat before carrying some of the gas canisters and other cargo on board. He gestured to Clara to bring her bags, which she did, the wheeled case bumping along the slats of the jetty while her stomach twitched with nerves. Arve lifted her luggage onto the tarpaulin, pulled the sides up so his cargo was covered, and threw her a life jacket. Once he had seen she'd fastened it properly, he held out his hand to help her on, waited until she was seated, and yanked the starter rope. Clara grabbed the side as water sprayed up around them and they left the island in their wake.

From the air, the mountains that made up the centre part of most of these rocky islands had looked dark and intimidating, but not huge; seen from the water's level, they looked enormous. The jagged edges of the rock were covered here and there by moss and occasional scrubby bush, but for the most part they were a volcanic black, almost navy blue, reflecting the deep dark water surrounding them. Friendly though he seemed, Clara was suddenly aware that Arve was now the only person between her and this vast landscape. She had not yet reached Maggie, and she was entirely at the mercy of a man she had met ninety minutes ago.

Måsholmen was becoming visible in the distance, but she had lost her sense of perspective: surrounded by so much sky and sea it was impossible to know how long the body of water would take to cross. And while the sun was bright, the air was cold. She was in the northernmost part of Norway; there was nothing beyond these islands until the desolate expanses of Svalbard, she remembered. And no one knew where she was. She had tried to check her phone incessantly during her last hour on the train, but to no avail, and she hadn't had a proper chance since. Her friends, her mother didn't know if she had arrived. And Simon might not even know she had gone. If she simply tipped into the water now, from an unscheduled boat, with Arve as the only witness and no passport to trace her, would anyone ever find out? Could simply disappearing be that easy? The nights she had thought about it, her heart pounding after another confrontation with Simon, seemed so long ago now that it felt like an option within her reach. The boat turned, throwing Clara to one side, pressed against the inflated edge and grabbing for a handle. Arve was looking out into the distance, one side of his beard dripping with seawater, which had just breached the edge.

Slowly, the island drew closer to them, the lighthouse becoming visible up on the rocks overlooking the shore. How would she get up there, she wondered as the RIB drew ever closer.

The boat lurched over waves as it approached, slamming back down onto the water's surface as it cleared them. Arve turned from his steering position to smile at her and give an encouraging thumbs up. While his back was turned, the sea surged higher than Clara had yet seen, lifting the front end of the boat high onto the wave before its descent and then its slam. Ice-cold water splashed up and over the sides and onto Clara. Her hair, already blown out of its ponytail, slicked across her face, leaving it fizzing with cold. The jacket, which had seemed like such an indulgence a few hours ago, had largely kept her dry, but one foot was sodden. She willed Arve to turn and smile again, reassuring her that they'd make it. He didn't.

Clara gasped and gripped the plastic handle on the side of the boat. The sea was churning, her stomach heaving – she no longer knew if it was a result of nerves or the constant motion of either the day itself or merely the last half hour. She had to make a conscious effort to breathe steadily, to stop herself from crying out or simply starting to sob. An inch deeper into the water, a handle held slightly less firmly, and she would have been tossed into the sea, she was sure of it. And she was equally sure that if she had been, there would have been no chance of survival. She had none of the hardiness that friends who had spent summers camping seemed to pick up, and none of the physical confidence she had envied in sporty friends at school. She would have had nothing to throw at the situation, and in that instant, feeling so small and so far away, she wasn't sure that anyone would even have noticed if she had been catapulted from the boat.

'I'm sorry about that one!' yelled Arve, over the noise of the boat's engine.

Clara gave him a pale smile and focused on the land ahead. The boat was slowing now, aiming for a battered-looking wooden jetty.

'A rough one today,' he said as he held out a hand and helped her across the boat and then up onto the pier. His beard was still dripping and his hand felt icy to the touch. Clara noticed that her own hand was shaking as she reached for his, her knuckles white. The ground felt unsteady beneath her feet; she had no idea if it was motion sickness of the dizzying effect of an hour spent wondering if anyone would realise, much less care, if she had simply slipped between the waves. The imagined scene replayed in her mind as she waited for Arve to begin the process of unloading her luggage and the boat's cargo, and she felt pathetically grateful for his kindness with every item he lifted. Once it was all off and the boat secured, he pointed to the wooden steps heading up and up to the base of the lighthouse. Time to get walking again.

Despite her panic, the trek up the steps with her wheeled case clanking behind her wasn't actually as bad as Clara had imagined. Yes, her heart now felt as if it might escape from her chest at any minute. And yes, she could feel that the back of her top was drenched with sweat yet again. But she had made it – albeit with Arve's help. She scraped her hair back, running her fingers through to try and smooth it into a ponytail. Arve stood at the threshold of what looked like a kitchen and shouted something in Norwegian. A moment later a small woman about Clara's mother's age appeared at the door. She was slim, wearing a close-fitting rust-coloured pullover, a pair of neat oatmeal slacks and felted wool slippers. She also had on an apron and was wiping what looked like flour from her hands onto it as she appeared at the door. Clara wasn't sure if the white in her hair was flour or natural flecks of colour.

'Hello?' she said, before looking up and seeing Arve standing next to Clara.

'Signe, hello,' said Arve. She glanced at him, clearly puzzled by Clara's presence. Clara went to open her mouth to explain that she wasn't a guest, but before she could, Arve had given her a hearty clap on the back and said, 'Don't worry dear Signe, this is my new friend, Clara.'

'OK ...'

'She is not staying with you; she is coming to visit her sister.' Signe frowned.

Clara's mouth kept opening to speak but Arve just kept going. She felt that she was losing control of the conversation, but she didn't know how to seize it back.

'She has hitched a lift with me and the gas canisters and I told her I was sure you would make her welcome.'

Signe's brow was still furrowed in confusion. She was looking at her hands, brushing them together to get the last of the flour off.

Clara took a deep breath and leapt in.

'Maggie ... I am here to visit Maggie.'

Signe's face immediately flicked up towards Clara. Her forehead was now smooth, her eyes wide open, her head tipped slightly back with curiosity. The jut of her chin made Clara anxious. She had been hoping for a welcoming smile and instead she was confronted with high cheekbones and pale, glassy eyes looking her up and down.

'You are here to see Maggie? The French woman?'

'Well, I suppose she is a bit French, yes,' Clara babbled. The conversation was spinning even further from her grasp now. In truth, Clara had never thought of Maggie as French at all, focusing instead on their shared English parent. Now it was dawning on her that perhaps Maggie didn't speak any English and she had come all this way to try and bond with someone she would never even manage a three-sentence chat with. Signe had said nothing else, continuing to stare intently, clearly waiting for Clara to explain further.

'We have the same dad. He's English, I'm English. But I think maybe Maggie's mum was French.'

'I see,' said Signe. 'I didn't know any of this, she has never spoken about her family.'

'Anyway, I have some news for her. And she is very difficult to get hold of!' Clara laughed nervously, while simultaneously wishing she could just stop and hold it together with just an inch of Signe's chilly calm. 'So I have come to visit her.'

Signe's head dipped a little now, and her voice was lower.

'Clara, perhaps you had better come in. You need to be warm before you make the journey.'

She looked up at Arve and thanked him.

'My pleasure, Sig,' he replied. 'I am glad you have our friend safe now – we nearly lost her out there.'

Clara turned back to check that she had heard him correctly. The expression on their faces suggested she had. Just how dangerous *was* this island? She had rather forgotten that there was more of the journey to go, and felt her heart sink at the realisation, just as she was catching her breath; she wasn't going to be staying here, enjoying the view, and eating whatever delicious pastry Signe had been making. Because the view *was* spectacular. The weather would have felt ordinary, gloomy even, back in England, but here, where the colours had the space of endless sea and sky on which to spread and bleed into each other, it was mesmerising. Blues seemed green and greens seemed blue, reflecting against each other as if someone were holding a giant mirror at the invisible horizon. In fact, the only thing that distinguished the point where sky dipped and turned to sea was the dark bumps of the rocky islands in the distance, strewn across the horizon like laundry thrown on the floor. Shards of pale sunlight were peeking through the low clouds, the stripes reflecting in the now still water. Clara stared out as far as she could, reluctant to absorb Signe's doubts. Or was it concern? Either way, she realised that in a few minutes Arve would leave, and she would be alone on the island, with just this woman and – somewhere out there – her sister for protection. What had she done?

She had no idea. But she had come too far to turn back now. She smiled at Signe and stepped into the lighthouse.

# Chapter 14

The warm mug had been in her hands for a couple of minutes before the tiredness hit Clara. Signe had welcomed her in and passed her a strong black coffee in a pale-blue enamel cup without even asking her if she might like milk.

'Take a seat,' she had said gently, inviting Clara into a cosy kitchen, furnished with a combination of traditional wooden surfaces and professional equipment. It smelled of cinnamon, coffee and warm yeast, and just sitting there on a bench at the window, overlooking the view below, made Clara's limbs feel soft and spongy, like proving dough. She wasn't even halfway up the structure, but she still felt miles above the ocean.

'Thank you so much,' Clara replied as she took the drink. She looked down at the mug lest her glossy eyes give way to tears. She took a breath, then asked, 'Is it far?'

'It is not too far; the island is not large. You simply follow the path around the coast. Some of it has track, but in parts you may have to clamber across the rocks, depending on the tide. I think it is too late to walk across the beaches now.'

'Will I know when I reach the house?'

'Oh yes, the house is very clear. There is a bit of a hike; I am not sure if Maggie has secured the path, but you can see the house easily.'

Clara sipped her coffee.

'And did you mention I was coming? When I called before?'

'Oh no. Your decision is private, I would not have discussed it. And we have a lot of enquiries about visits here which come to nothing. Some people see the website and want to visit, but then they realise how far we are, or how remote, and they decide against it.'

'I see.'

'Why don't you leave your case here and take what you can in your rucksack? You are welcome to do that, and return when you can. Once you are beyond the lighthouse, there is nothing until you reach Maggie's house, so it would be best to travel light.'

'Oh, thank you.' Clara put her hand across her chest, touched by Signe's kindness. 'I am so nervous.'

'Don't be,' said Signe. 'I used to do that walk several times a week as I was growing up.'

'I don't just mean about the walk.'

'Well, you have shown admirable commitment in making it this far.' Signe's eyes were soft. She seemed like someone who was not used to encouraging others – but only because she rarely came across people who doubted themselves. Perhaps she mostly knew people who were like the woman Clara had always wanted to be – rather than the woman Clara feared she was. 'I do not know Maggie well, but she has always been kind and courteous to me. I cannot imagine she will not welcome her own sister. You have been under the same stars all this time, and now you are just a little closer.'

'Thank you. I hope so.' She smiled at Signe, then looked out of the window again. *Under the same stars.* Clara felt pathetically small.

*

The path was less a path and more a slim groove along the grassy side of the rock face. At first, Clara hadn't been able to see it at all, but once she had spotted its start, tucked away at the end of the lighthouse's small garden, it was almost easy to follow.

The hillside was green on granite. Tufts of rough bouncy grass sprouted up from dirt which seemed to be only a few millimetres deep before it gave way to the purply-black stone of the mountainside. Its surface was irregular, some chewed at by the wandering sheep that Clara could see in the distance, but there were shaggy mounds of longer grass too, some of which flopped right over onto the path itself. Wide enough for two parallel feet but not much more, it looked only slightly larger than the sort of gouge Clara used to make in her wooden desk at school with an old biro.

Only fifty metres ahead, round the bend of the cliff, the path was barely visible. So she tried to keep looking at her feet, concentrating on where she was, rather than where she was going. She could see how close to the edge it was, and how far there was to fall if she put a foot wrong. Her legs were tired after the journey, and as the walk continued, her ankles were starting to tire, worn out by having to constantly adapt to the rocky surface. The slight shake and judder of her ankles started to increase, step after step, and she had to will herself to stay steady, stay strong. One stumble and she would drop a few hundred metres down, past the point where the soft landing of spongy grass ended and it would instead be nothing but rocks. Rocks and then ocean.

She couldn't look to her left without feeling her head reel back, dizzy with images of herself tumbling towards the sea, bouncing from back to shoulder to thigh and back again. Didn't dare to look ahead lest the panic about how much further she had to go set in. So she tried to keep her head down, following foot after foot, letting her heart rate try and find a pace with her steps.

*Just keep going,* she whispered to herself. *Left, right, inhale, exhale. Left, right, inhale, exhale. Left, right, inhale, exhale.*

But her thoughts kept running away from her. What would happen if she fell? Would anyone ever know? How long would Signe leave it, assuming she had made it to Maggie? Would she ever check? Or if she fell would she simply lie at the bottom of the cliffs until the waves took her? How long does it take to die from a broken leg? And what would her dad have thought if she did that? If she failed in getting one simple message to just one person?

The thought of her dad sent her thoughts racing in another direction – why had he done this to her? Was it some sort of prank? A practical joke that just wasn't landing right because, well, because he was *dead*? And it was only that thought – his being dead – that galvanised her.

*You're here because he can't be. Honour that.*

*Honour it, honour it, honour it.*

She started to whisper those two words to herself. She was at least still here, and able to do this. It didn't have to be fun, she just had to get through it. To survive. She paused, took a deep breath, adjusted her rucksack, which was now sticking to the growing sweat patch on her back, and looked up at the sky.

A couple of hundred metres later the land had curved so far behind her that she could no longer see the lighthouse: she was in limbo – beyond the lighthouse – what she had left behind now as invisible as her destination. *But you're onto the next bay,* she told herself, *you're working your way along the north edge of the island, just like Signe said.*

She could see that the path was starting to head further

uphill here, to make it up and around some grassless patches of nothing but sheer exposed rock. Jammed into the side of the path were a few steel rods, and looped between them a length of steel chain. At first she thought they were there to prevent falling, to hold her in, before realising that they were more useful for hauling herself up the path.

After a few steps she found that rather than stepping up and using the chains for guidance, she was grasping the chains on either side of her and pulling herself up where the path had changed from scrubby track to huge granite steps. She had to position her leading foot at mid-thigh height before yanking to get her body up and onto the next step.

Sweat now covered the whole of her back, and her feet were damp with the effort of having to grip the track with her boots. Her hair, still plastered to her skull in the ponytail she had put in after the boat ride, was starting to feel itchy with saltwater and sweat. She wanted to cry, to call someone to help her, to see a helicopter hovering into view, come to take her away. But there was no one. She was alone on a huge lump of rock, as far from anyone she had ever loved as she had been in her life. And yet ... and yet perhaps around the next bay there was a sister, unknowingly waiting for her. Under the same stars.

So she kept going. Knees aching, thighs burning, ankles wobbling. And just as she had fully convinced herself that she could only make it a few steps further, the path turned and then plateaued. And there, across the next bay, sitting on the rocks above a perfect white sandy beach, was a small blue-and-white house.

*Maggie.* She whispered it, the name immediately whisked away by the wind. *Maggie.*

# Chapter 15

It seemed impossible, but she could see her sister's house. Right there! The place where her father had never managed to reach her. And now she was within walking distance of it. Clara held onto the steel railing and threw her head back, whooping into the wind, feeling her voice vibrate through her entire body. For the first time, she believed that she might actually make it.

She sat on the side of the path with her feet resting on the rocky steps and looked out over the bay and the sea in the distance. It was early evening now, but the light was not fading, merely dulling a little behind the haze of cloud. She took her rucksack off her back and pulled at her T-shirt to get some air up and around the area where the fabric was clinging to her wet torso, then opened her bag and took a few sips from her water bottle while trying to take in the view.

On the one hand it was incomprehensibly enormous, the sky and sea overwhelming, almost filling her field of vision. But on the other, now that she had stopped for a minute, she could make out details in the landscape. The lichen on some of the rocks around her, almost neon green. The small candy-pink inner-ears of the sheep she had passed from time to time, twitching as they wandered aimlessly. And there were scrubby plants in the distance – small patches of grass, some topped with white puffy clouds which made her think of the images of cotton fields in the Deep South she had studied at school. They waved in the wind, tiny, incongruous powder puffs against the rock.

After a few minutes and half of her water, Clara began to wish she had never stopped. The sweat was starting to dry on her, making her shiver in the wind. And her muscles were now throbbing where they had done the heavy lifting of getting her to this height. She felt a sort of giddy exhilaration that she had made it this far. Finally, she had completed an expedition of her own. Well, nearly, she reminded herself. Was the air a bit thinner up here? Or was it the tiredness? Either way, the combination of excitement and anxiousness had left the tips of her fingers fizzing, a slight dizziness creeping up on her. But when she looked down at the little house, its cheery cornflower-blue front and the bright white window frames looking out onto the beach, she knew she had to keep going: she couldn't give up on her dad now. And anyway, how hard could this last bit be? She had done the treacherous section, after travelling for two days. Now she was almost there: family.

Clara took a deep breath, wriggled her toes in her stiff boots and stood up. She tried to visualise her feet crossing the sand, her hand knocking on that front door only a mile away. She imagined Maggie, opening the door, her face breaking into a smile as Clara explained who she was. She pictured her welcoming her in. Perhaps she had enamel mugs too. Perhaps she swapped recipes with Signe from time to time and could also make the sort of cinnamon twist Clara had seen in the lighthouse kitchen earlier that day. Perhaps tomorrow morning they would be sitting on the beach together, toes in the water, enjoying breakfast. Perhaps.

As she hoisted her rucksack back round onto her back, she also tried to imagine her father. Him, writing the letter that she had just checked was safely in the top of her bag, folded carefully in the plastic folder in which she had placed it for protection. Clara tried to imagine him somehow watching her now, willing her on, willing her to make the final part of her journey. But all she could see was a memory: Dad, flipping that small biscuit into his mouth in the Place des Vosges. Grinning at her and encouraging her to live a little, to try new things.

She thought heading downhill would have been easier, but it turned out to be harder going trying to balance herself with the big drops between the rocks. Her bag seemed to be getting heavier, the new position of her water bottle rendering her balance a little off. She clung to the steel chains that made the loose barriers, at one point losing her footing and swaying perilously over the edge, her knuckles white and her feet trembling. She turned and tried to do some of the steepest parts backwards so that her bag wasn't creating quite as much imbalance. It pushed the pain down to her feet though, her ankles screaming each time her weight landed on another step.

The threat – as well as the constant mental image – of falling over the side hovered over her with greater urgency the closer she got. When the path finally seemed to flatten a little, she turned to face forwards again – only to realise that while her back had been turned, the tide had come in, and fast. The water had been encroaching while she was having her rest, but when she had been fiddling with the letter, her water bottle and the fastenings on her bag, the bay had seemed impossibly far away. Now she realised that it hadn't been – and that the water hadn't had any real distance to move to cover almost every inch of sand.

She was too scared to hurry, and too tired to rush even if she had wanted to. But her heart sank as she realised that instead of her final steps being a couple of hundred metres across pristine white sand, she was going to have to scramble around the huge granite boulders at the back of the bay, hoping that the seawater wasn't going to envelop them too.

The sea was close now. Its tangy mineral smell was in the air, foam from the waves slamming on the shore and creating a mist which left Clara's face damp, as if she had been using the sort of facial spray she longed to be able to afford while dawdling on beauty sites online. The lines between sky, sea and the shoreline were starting to blur, the rocks increasingly slippery from the sea spray, glistening black as the path petered out and she was left at the point where all three met.

She saw a glint of light flashing between two rocks and leaned forward to see what it was. A bottle? She reached forward – perhaps this was the moment she found a message! But no, it was an old vodka bottle, and its lid, complete with a logo in Cyrillic font which meant nothing to her, was still screwed on. The glass was worn by the sea; it must have been in and out on the tides a few times. Clara imagined a Russian sailor tossing it overboard after a long night, hundreds of miles away, with no idea that a young woman so far from home would be the next person to see it, or even touch it. She rolled the cool glass between her palms for a moment, soothing the red-raw patches where she had been gripping the chains for dear life. Then she dropped it softly down between the rocks where she had found it. Her appearance might be a shock for Maggie. The least she could do was not turn up with litter from the beach in her hands.

The water was still coming in, so Clara had to scramble

around the rest of the beach until she was on the far side of it, approaching what looked like the edge of Maggie's property. The daylight outside was still dimming but it looked as if there were no lights on inside. Clara was so close she could probably shout and be heard if she timed it between the crash of the waves. The rocks had given way to a smoother grassy slope on which the house was sitting. It was a cheerful blue, with bright white window frames and front door. It was a different colour scheme from the red or yellow huts she had seen from the train or once she had been on Hestøy. Had Maggie done it herself, knowing that she didn't need to pander to tourists on this remote spot? Or had it simply been bought like this? The house was unlike anything she could have imagined – in the context of the island it was tiny, standing all alone facing towards the Arctic. What must it feel to wake up here on a grizzly Monday in January? But it also seemed like an achievement of such a magnitude that Clara felt almost breathless. Maggie had the run of all of this – the ocean, the cliffs, this sky that seemed to unfold further and further each time Clara looked up. She had so much.

On the grass on the far side of the house there was a solar panel about the size of a large double bed, facing out to sea, its glass glinting in the last of the opalescent sun. The nearer side seemed to be divided into a vegetable patch and some flowers, and behind, before the rocks started again, there seemed to be a chicken run. But inside the house there appeared no sign of life.

Clara was nearly at the door now. She tugged at her clothes, trying to straighten them, to make herself look a little more presentable. This was it, the big reunion. She shook out her ponytail with trembling hands, running her fingers through her hair and tying it back afresh, as neatly as she could. Finally, she raised her hand and knocked on the gloss white wood of the front door.

Silence.

A pause.

Clara looked down at the back of her hand, flexing her fingers in and out. There was mud from her trek across the rocks, her short nails were dirty. She listened. Could she hear movement in there? It occurred to her that she might have frightened Maggie, who of course would not have been expecting anyone.

Clara took a breath.

'It's safe!' she called out. 'I am safe! I have walked from the lighthouse – Signe knows I am coming to visit you.'

Silence.

'I am so sorry if I startled you. I promise I am safe!'

This time, she heard shuffling. Then keys in the door. And slowly, the white door opened, a crack widening towards Clara. A face appeared. The face she had thought about so much for the last few weeks. Yet still the face of an absolute stranger.

Maggie's pale grey-blue eyes looked out from above wide, high cheekbones. Her skin was darker than Clara's, and darker than her father's. She had a sprinkling of freckles across a neat nose; her face seemed healthy, if slightly weather-beaten. She had a strong jaw, jutting slightly defensively as she looked out at Clara. The only thing Clara recognised was her long dark hair, which had the same cow's lick kicking out from a rough side parting. It was just the same as the hairstyle of the women whose passport Clara had in her suitcase back at the lighthouse.

She saw nothing of her father. But who else could she be?

'Hello, I am your sister. I have come to find you.' Clara smiled, waiting for Maggie to return the gesture.

Instead, her hand flinched, moving from the door handle to her chest in shock. Clara watched the gesture with widening eyes. Because there, resting on her chest, was a hand almost identical to her father's. The same wide fingers, the same defined wrinkles at her knuckles, and the same wide, square fingernails that she had just seen on her own hands too.

Maggie's hand had given her away, but her face remained unmoved.

'I don't have a sister.' Her voice was slow, deliberate, as if she had been waiting to make this clear.

And with that, the hand that Clara knew was her own flesh and blood moved back to the door handle and started to close the front door.

# Chapter 16

After a pause which had felt like an hour, suddenly things started to move too quickly. Clara tilted her head, trying to maintain eye contact through the fast-closing door, talking incessantly in an attempt to keep Maggie engaged.

'I *am* your sister! Ben's daughter! Ben Seymour! He has sent me here with a message for you! I am so sorry to have startled you ...'

She realised that she had not explained that Ben was dead, but nor could she bring herself to blurt out news like that into a slamming door. Her father deserved more than that and so did Maggie. Everything was unravelling and she was too tired to keep up with any of it.

'Please! I am not here to upset you!'

But her voice was drowned out by the noise of the window shutters either side of the front door being brought down fast. And now she could see them starting to close at the windows running along the west side of the house, facing her. It hadn't even occurred to her to look into the house before she knocked, and now she was being shut out of it. Clara ran along the west wall, trying to keep up with the pace at which Maggie was working inside. She saw her sister's hand, and the neat knitted sleeve of a patterned sweater, reaching for the final blinds. The entire wall was now closed to her. Maggie was hiding herself from sight, as well as from communication.

Clara darted around the edges of the house. She tried to avoid the plant beds in the garden to the side, but tripped on the terracotta pots holding scrubby mini-bushes of garden herbs lined up along the small path. She stumbled and fell, slamming the heel of her hand into the earth and trying to brush the dirt off onto her jeans. She realised she had no idea which room was which inside the house. Was that the kitchen, looking out onto the herbs? Where would Maggie be heading now? Why should Clara have expected that this would be her welcome? They were *sisters*.

Dusting herself down and adjusting her rucksack, she crept around to the back of the house, where she had seen the chicken run as she approached. She had just about beaten Maggie.

The rear windows were large – the same size as the two that were either side of the front door, looking out to sea. These ones wouldn't have nearly the same spectacular view, but they did afford Clara a crucial glimpse into the house. She could see that most of it was open plan – a large wooden-floored living area scattered with rugs, with kitchen units running the length of the left side of the building and through to the windows by the main door. She could see internal doors off to the right and wooden cupboards surrounding the kitchen units against the wall to the left, where she had stumbled on the pots. And beyond them was a staircase, up which she could see the dark grey boots of her sister, slowly walking. It looked like there was a mezzanine sleeping space up there, with the circular window from the front of the house above the bed, looking out to sea.

Clara had no idea if Maggie knew she was still there, peering in. Maggie had made her point and retreated from view; from this angle there was no way Clara could make out any more than the end of a bed or sofa up there on the mezzanine. Whether Maggie cared or not, Clara was still peering into her space, and it felt wrong. But she wasn't ready to give up yet – and there was nowhere else for her to go.

She unhooked her bag from her shoulders and rested it on the grass at the back of the house. She pressed her face as close as she could to the glass of the window and cupped her mouth with her hands.

'Maggie! I'm so sorry to frighten you like this. I am not here to upset you, I promise. I have travelled from England; I've been so excited to meet you.' Urgh, the pathetic whingeing tone of her voice.

*This is too much about yourself*, she thought, *say something about her* . . .

'There is some news for you. And Ben – our father – wanted me to see you to deliver it. It seemed like the right thing to do to deliver it in person. I don't know what to do . . . can you come to the door so we can talk? I *will* go back as soon as I can if you want me to.'

Silence. Not even any movement from up on the mezzanine. She had to try and get Maggie's attention somehow.

'I am *so* sorry to do this this way . . . but Ben is dead. Our father is dead. There are documents and information he wanted you to have. I thought you should know. I thought you should have these documents yourself. I've brought them for you. They are back at the lighthouse . . . '

Nothing. Could Maggie even hear her?

The wind was picking up now and the light was shifting again. Cloud cover was almost complete but there was also an eerie sort of dusk falling. It was as if the sky was heading less towards darkness than a murky filter: a different light, rather than less of it.

'Maggie? Can you hear me? I am so sorry to ambush you like this ... I messaged you, and called the lighthouse ... but I can see that that wasn't enough.' She sounded pathetic now.

Clara slumped onto the grass. She leaned her back against the house's rear wall and put her head in her hands, palms pressing into her eye sockets in a desperate attempt to wake herself up, to find some sort of inspiration for how to break this deadlock.

Here she was. On exactly the sort of mission, the kind of exciting adventure she had told herself she had always longed for, and she had failed. She had turned her back on her life, closed doors she could never reopen, caused immeasurable pain, and for what? She unzipped her jacket pocket and pulled out her phone. No reception. Of course. She wanted to howl with frustration.

She opened the top of her rucksack, looking for she-didn't-know-what. Something to open the door with? Something that would win over her sister? Something, anything. She took a sip of her water and, as she did, she saw the plastic envelope in which she had put her father's letter.

She hadn't really known what to do with that second copy, the proof of her father's belt-and-braces approach not just to life but his own death too. It was only as she packed the rest of her travel documents that she thought to protect this version, to carry it as a form of ID for anyone she met along the way who might know Maggie or be able to help find her. At no point had she thought that she would have to let Maggie herself see the whole thing, but now it looked like it would be her best chance. She pulled it out of the top of the bag and tried to flatten it as best she could before walking back around to the front of the house. She tried to push the letter under the front door but the neat weatherproof seal around it was entirely flush to the front step.

Of course it was. You couldn't live in a house facing the Arctic if you had a gap beneath your front door. Clara bit her lip in frustration, taking a slow breath in – reluctant to let go of her letter but painfully aware that this might be her only way of proving who she was to her sister.

Gripping onto the plastic as it flapped and fluttered in the breeze – which, it turned out, was now becoming more of a gale – she walked down to the edge of the rocks above the bay. She felt around, trying to dislodge a stone that seemed strong enough to hold the letter down safely, but was light enough to carry to the doorstep. There was nothing that would even nearly work. These rocks were enormous, as if a giant had tired of some building blocks and let them fall, distracted by a shinier toy.

She kicked the rocks, her frustration now less fiery, something closer to desperation. As she turned back to the house she spotted the plant pots and realised her answer had been there all along. She headed back, grabbed a sturdy looking thyme bush, carried it around to the front of the house and plonked it on the letter, flat against the doorstep in its plastic folder.

It seemed likely that Maggie was still in the mezzanine area just above where Clara was standing, so instead of shouting into the shuttered windows, this time Clara tried to cup her hands and shout up to the window above her, high up in the blue gables.

'Maggie! I've left the letter for you. It's down here, the letter from my dad. So you know that I'm me. I *am* me! And I didn't come here to upset you. But … I can't leave, so if you change your mind and want to talk, I will be here, waiting.'

And having heard her own voice say it, Clara realised that this was what she would now have to do.

For the first twenty minutes, Clara sat on the doorstep, convinced that Maggie would appear imminently. But there was no sign of movement from the house at all. Slowly, the adrenaline that had got her this far, round the island bay after bay, started to seep out of her like the tide. She wasn't going to get her Hollywood ending, the result she had been naive enough to assume would be hers if she could just make it this far. Even if she waited all night, the moment she had dreamed of had already passed. All those feelings: slowly, they were just being replaced with exhaustion.

Clara moved away from the house and back to the grassy area above the shoreline. She just didn't have it in her to make it back to the lighthouse right now, and she was too scared to do it at high tide. She was pretty sure that there would only be a few hours of darkness at this time of year, so she decided to wait until the tide started to recede before deciding what to do. For now, she busied herself taking her waterproof coat from the rucksack and laying it on the ground, then finding her second jumper and wriggling into it as best she could over the clothes she was already wearing.

She sat watching the waves rolling out ahead of her, wondering what they would hit next. A boat? An island? The sea reached as far as the horizon then followed it over the curve of the earth. She had no idea what lay that far. Ice?

There wasn't much water left in her bottle, but she had a few more sips from it, as well as some of the nuts she had bought at Trondheim station what seemed like days ago. She tried not to look over towards the house as she sat there hugging her knees. She wanted to let Maggie see that she had meant what she said: she hadn't come to frighten her, but she couldn't leave

155

the island either. But it was hard to resist, and from time to time she looked across, just to check if the letter was still there, under its plant pot.

And at last, after nearly two hours, Clara saw the front door open a crack, and then that same forearm creep out. Maggie deftly nudged the pot to one side with the toe of her boot, and grabbed the letter. It was a matter of seconds, the movement barely a flutter, but Clara felt as if the air itself had changed its density in that moment. Surely this was it? Time to be welcomed in!

But the door stayed shut. Even worse, as the light dulled even further, she saw from the edges of the shutters that lights inside were being turned out. Night was drawing closer. Still no proper darkness, but the sort of grey pallor that Clara associated more usually with waking at dawn suffering from a murderous hangover. The sort of light that Simon had so often come home in, a prelude to some of their worst arguments. The same clammy desperation that she felt then was starting to claw at her now. She couldn't just sit there, letting it settle over her. She had to keep moving, keep shaking it off.

Painfully aware that she could be seen from the house – the circular window had no shutters – but desperate not to just sit in torment, she shuffled on her haunches across the rocks towards the water's edge. Then, perched on a rock, she took off her boots and socks, leaving them perched on a level higher than her, and dipped her feet into the sea.

The cold hit her like an electric shock. It was as if the water wasn't just on her feet but in them. She had been shot through with cold, her entire body contracting at the change her feet felt. Clara gasped before exhaling slowly, letting the pain of ice water move across her feet and up her lower legs. Yes, it was pain, but at least it was sharp, shocking, a change from the dull ache of the walk there.

Galvanised by having survived a partial dip in the Arctic, she wiggled her toes in the breeze before scrambling back up to her bag, digging out clean socks, a spare T-shirt and her sponge bag. As fresh warm blood made its way to her newly cosy feet she felt honey-sweet dopamine hit her system. But she was also aware that they were swollen with blisters, and simply couldn't face looking to check. She stripped her top half, put on the fresh T-shirt, and layered up the rest of her clothes before shoving the dirties to the depths of her bag. She smiled, sitting in her little camp, wiping her face with micellar water on tissues and brushing her teeth with the very last of her drinking water.

Next, she unclipped a biro from its slot in the bag and ripped a page from her new travel journal. It took her twenty minutes of scribbling, writing and rewriting, crossing the odd word out and then trying to colour in a dark blue box to hide what it once said, but eventually she completed a note to her sister.

Dear Maggie,

I have come to talk to you. I have not come to upset you. But I won't let our father down. I have come too far.

He loved you so much that even when you lost touch, instead of just writing a will and pretending his past had never happened, he wrote to me and asked me to find you. I wanted to respect your desire to be alone, but he clearly felt he could not keep your life a secret from me either.

I have no other siblings, only you. I have spent my entire life dreaming of having a sister, never imagining that I had one all along. I hope that we can meet, if only for me to pass on to you the documents and memorabilia that our father wanted you to have.

I will understand if you want no contact beyond that.

But I have an open-ended ticket — and more than that,

I have lost my passport and am waiting for news of documentation so that I can travel home. Signe knows where I am, and I hope that I can stay with her if you need some time to think about all of this.

I am your sister, and I will never forgive myself - and I suspect you and Dad would never forgive me - if I give up on trying to engage with you now. I will not leave Måsholmen until I know what your decision is. I do not think I can make it back to the lighthouse tonight, but I will go tomorrow if I do not hear from you. For now, I hope you can accept that I will be here, in your bay, for the night.

With lots of love (and hope!)

Your sister, Clara xxx

Clara shoved the note into the back pocket of her jeans, packed up her rucksack neatly, and gingerly made her way back down to the front door where she put the plant pot on it, hoping that the sea spray would not reach the biro ink before Maggie came to collect it.

She checked her phone again: still no reception. She tried to recall the point at which her phone had stopped having any. She had turned her phone on at the lighthouse, and seen some bars appear on screen, but not been alone long enough to see if any messages had arrived. Now, nothing – no messages had come through, and no messages would. She barely had any battery left either, her anxious flicking and scrolling, as well as presumably the device's constant searching for a mast, meaning that it was almost out. Did she have it in her to walk that far back along the trail again? Was it even worth it? There was no other option if she wanted to let anyone back at home know where she was and what she had achieved.

Slowly, she picked her way back over the rocks and towards

the path she had arrived on. The water was behind her now, she would just have to avoid thinking about it. *You don't have to go all the way back*, she told herself. *Just get to some reception before your phone dies.*

The light was dimming ever further. She was having to look carefully where she was putting her feet, and as the light started to seep away, the noises on the island seemed to get louder and louder. The tide was definitely on its way out now, but the wind had rendered the water choppier. Where it had been rippled blue silk on the way to Maggie's house, now the cresting waves left foam on the surface. The silk was torn wherever she looked … when she dared to.

Clara walked for nearly an hour, stopping and checking her phone for reception every few minutes. It was boring, slow work, but she was so tired and so terrified of stumbling and falling off the path that she was taking it almost comically slowly. Dropping the pace like this allowed her to listen to as well as look at her surroundings. There were birds circling at points, the wind whistling through the thick steel links which made up the chains she was gripping, and the steady, soporific sound of the sea.

After about an hour of walking in this almost trance-like state, she started at the buzzing sensation on her hip: her phone. She stopped as soon as she could and pulled it out of her pocket to see that she had a couple of bars of reception. She must be close enough to the lighthouse to pick up a little of whatever signal they had there. She sat where she had been standing, plonked in the middle of the path, her arms around her knees with her phone drawn up to her face, and looked at the messages.

She swallowed as she saw that there were seventeen texts. So he had realised she was gone. She realised to her horror that her first instinct was to look over her shoulder.

When are you back?

What time you getting home?

Fucksake call!

Jesus did you even come home last night?

Where are you?

And so they continued. Clara couldn't take them all in, her heart thundering away in her chest as she realised that she had finally done it. She had finally stood up to Simon. She saw herself sitting at her dad's kitchen table, biting her lip as he turned to stir the gravy for their last ever Sunday lunch. He had been chatting away about work, while she had been trying to start the impossible conversation. Admitting how much she wanted to get out, how much she now needed to. How much she had let him down by getting herself into this situation. And now, prompted by his death, she had finally done it – but it had left her here, on the edge of a mountain, not welcome to go forward and not able to go back.

In the absence of the conversation she had promised herself she'd have with her dad, at last asking for his advice, but never been able to, she had taken his request to visit Norway as a sort of sign, giving very little consideration to the consequences of leaving home in the way that she had.

But she was here now, and he would not find her. So, playing for time while she tried to decide whether to reply to the messages – if only to stop them from continuing and using up further phone battery – she sent the same message to three names: her mum, her Auntie Liz and Nikita.

Hi there, I have made it to the island and I have met Maggie! We haven't spoken at length, but I have found her. Am on the island where she lives, and it *is* very remote, but I have found somewhere I can stay. I lost my passport en route though and am waiting for replacement documents – govt website worked as fast as ever, obvs.

Hope to speak to Maggie more tomorrow, will let you know. There is v little reception though, so don't worry if you don't hear. Miss you, speak soon, C xxx

Then, finally she took a deep breath and typed.

Hey, Sorry we didn't have a chance to talk properly before. My dad has died, and I decided I just had to get away for a bit. Just staying in the countryside a little while. Let's chat when I'm back – I won't be gone too long, just needed a bit of time to get my head together. I know the last thing you needed was me moping around while you're so busy! Miss you, babe. Love you, Cla xxx

She hated herself for trying to appease him, apologising for the burden of her emotions even from the other side of Europe. But there was a tiny part of her that was proud for having kept her secret grief to herself for so long. She had long known that her having large or 'unmanageable' feelings made Simon feel threatened, a little less important in her life that he'd like to be. So she had used his late nights and her early mornings to hide behind, telling herself that there simply hadn't been the right moment for a chat like that. And now, even at the other side of the continent, she was still careful not to let him know where she was. I *am* in the countryside, she told herself,

161

determined not to lie to Simon, but desperate not to be found either.

When she raised her eyes from the blue glow of her phone she realised that night had now fallen on the island – as far as it ever would. If she had been in London, wandering down Tooting High Street on her way back from the pub or the common, it wouldn't have seemed that dark. It would have been the sort of balmy summer's evening light that she associated with long teenage nights sitting around in pub gardens or local parks. Bikes thrown to one side, cigarette scent barely noticeable in the summer haze, shoulders chilly as the sun goes down. Dark, but not really dark.

But here, there was no artificial light. There were no buses rumbling by, illuminated from within, there were no neon shop signs advertising chicken shops or late-night chemists, there was no street lighting clicking on at a preordained time. Clara could really only see where the path was if she used her phone, but she only had 18 per cent battery left: there was no way that would be enough for her to walk back with the torch function on – and it was impossible to hold on to the steel chains with both hands and keep holding the phone. But she couldn't stay where she was: she was utterly exposed, and if she did somehow manage to fall asleep, shifting position while unconscious might send her rolling off the island and down into the sea.

She devised a system of carrying the phone in her mouth, her breath noisy as she tried to grip it with lips rolled over her teeth, her head tipped slightly back so that the torch illuminated her path. She could only take a few steps at a time, trying to look ahead to where she might need to step if the phone eventually died. Each painstaking step was a balance between taking it slowly enough to feel safe but getting within sight of Maggie's house before the battery went, leaving her all alone in the dark.

Added to this, each metre she passed moved her further from reception – from being able to either receive a reply from any of her loved ones or to call for help if she needed it. And she suspected Maggie had no phone.

The return journey had already taken almost twice as long as her original walk out. The sheep in the distance were now sound asleep, distant grey wool puffs on the mountain edge. Even the gulls that had been swirling so noisily were now tucked away in their nests. How could Maggie stand this? How could she bear to be so alone, so vulnerable? What had happened in her past to make this preferable to any sort of contact with others at all? Did she never look up to the stars and wonder at what all the others beneath them might be doing?

Sleepiness was starting to nip at Clara, clumsiness snatching at her as she struggled to lift her now-heavy legs high enough to navigate the path, even when she could see it clearly. The all-consuming desire to sleep was only kept at arm's length by sheer terror. Finally, when she made the final curve and saw Maggie's bay, and her house on the far side, the relief was so enormous that her adrenaline seemed to stop working. The small round window, its tiny light leaving an illuminated stripe on the door below, seemed welcoming, despite Maggie's earlier response. And, as Clara followed the path, winding her way around and down towards it, she finally stumbled and tripped.

She fell on the path just as it was plateauing, before the scramble down to the water's edge. The ground was cold, but Clara didn't care. She was exhausted, but the fear of falling, which had kept her awake for so long, now felt irrelevant as she lay there in the dark. I just need a little rest, she thought. And she closed her eyes, letting the lapping of the waves lull her into oblivion.

# Chapter 17

The swish of the waves was so loud that Clara woke, heart pumping, sure she was about to be washed away. The adrenaline was back, as if she'd been shot through the heart. She tried to sit up, but her joints were stiff, she ached everywhere.

She blinked, flickering eyes making the light flash as she stared at the sky, and realised where she was – at the end of the path to the lighthouse, where the grass levelled above the rocks and then the bay just below. The tide seemed to have gone out and was now on its way back in, almost the same level as it had been when she had arrived at Maggie's house the night before.

Clara heaved herself up, realising that her feet were sharp with pain, and began to piece together how she had ended up here, on the side of a remote island, with a dead phone and absolutely no idea what time it was. She remembered falling when her attention started to slip as she reached the end of the path around Måsholmen. At the time she had only intended to rest for twenty minutes, but instinct told her that more time had passed – she had noticed that the activity on the island seemed to have stilled as she was walking back, but now there seemed to be more of a hustle and bustle. She could hear a sheep's bell somewhere, and the birds were up and busy once again.

The light had consistently been confusing, making dawn seem like dusk and vice versa. Now, there was an utterly clear and cloudless sky, beneath which she could see the sea as far as there was sea. There was none of yesterday's haze making the two seem indistinguishable: a clear line separated the pure blue of the sky from the emerald-tinged flatness of the sea. It was the kind of morning that she more usually saw on social media, with looping cursive written over the top of it, promising the reader that today was a day where absolutely anything was possible.

Except in Clara's case she felt the opposite. Slumped over her tired knees, feet stinging and eyes gritty from dust, sand and lack of sleep, it was as if she had reached the end of the road. Possibilities weren't endless, they were over. It was time to go home as soon as she could.

This thought passed through Clara like a shiver. Suddenly she started to shake, unsure if it was the cold or the intensity of the loneliness she felt, realising that she had come all of this way, done as her father had asked, only for it to change nothing at all. She was still stuck, still *her*. Directionless, without a father, and with nothing gained from this stupid, foolhardy mission. Only now she had to face what she had left behind.

She put her head between her shoulders, crouching over the path, staring numbly at the rock poking out from between moss and grass as she tried to steady her breathing. Slowly, Clara raised her head, looking over towards the house, and saw a small metallic Thermos flask a few feet ahead of her on the path. It certainly hadn't been there last night.

She looked more closely at the house, and saw that the last note she had left was gone from the doorstep. Not only that, but the shutters around the house were now raised, just as they had been when she had arrived yesterday evening.

Clara reached for the Thermos, instinctively looking around her in case it had been left by someone nearby. She sniffed at it, but it gave no clues as to its contents. Slowly, she unscrewed the lid; wafts of piping hot coffee hit her face. The smell was in such contrast to the briny sea spray that it seemed almost indecently intense. She took a second inhale, just to savour the steam pouring out of the lid, letting it ease the dryness in her eyes, then, with shaky hands, took a sip. Immediately, the hot liquid began to warm her from the core. She poured some into the lid, and drank it down gingerly.

She could tell that the coffee was strong, but instead of it making her feel jittery, like a black coffee would if she had one in the office, or after dinner, it had the opposite effect. There were three cup's worth in the Thermos, and she drank all of it, replacing the lid between each one. The gesture of kindness that Maggie – surely Maggie? – had made in leaving it for her warmed her anxious heart. This made her feel sleepy, as if her muscles might stop working entirely.

Clara lay back down and curled onto her side, watching the sea. The beach looked strange from its side angle, a screensaver on a laptop as she lay watching television. The brightness made her eyes droop again, and she began to feel as dozy as she had last night. She couldn't quite make her thoughts coherent; they didn't seem to be following each other in any manageable order. Plans wouldn't form while she was trying to order them – instead, a tidal wave of emotions seemed to be overtaking her.

Up until now, she had been carrying what felt like small, cold stones of grief inside of her. Little pebbles of resentment at being left by her father, or loneliness as she tried to inhabit this larger space that the world seemed to be without him, constantly

166

needling at her like shingle through the soles of an old pair of shoes worn at the beach. Not quite visible but pressing at her with every step.

But here, as she stared out to sea with watery eyes, this shingle now seemed to have turned into a liquid torrent of sadness. And suddenly it was bubbling up, threatening to spill out of her as she lay there, trying to rest.

Flashes of physical memories started to crackle away as if shot on an old phone: her father, curled around her five-year-old self as she tried to sleep in her childhood bedroom, noises outside the window frightening her. His rough hand outstretched for hers as she stood on a stepping-stone in the pond in their local park. The breadth and warmth of his chest as they hugged that Sunday night, the day before he had died. Rubbing her back reassuringly, he had promised her that her path in life would reveal itself to her in good time, and that he would always be there for her until then.

But he hadn't been.

And before she knew it, she was wrapped into a tighter ball, emitting huge racking sobs, eyes and nose streaming, howling for the grief she felt at the realisation that she would never feel that human warmth from her father ever again. That no one would ever have faith in her the way that he did. And that she had wasted it when she'd had it – too ashamed to admit she needed to leave, too afraid to stay.

She scrunched her eyes shut tight to stem the tears, and tried to wipe at them with the edge of her fleece, which she had pulled down from under her rainproof coat. The biggest of the sobs were passing, leaving her with heaving shoulders and laboured breathing as she attempted to get herself under control. Then she realised that a shadow had fallen over her.

Unfurling herself, she looked up. Standing right there,

towering over her, was Maggie. She seemed to have appeared silently – or at least quietly, relative to Clara's crying fit. Wearing thick cotton workwear trousers, a sage-green knitted round-neck jumper and the same dark-grey boots that Clara had seen disappearing up the stairs last night, she was just standing there, peering down at her soggy wreck of a sister. One hand was over her eyes to protect her from the glare of the sun, dark hair falling either side of her face; her eyes, nose and mouth were just shadows beneath the swaying hair. In that moment Clara thought she looked like something from a horror movie: featureless, expressionless, silently watching.

Clara wiped her eyes again. *She could kill me right now if she wanted*, she found herself thinking. *She could just tip me over the side of the mountain and pretend that it had happened in the night, that I had never made it at all.*

Just as that thought was truly starting to sink in, the fear gripping her tight, Maggie shifted, shaking her hair behind her shoulders and leaning down to pick up the Thermos. As she stooped, sunlight hit Clara, dazzling her for a moment. Suddenly, Maggie was transformed. Her dark hair, now running down her back, was flecked with strawberry blonde, and there was that tell-tale smattering of freckles. The light caught the fuzz of her jumper, and Clara could see that it was made from fine, soft wool. Maggie tipped her head slightly to one side, and asked in her low, serious voice, 'Did you drink the coffee?'

'Yes – thank you so much. I was so cold.'

'I can imagine. I think you need to come with me.' Maggie's face remained still, almost stern. Was there a trace of a French accent there? Or was her slightly stilted manner simply that of someone who had not spoken to anyone for weeks, or maybe even months.

The optimism Clara had felt the night before, the

determination to make a connection, was now gone. She still felt something closer to fear. Fear and a terrible sense of solitude, keeping her voice in her throat as she tried to decipher Maggie's closed expression.

Then Maggie extended a hand. A hand that Clara recognised again, dry, with those familiar deep grooves, and wide flat fingernails. Her father's hand. Her hand.

'Come on, you need a proper shower and some rest.'

Clara let her sister help her up, and Maggie bent and picked up the rucksack. Clara winced as she realised that the pain in her feet was not just a muscular ache but the sharp, broken-glass pain of fresh, ready to burst blisters. She remembered dipping her feet in the salty seawater last night, before simply shaking them dry. Suddenly, the pain made perfect sense: her feet felt as if someone had thrown a handful of rock salt into her fresh socks, and yes, that is basically what someone *had* done. Her.

She must have winced.

'Don't worry, we can deal with those too,' said Maggie, looking over her shoulder as she headed across the rocks to the far side of the beach. She moved with a sureness that Clara could never imagine achieving, no matter how long she lived here. As nimble as a goat, Maggie seemed to know exactly where to put feet then hands as she scrambled down, turning occasionally to lend Clara steadying support. At times, she even put both hands out, enabling Clara to hobble down, gripping onto her like a sort of human walking frame. Clara was terrified of bringing an abrupt end to this kindness, and didn't dare bring up the previous evening's high emotion, so their conversation was restricted to a handful of 'Here's, 'Thank you's and 'Watch your footing's.

As they approached the front step, Maggie stopped, at first stomping her feet to shake off any residual sand from the edge of the beach, then looking at Clara. Her face was wide and clear, quite unlike that shadowy figure who had been so frightening half an hour ago. But her stillness, her self-possession, still made Clara nervous.

'You need to rest, so you can stay here. We'll get the blisters taken care of, get you some sleep and some food. But I don't want to talk about the past. I don't want to talk about your father. I don't want to talk about any of it. Måsholmen is a place where the past is of no consequence to me, it is a place where the present is everything.'

'OK,' said Clara. More tears were starting to rise in her throat. She was so pathetically grateful to be safe, but utterly confused by Maggie's absolute refusal to engage with her as a sister.

*Your father ...*

*He's* your *father too*, Clara wanted to say. But she stopped herself, nodding like a small child. The relief at being invited into a house she had been entirely shut out of only twelve hours before, combined with the exhaustion from the journey, left her feeling limp, barely able to object to anything at all.

As Maggie opened the huge front door, Clara saw the house from the opposite perspective from yesterday when she had peered in through the French windows; it was as if she were looking at a flipped photograph. The interior was warm wood, huge beams running along the length of the room. From the hallway, she could see the kitchen units running along the west side, and the windows, she knew, looked out on the vegetables and herb patch. At the far end, on the sides of the room not clearly visible from outside the French windows, were an orangey corduroy armchair and a battered leather sofa with some elegant woollen throws draped over its back. A log burner stood in one corner, next to a basket of logs.

Above the stove a selection of cooking and dining essentials were arranged carefully on thick wooden shelves. Some simple pots and pans, an orange cast-iron casserole dish, and plates, bowls and mugs – two of each, in earthy tones. There was a clean terracotta flowerpot with various spoons and tongs next to the stove, and cork-lidded glass jars were arranged on both the shelves and the worktop. Coffee beans, small white and yellow flowers, rice and various other bits – some familiar, others not – were held within. The room smelled of warm bread and, perhaps, leather. Clara wasn't sure. It was in many ways an Instagram log-cabin fantasy, but there were too many signs of genuine, unstyled life for it to truly hit that mark.

While Clara was standing on the threshold, taking in everything from the laundry drying in the sunlight to the bread left on the side, one slice taken from it, Maggie swung the rucksack off her shoulder, grabbed an enamel bowl from one of the kitchen cabinets and stalked off into what Clara realised was the bathroom. There was the sound of running water, then Maggie returned with a bowl, which she set on the ground before the armchair. She reached for a glass bottle on the side, before beckoning to Clara.

'Come here, you need to soak those blisters.'

Clara walked over, wincing in pain. She reached the chair and bent over to pull off her boots before Maggie urged her to sit, and set about helping her boots off. Then she poured a glug of apple cider vinegar into the bowl of warm water and invited Clara to put her feet in it.

'It's antibacterial,' she said plainly. She was kneeling at Clara's feet, turning them over in her hands gently, before nodding to herself. 'You're going to need to stay a day or two until these have healed up. You can't walk with feet in that state, they'll just get infected. I've made up a bed for you, and I'll help you back to the lighthouse as and when.'

Clara nodded. Maggie placed each of her feet into the enamel bowl gently before standing up. Once again, she loomed over her sister.

'But please remember, this isn't a favour. It is about survival.'

Clara nodded, her eyes watering as the vinegar water reached the torn skin flapping on her heels and on the crease of her big toes where her new walking boots had rubbed. She couldn't imagine ever getting those boots on again, let alone making the walk back to the lighthouse. But in that moment, as she watched Maggie hang up her coat next to hers on the rack by the door, she simply didn't care. She was just happy to be safe. Within seconds she was asleep again.

It was several hours before Clara woke up. She had a woollen blanket over her lap and felt as if her legs were made of liquid honey. She kept her eyes closed for a minute, letting the smells of the house take over her as she listened to her surroundings. She could hear the sea, of course, and some distant gulls. And there seemed to be the hum of an oven going, which hadn't been there before.

She opened her eyes and peered around, with no idea what time it was. There was no sign of Maggie, so Clara took the chance to scan the room in a way she hadn't dared to before. Some things were more luxurious than she had imagined – the armchair she was in, for example, and the soft wool of the knitted rug over her lap, which looked like the sort of thing she would see in the windows of South Kensington design stores. But others were rustic in a way that Nikita would definitely have raised her eyebrows at – a heap of carrots apparently just plucked from the ground, covered in mud and far knobblier than a set designer would have let anyone get away with.

What struck Clara was that there was barely anything there which did not have a purpose. There were jars full of screws, a fishing rod leaned up against the wall by the front door, and some gardening utensils by the French windows leading out towards the vegetable patch. She thought she would see it left on the heavy wooden table in the middle of the downstairs space, but there was absolutely no sign of the letter from Ben, nor her own scrawled letter from the night before.

Just as Clara was craning her neck to see what was behind the doors on the east side of the house, Maggie reappeared from the French windows, her hands covered in soil.

'Oh, hello,' she said, dumping a small bunch of beetroot next to the carrots. 'Welcome back to the land of the living.'

'Hi,' said Clara. She pressed her hands into the arms of the chair as if she was going to stand up and leave. Then it hit her: she couldn't leave. She had no way out. She was here, relaxing in Maggie's home, just like she had dreamed of yesterday. Only she wasn't relaxed.

Instead, she was trapped.

# Chapter 18

Yes, she was trapped, but to her relief, Clara realised quickly that her sister was keen for her to make a safe recovery. She showed nothing but kindness and attentiveness to Clara and her ragged feet, and before long she saw the forbidding woman that she had come so close to fearing start to fizzle away, aspirin in a glass, leaving a clear-eyed and kind-hearted woman in her place. Yet Maggie remained a woman with an unerring ability to steer the conversation back to a few choice topics, none of them even close to what Clara had dreamed of or intended. Clara couldn't deny the kindness in her sister, but nor could she deny that it wasn't manifesting in the ways she had hoped. And she knew that to try and change that could put her survival at risk; she *had to* keep to her end of the bargain, not daring to mention their shared parenthood, or anything that Ben had asked her to discuss. Still drawn to this strange woman, she was prepared to play by her rules in order get closer to her. She just wasn't sure if it was ever going to work.

In truth, it did not seem like too much of a sacrifice at first. She was so wrung out by both the physical and emotional rigours of the journey – and what she had left behind – that she was content to rest, and to watch how Maggie's solitary life at what felt like the end of the world worked on a day-to-day level.

It did not take long for her to confirm that the mezzanine level above the wooden staircase at the front of the house was indeed where Maggie slept, in a little eyrie looking out to sea. On the east side of the house there was a small bathroom, and a second bedroom of sorts. It was obvious that until Clara's arrival it hadn't been used for that purpose, set up instead as a sort of creative den. There were flowers drying on a shelf by the window, jars full of various herbs marinating in oils and coloured liquids, and one entire wall had been given over to fifty or so wooden cubby holes, each stuffed with yarns of different colours, textures and thicknesses. There was a strange spindle type thing, wool wrapping its four corners, a shelf of books and papers, and a selection of half-made knitwear on a small desk opposite the wall of shelving. Tucked in one corner was some fabric and thread, as well as a small toy animal covered in the sort of granny-ish Liberty fabric that she had seen on her mum's make-up bag. But most of the room was devoted to knitting. Wooden needles attached to pieces of plastic twine were hooked over studs on the wall and almost everything was labelled with letters and numbers which meant nothing to Clara. Next to the desk, below the wall studded with hanging knitting needles, was a large battered sofa, which Maggie had pulled out to make Clara a bed.

On her first night there, Clara was too timid to ask about the contents of the room, and far too nervous to touch anything. Whether it was a hobby grown out of hand or simply her way of clothing herself, it was obviously a working system that Clara dared not interrupt. So she let Maggie lend her a T-shirt and some thermal leggings, and kept quiet, grateful for the spare quilt Maggie found and the warm sheep's milk she handed her before bed.

The next morning she had eased her feet anxiously out from under the quilt, nervous about standing – let alone wearing anything on them. The blisters *were* drying out, but slowly. They still had the clear ooze of skin that was desperate to heal if given the chance, and it was obvious that putting her boots back on would return her straight to the previous day's agony.

Clara crept out from her room, unsure what time it was or whether Maggie was up, and found her sister standing at the wooden kitchen worktop, stretching out dough from a metal bowl and folding it over on itself, while coffee simmered on the hob.

'Good morning,' she said, with that same half smile from the day before. 'I hope you slept well.'

'Oh yes, thank you so much, I didn't realise how exhausted I was until I woke up feeling so much better ...' Clara had started burbling before she realised that Maggie hadn't actually asked her anything. She had turned her back and was pouring coffee into a mug. After passing it to Clara, she crouched at her feet, examining the blisters.

'They certainly need more air,' she stated.

After a strong coffee and slice of buttered sourdough each, Maggie announced that a walk would help, explaining that 'I just need to pick some bits.' She lent Clara a pair of sandals – a sturdy sort of affair that Clara normally associated with middle-aged women spending a day's city sightseeing. But the straps fell in exactly the right places, allowing her feet to breathe while keeping her soles safe, so Clara, profuse chat and gratitude still babbling from her like a brook, followed her sister out of the house, prepared to go wherever she was going.

They headed up a path on the opposite side of the house,

the side onto which 'her' bedroom window had looked, which had been out of view on her initial approach to the island. The path was a consistent uphill incline, not as intensely steep as the walk from the lighthouse had been at points, but, well, somewhat relentless compared to Clara's usual trudge home from the office.

She glanced back at the cottage, fishing ropes and net-covered glass floats looped and hanging against the side wall, and wondered when they'd be back. She was, once again, entirely at Maggie's mercy. Maggie lent her a hand from time to time, helping her when the path narrowed or grass sprouted over the track, potentially scratching her blisters. But as they walked, the air made her injuries start to feel fresher than they had done. And after almost half an hour, the incline had led them to a greener, lusher part of the island, up and behind the house.

Maggie paused, removing a metal flask from her bag and taking a sip of water before offering the same to Clara. She seemed to know exactly what she was looking for, her eyes scanning the landscape.

'What are we after?' Clara had asked, as casually as she could manage.

'I'm just checking on some berries, seeing how they're doing, when they might be ready, that sort of thing.'

'I see.'

'And I want to pick some other bits, if you are doing OK. If you can make it up there, you can see down towards the other side of the island.'

'Yes, I'm fine,' said Clara. She was tired, but she was also desperate not to let her sister down. They continued along the path, heading for what looked like a peak.

'The path is so neat,' remarked Clara. 'Who else comes here?'

'No one really,' replied Maggie. 'Well, occasionally guests at the lighthouse take a long walk. But it was me who created this path, and it's me who takes care of it.'

Clara watched her, stepping steadily forwards, and imagined Maggie gently, firmly, cutting back the grass, choosing which way to let the path take her, tending to it year after year while she ignored messages from her own father. It was unfathomable. But as she watched her own feet, step after step, she could not deny that is what had happened. That these had been the choices that Maggie deemed best for herself.

The walk became tough after a while. Clara's legs felt wobbly after the hike from the lighthouse and the night spent outside, but as they continued at an even pace, she was glad of the chance to stretch out her legs, of the space to let her mind wander and try to process the situation.

Without the panic she had felt when she had first arrived on the island, she was now able to take in more of the details around her. The air was a heady scented mix of sea spray and pine sap, the sort of thing that expensive candles in the bathrooms of smart restaurants tried so hard to recreate. And the path was becoming less scrubby, more dotted with colourful little flowers as the grass alongside it became greener.

Maggie crouched at the side, her hands rifling through the undergrowth with the same confidence Clara had seen in chefs in open kitchens at restaurant openings.

'What are these ones?' asked Clara, pointing to pinky-purple shoots sprouting up from the grass, reaching for the sky.

'I don't know what they are in English,' said Maggie. 'I have never been here with anyone English. Here, they are called *geitrams*. We might get some on the way back – you can eat the shoots as a vegetable, and the flowers make teas and syrup.'

A burst of energy surged through Clara, a sensation exactly

opposite to that which her mother always referred to as 'some-one walking over your grave'.

*We*!

Hearing that word for the first time felt golden. She hadn't realised she had been yearning for it until she heard it. She was part of a plan, with Maggie. The buzz kept her going as they walked a little higher, Maggie explaining that she was checking to see how the blueberries were doing, as last year had been very bad for them. And that she was keeping an eye out for cloudberry flowers, which were rarer, but should be appearing around now.

Clara tried to look out for cloudberry flowers, before silently admitting to herself that she didn't know what cloudberries were, let alone their flowers. She longed for her phone to work, so she could pull up an app and start scouring the grass for flowers. But there was no reception, so she just had to keep looking, absorbing, trying to process everything that she saw. As they walked, she heard gulls closer than before, and even spotted a puffin.

Just as she lost herself in this train of thought, Maggie turned and looked at her. She was pointing down towards the other side of the island. To the left were steep cliff faces, noisy water churning below and then a small land mass, which was basi-cally an enormous, uninhabitable rock, just beyond it. 'The maelstrom!' shouted Maggie. She indicated the water between the two islands. A gull shot up behind her, calling to its neigh-bours on the cliff.

'Oh wow,' said Clara. She still wasn't entirely sure what a maelstrom might look like, despite having researched the mean-ing of the word only a couple of days ago. Oh, for ten minutes with her phone and some Wi-Fi! Should she be scared of it? She didn't dare ask, but the roaring of the water suggested yes.

'This is as far as we should go today,' said Maggie. 'But it's a good spot to get your bearings on the island, isn't it? It's a neat little gap right here beside the highest point.'

Clara nodded, slightly dizzy at the volume of sky she seemed to be surrounded by.

'But look, before we go … ' Maggie, a good few inches taller than Clara, put her hands on Clara's shoulders, manoeuvring her to face the way they had come.

'My house … ' she said softly, her face bent to Clara's ear. There it was, the little blue house, perched on the edge of the bay, its crisp white window frames bouncing light around the windows.

'The maelstrom,' said Maggie, turning her to face further east, then, as she turned her 180 degrees to face into the island, 'and the forest'.

They were just high enough to peek over the top of the ridge and down over the other side, in the valley that comprised the centre of the island, were the trees. A forest!

'A secret forest … ' Clara found herself whispering. Because that is what it looked like. Tucked away in the deep valley between the dual mountain spines of the island, peeked at from this strange soft gap between two peaks, there it was. A secret forest of dense, vivid trees, as if put there by a child absent-mindedly playing with their train set.

'Yes,' Maggie whispered back. Clara's head whipped round – she hadn't realised Maggie had heard her. She had barely realised she had spoken out loud. The trees were rustling slightly in the breeze.

'It must feel like it's all yours,' said Clara.

'It does,' replied her sister. 'I have lived here over a decade now, and I could count on one hand the number of times I have ever come across anyone else in there.'

There was something about them being able to avoid eye contact, staring down at the trees below, that allowed for this brief moment of connection. Maggie wasn't able to make a point of avoiding Clara's gaze, not while they were both watching something else, their hair flailing wildly around their faces.

'It's not a large forest, but it's big enough for me.' Maggie's eyes were soft, a gaze Clara had not seen thus far.

'Do you go down there a lot?' asked Clara.

'Oh yes. I get a lot of my food there.'

After seeing the chic, well-equipped service kitchen at the lighthouse, Clara had assumed that Maggie ate imported food, perhaps spiced with the odd juniper berry or some such. But now it dawned on her that Maggie ate a lot of what the island provided. How barren it had looked from that approach on the boat, the granite slab of the mountains echoing the black chop of the sea below. How well this little island had hidden its secrets. Clara longed to ask more, but didn't yet dare. Did Maggie eat foraged food because she liked to or because she needed to? What did she even do for work? Did she work? Or did she have money? And – above all – how could she find these things out without upsetting her. She thought about simply asking, but the image of a startled cat, spine up, fur out, passed unavoidably through Clara's mind.

As if she knew what Clara was thinking, Maggie gave herself a quick shake, pushed her hair from her face and said suddenly, 'Right, we need to get you back. I don't think the asparagus will be ready yet. Not until next month. But we can get some *geitrams* shoots.'

'Where would you get asparagus from?'

'The edges of the forest. There is some wild garlic down there too, and onions. And mushrooms of course. But not today.' The dreamy tone was gone. Back to business.

Maggie turned and led the charge home, Clara's mind fizzing with all that she had learned in what had only been forty-five minutes out of the house. On the way back Maggie paused to pick dandelions and some of the pink *geitrams* shoots, as well as to point out the spot where she hoped some cloudberries would reappear.

When they returned home, she told Clara there was work to be done in the garden, and Clara offered to help her. After a cup of coffee on the beach, they got to work digging, sorting, planting. Onions and beetroot, Maggie explained, and they wouldn't take too long. Clara nodded, and did as she was told. She got to work in the soil deep in thought, desperately trying to work out how she was going to talk about something other than the practicalities of island life with her sister. It didn't take long before the monotony of the work began to frustrate her. Hacking away at the soil silently, developing a crescent moon of dirt underneath each of her nails. She remembered a Sunday afternoon helping her dad in the garden, probably ten years ago. The same sulkiness had beset her as she plucked at weeds as per her father's instructions. The same spongy part below her kneecap fizzing with frustration, desperate to kick out in boredom. Then, she had merely felt trapped. She had committed to an afternoon in the garden in order to 'earn' a trip to the cinema, and it had been over soon enough. If only she had known how few afternoons in the garden with her dad she had had left, she might have enjoyed it a little more.

Now, as she burrowed her fingers into the soil to make space for the seeds she was planting, she was *actually* trapped. And she wasn't just trapped: every time she felt she was close to making a meaningful connection with Maggie, she was quietly reminded that, essentially, she was unwanted on the island. An inconvenience until she could get back to the lighthouse, check that her travel documents were ready, and be safely dispatched again. The absolute lack of control over her situation left that same soft part of her knee itching to kick again in exasperation.

She felt a pang of longing for the convenience of London life. A bus app that would just tell her exactly how many minutes she would be waiting at the stop, a taxi app on which she could follow the tiny black car as it moved, street by street, to her doorstep. A warm bath listening to a podcast, messaging a mate, the phone perilously held over the bubbles. But just as she imagined that taxi ride, that warm bath, she saw her hand putting the key in the door to the flat, shaking, and realised that no matter how much she wanted not to be here, scrubbing around in dirt, worrying about oozing feet and wobbly paths, home was not an alternative either.

Just thinking that word – home – reminded her of how ephemeral the idea of home had turned out to be. What she realised was that she wanted the reassurance of an afternoon with her father. She remembered him carefully picking small courgettes from the tiny plot at the end of her childhood garden. The pride in his face as he returned to the kitchen with his little wicker basket full of vegetables. She looked up and saw a whisper of that expression on Maggie's face as she stared in concentration at the edge of her vegetable garden. Where had Maggie been that day that she had spent in the garden with her dad? Was she already living here, immersed in the land, letting it soothe her the way that those afternoons had seemed to soothe their father? It would seem she had been.

While she had been churning through these thoughts, the repetitive motion of the digging, the sounds of the tide drawing in and the sheer physicality of her task in hand seemed to have eased the frustration nagging away at her. Panic – *there's nothing I can do!* – was slowly turning to *Well, there's nothing I can do.* By the time the seeds were all in the ground, Clara was resigned: she was here until she wasn't. And that couldn't be too bad, because despite her sister's resistance, she still felt that pull towards Maggie. No matter how little it might be reciprocated right now, Clara felt a stubborn determination that one day it might be.

They worked through what Clara would have considered lunchtime, and by what seemed like late afternoon, Maggie headed indoors to the kitchen and pan fried two large chunks of fresh cod in a skillet alongside the *geitrams* shoots and thyme from one of her herb pots. She also roasted some beetroot slowly in the oven which she now sliced, tossed in oil and some thyme from the garden, and slid onto a plate next to the fish and greens. Clara sat watching her, the steady, confident way that she moved. It bore little resemblance to her own haphazard cooking, ingredients half-remembered and techniques copied from the glow of her phone as she tried to recreate YouTube videos or lightning-fast TikToks.

The food itself tasted unrecognisable from anything she had had before. The cod was meatier than any of the supermarket fillets she had let sit at the back of the fridge before eating on a gloomy Monday night, and tastier than at any of the restaurants she had been treated to. The *geitrams*, something she would have walked past, dismissing as a weed, were fresh and crisp. A treasure that might otherwise have been hidden from her. When she finished, thanking Maggie profusely, she felt well – nourished, even. Her usual bowls of solo after-work pasta left her feeling sleepy, often so sleepy she could barely be bothered to put herself to bed after a day in the office. This felt different though. She *wanted* to go to bed. And when she yawned, looking out of the window and wondering what time it really was, Maggie saw her exhaustion and recommended that she head off to sleep.

The next morning, Maggie took another look at Clara's blisters and declared – to her surprise – that the following day Clara would probably be able to wear her boots again. They could walk back to the lighthouse. The plan seemed so simple: they would spend the day together, then Clara would head back to Signe's, with Maggie's help. They would log on to Clara's email, sort out and print the replacement travel documents required by the UK government in place of a passport, meaning Clara could head back to Hestøy on the weekly boat that Arve ran for Signe.

Maggie explained this to Clara with a briskness that was never rude – but was nevertheless dripping with visible relief. Clara admitted to herself that she had been naive. Why had she assumed that her sister would welcome her in, unquestioning, for an unlimited mini-break? Because she had wanted it so much? Or because she had been seeing life through lenses smeared with grief and just wanted to get away, anywhere, anyhow? Either way, she did not foresee the way that Maggie looked at her as she brushed the flour off her hands onto her apron that morning, making her announcement then turning away with a contented smile. As soon as Clara was safe to travel, Maggie was telling her that she would.

Clara said nothing, quietly going to the spare room where she had slept and looking down at her rucksack, slumped on the floor by the sofa bed. She was there for one day. One more day. How could she use the time? What would her father want her to do with those hours? What did *she* want to do with them? And what the hell would she be going back to?

She stared out at the sea, trying to take in how far she really was from anywhere she had been before. She wanted to steel herself, to summon up some wise words from a novel she'd read. But instead, her heart seemed to be wandering off into despair, clothes dishevelled and hair askew – while her head was desperately trying to keep the conversation aloft. What would Nikita say? Well, she figured, Nikita would probably tell her to just do what she wanted to. *This is the adventure you always said you were waiting for,* she remembered her friend saying as she had driven her to the airport. *Use it, don't let it use you.* Her stomach churned with anxiety but there seemed little else to do than just that.

'Would it be possible to walk up to see the forest again today?' Clara asked Maggie. 'It was so beautiful, and this morning's weather is even clearer than yesterday's.'

'I don't see why not,' said Maggie with a smile.

Clara couldn't quite believe that her wish had been granted so easily, and when Maggie packed two sandwiches made with her fresh bread and handmade jam, Clara felt a tingle of excitement. Maybe this was it, the moment she became one of those women who really lived a life of Instagram inspirational moments and mug-based motivation – taking up space in the room; being the change she wanted to see; living, laughing and loving! Yes, she had expressed herself clearly and she had been *heard*. This *was* the adventure she had always wanted.

They made it up to the viewing point faster than yesterday. Clara's feet felt noticeably fresher and her legs were now both stronger and more accustomed to the path. When they reached the spot, they sat, side by side, and Maggie opened a flask and poured coffee into two small tin mugs.

If anyone saw us now, they would probably *know* we were siblings, thought Clara. She imagined what they looked like from behind, side by side, sharing their coffee. Proper sisters.

'Thank you,' she said with a smile, turning, trying to catch her sister's eye.

Not a chance.

Maggie looked resolutely forward, so all that Clara could see was the side of her face, further obscured by hair blowing across it in the wind.

'Is it easy to get down there?' she asked.

'Relatively.'

'Could I do it?'

'Not today, I don't think. But in theory you could.' Maggie's stare was still straight ahead.

Clara pushed her fingernails into the palm of her hand. She had to keep going, even if Maggie kept batting her away.

'When did you first go?'

'Years ago.'

'When you first lived here?'

'Yes, it wasn't especially long before I paid the trees a visit.'

Paid the trees a visit. She talked about them as if they were her friends. She had no one else around, Clara supposed. She took a deep breath.

'When did you arrive here?'

'Over ten years ago now.' Maggie was still avoiding her eye-line. Maybe this was what had given her the relative confidence to talk, or maybe it was her way of trying not to talk.

'Why here?' and quickly, while she still dared, 'Just because it was far away?'

'Well, there was that ... ' Maggie was smiling a little, but her eyes were still firmly on the trees below. Clara watched some birds circling above them.

'Seriously ... '

'I was working in a bar in Paris, and I had a Norwegian boyfriend. His father had a company not too far from here, in Lofoten. We came for the summer, we worked – it was a guided kayaking thing – and I stayed.' A small shrug. It was the longest unbroken time Maggie had spoken for since Clara had arrived.

Clara stayed utterly silent, reluctant to break the spell. 'We had broken up, but I couldn't go back to Paris. Not … '

'Not?' Clara bit her lip, furious with herself at having interrupted. The possibility that Maggie had run away in the same way that Clara just had was too intoxicating though.

'I just couldn't.'

'Wow, I would love to have lived in Paris though.'

'You never lived my life.'

'What do you mean?'

'It doesn't matter. You have just had a very different life.'

And just as Clara saw a thick duvet of cloud appear out of nowhere over the island, so Maggie's face darkened too. Her eyes narrowed a little, her mouth set firm. The sunshine firmly hidden from view.

# Chapter 19

They walked home in silence. When Clara attempted chit-chat, a hum of anxiety growing louder within, Maggie answered in monosyllables, looking into the distance. That steadfast firmness of tone Clara had heard once or twice when she had asked quite enough questions at the doctor's and the GP was trying to ease her out of the door.

When they got home, Maggie suggested Clara take a nap. Clara lay on her back in the spare room, listening to her sister tidying and sorting in the kitchen, before straining her ears for any clue as to what Maggie might have been doing while the room beyond the door fell silent. There was nothing, and before long her thoughts turned inwards to the choices she had to make about her return. She had not yet had the confidence to tell Simon that she hadn't planned to return home, but with every day she stayed on the island she knew that any understanding on his part would be curdling into rage. And she hadn't really told either Nikita or her mum that she didn't want to go back – or why. She had just left, like a coward, in the hope that the trip itself would provide some answers. Without her dad to blame, and with the mission he had set her almost accomplished, Clara realised that her plan to just keep hoping that someone else would sort everything out was starting to look foolish. She wasn't naive enough to have thought she could just turn up in the middle of nowhere until Simon – what? Disappeared? Stopped asking where she was? Moved away himself? But, yes, she tentatively thought, she had perhaps assumed that finding a connection elsewhere in her life might ease the more immediate ruptures. Or at least make them less her responsibility to deal with. This endless loop of self-recrimination continued, various scenarios squirming in her mind without any of them presenting themselves as a solution, until she dozed a little. The birds' squawking outside was the only thing louder than her own thoughts.

When she woke up, the sky had cleared and there was some food left out for her on the kitchen worktop, alongside a note which simply said *I have gone for a walk. Back later.*

Clara held the notepaper between finger and thumb. It was the first time she had seen her sister's handwriting, but she had no idea how to translate those loops and lines into any insight about her. She knew that she had pushed her luck earlier; she had peeled back something that Maggie would rather remain sealed tight. And now, she had mere hours before she would be heading off the island. This bond she had longed for her whole life without ever realising it now seemed further out of reach than ever.

At first, it was relaxing being in the cottage alone. For the first time in a couple of days, she wasn't scared of saying something that might upset Maggie. For an hour or so, the tension trickled off her – she could just be, staring out at the sea, replaying events in her mind, pondering what her next move might be. Her phone, her job, her real life: against a clearer sky they all seemed once again like problems she could deal with a little later down the line. She was sure her mum would let her stay for a bit. It might even be nice to spend time with her, Clara thought, recalling how fragile she had looked at the funeral. And maybe she could even sort things out with Simon, now that this impromptu trip had shown him that she had a bit of backbone. And anyway, these were calls she could make later, on the long journey back to the UK. For now, all she had was what was here, for the twelve hours until she left.

But Maggie didn't return after a couple of hours, and slowly the situation became unnerving. Clara had no idea where she was, and even less of an idea how to look for her. The wind began to pick up outside. The house was small, well sealed, and felt snug, but the ghoulish howling slowly became insistent. The eeriness of such an autumnal noise was inescapable while the grey sky overhead seemed reluctant to get dark at all.

Clara made herself some coffee and dug a pen out of her bag. Perhaps, she decided, what she ought to be doing was some earnest 'journaling'. People who wrote wise and reflective things on social media always seemed to have some sort of diary on the go, and this was just the sort of trip she would want to tell future generations about. So she found the notebook she had brought with her for just this purpose, and sat cross-legged on the floor at Maggie's coffee table.

But the pen remained poised at the page. What could she say about someone who was giving her so little of herself? She drew doodles in the margin, swirling spirals, little bunches of *geitrums*, a puffin's beak against the back of a capital 'M', crenelations around the edge of the page.

Why couldn't Maggie tell her what their dad had done? What could be so bad? He wasn't a criminal, and he had never seemed a cruel man. Why would he have sent her out here if he had a darkness to him that was so awful?

Clara made some anodyne notes in the journal and stood up, reluctant to admit defeat. She put on the sandals Maggie had lent her, wedged the front door open with a boot and walked out onto the beach. She stared up, to the path she had arrived on, and the less obvious one they had taken up and towards the woods. No Maggie. No sign of her as far as the eye could see, in any direction. The anxiety pumped tiredness and jitters into her in equal measure. After a couple of lengths of the beach, her hair going wild in the breeze, she turned to return to the house. But as she looked up, she remembered the higher path, heading in the opposite direction, towards the maelstrom. She wandered up, until she could see a little way along it, some instinct telling her to follow it just a little further.

She had been right. There stood Maggie, not far from where she had pointed out her bearings on the island yesterday. Only this time she was much further down the path. Much, much closer to the water.

At first Clara thought her sister was trying to shake her hair out in the wind, to stop it from flapping around her face. Then she realised that she was actually sobbing, her shoulders heaving up and down. And she was still walking. Closer and closer towards the water.

Clara froze. She didn't dare shout in case she startled Maggie, who was ever closer to the edge, looking down over the maelstrom. What if she fell? So she waited, transfixed, watching her sister cry.

She couldn't leave. How could she abandon someone sobbing, at the most perilous point on the island? But could she stay? Just watching like this? Maggie had left the house in order to be alone. She hadn't wanted to be visited in the first place. And now Clara was creeping after her, watching her every move. To leave would feel like neglect, to stay like a betrayal of trust. Yet she remained rooted to the ground, watching as Maggie's shoulders slowly stilled and she stood, staring, before sitting on the ground at the cliff edge.

There was grief in the way she was bent towards the wind, letting it lash at her face just as Clara was trying to shield hers. Why can't she just talk to me about it? thought Clara. Surely that has to be better than *this*? Surely she knows how dangerous this is? Is it what she wants?

So Clara stayed, watching, unsure of what she could helpfully do, but not daring to leave either. She only realised how wrong it was to have been staring like this when Maggie moved, leaning as if to get up, and Clara leapt up, and scurried along the path away from her, desperate not to be caught in the act of watching. She hurried home, battling the gale all the way, expecting Maggie to call after her at any second. But she never materialised. Was she gone? Or still out there?

Clara felt a fool the minute she closed the door behind her – wedging it open had let the wind in, scattering paper across the coffee table and making the whole house cold. She tidied up what she could, replacing some of the papers which had been swept across the living area to the desk, spotting as she did that her note – and her father's – from the night she had arrived had been carefully placed underneath a glass ball, one of the round floats from outside, unleashed from its netting. As she adjusted the glass to still some of the paper, she noticed a second letter in her father's handwriting. Not a letter she recognised, despite the familiar loop of his script.

For a moment or two Clara considered not reading it, suspended between a sense that it was the wrong thing to do and the fury that there had been correspondence between the two of them that she had not been told about. But she had gone so

193

far already this evening, and she was feeling reckless, knowing that Maggie could return at any minute ...

Clara grabbed the letter and read it standing over the table, one hand on the glass. The contents were largely inconsequential: her dad sending Maggie love, saying how much he missed her and how he hoped she was getting on OK up in the Arctic. But Clara barely read the second half of the page, scanning his handwriting as her eyes misted with tears and she felt a sort of heartburn in her chest. She no longer felt guilty for trying to keep an eye on her sister. Instead, jealousy seemed to singe her spirits. All this love, all this attention, and Maggie had been treating it as surplus. All those hours Clara had spent longing for a little more time with her father, an extra weekend as a teenager, another Sunday afternoon walk when she grew older, just a couple of extra hours to try and bend the conversation around to the truth of how her relationship with Simon was unfolding.

So many times she had wondered at how her father had felt so comfortable with the idea of Simon as a Great Guy. He'd fallen for the wine Simon would bring over on the rare occasions they went for a meal with him. He had been so visibly relieved that Clara 'had someone'. He had just eased himself into the whole set-up as if it were his battered leather reading chair. For so long Clara had seen this as a failure of communication on her part, but as the burning in her chest grew, she now saw it as his attention being diverted. How could he have been paying full attention to *her*, when he'd been writing his begging letters to Maggie? What a pitiful waste.

A hot tear fell as Clara blinked, and landed on his signature, blurring the letters but leaving his three neat kisses intact. She put the paper back under the green glass and wiped her eye.

Clara wrapped herself in a rug and curled up on the sofa,

listening out for any sound that Maggie might be back. She lay like this, in a heightened state of alertness, until the light performed another of its unreadable shifts. The sky was grey, but it was far from dark. Perhaps it never was.

# Chapter 20

The following morning, Clara woke up in the living room, the light the same as the night before, but the atmosphere in the room very different. There were some fresh wildflowers in an enamel jug on the coffee table, and the glass float that had been being used as a paperweight was nowhere to be seen. There was also no sign of the letters.

The oven was on, and the room was already starting to smell of fresh bread. It was clear her sister was back. But seconds after the relief of knowing she was safe came the uneasy shift in the pit of her stomach on realising she wouldn't know what mood Maggie was in. Or what to say to her about the letter she had found. And that this was perhaps the last morning they would ever spend together.

Clara unwrapped herself from the rug and stretched out her back. She ran her hands through her hair and made a promise to herself to try to keep the mood breezy. To keep Maggie feeling safe. But when she came in from the side door to the garden, Maggie's face was bright, a vision of nonchalance. Clara was wary but went along with it. She didn't ask Maggie where she had been, or why she had not returned for so long. She didn't reminisce about her time on the island. She didn't probe any further about Paris, or their father, or any of it.

Instead, she packed up her things, took a last look out of the windows to the beach and reminded herself that she had yet to deliver the envelope of memorabilia to Maggie. She'd do it at the last minute, she told herself. Less pressure. They left not long afterwards, taking the path back to the lighthouse. This time, she tried to cherish every step, to recast herself as a travelling hero who would enchant future grandchildren with tales from the North.

'It was beyond the lighthouse that I found my sister!' she imagined telling enraptured grandchildren from the comfort of her future home. She was no stranger to imagining these perfect future scenarios as a way of easing the path through the challenges of reality. More than one evening of conflict with Simon had ended with her imagining telling these same fabricated grandchildren about how much they loved each other, how long they had been together. As another hour passed, it occurred to her that she was yet again having a relationship *at* someone rather than with them, but she shoved the thought away, focused on the big handover, and kept putting one foot in front of the other until there was more of the path behind her than in front.

They were close now, and Clara knew that they had passed the point that she'd walked in order to send her text messages on her first night. She hadn't even received any replies as the phone had run out of charge not long afterwards. Despite discovering that Maggie's house was powered by two large solar panels at the east side of the house, she had been too nervous to ask if she might recharge it. Part fear of being contacted, the buzz of all those messages arriving still humming in her ears, part fear of asking a favour too far of her host. And part, she now realised, because she had simply started to forget about the device once the squawks of its insistent notifications had been replaced by those of gulls.

They walked for well over an hour in silence, the brisk breeze providing a convenient reason for Maggie not to chat. Clara still bristled at the endless quiet, but eventually let her feet find a rhythm that eased her ricocheting thoughts as they followed the path around the curve of the rock. Slowly, just as Clara began to wonder if she had misremembered the journey entirely, the lighthouse peeped into view. Its cheery red and white paint was immediately clear against the dark grey on which it sat, and Clara's heart quickened a little at the thought of seeing Signe, and showing her that she had made it there safely, and found Maggie – she had done what she'd come to do. This tiny burst of confidence, this realisation that she hadn't entirely failed, gave her the nudge to go even further. What could she lose by having one last try?

Clara took a couple of larger strides until she was closer to Maggie than she had been for most of the walk. They were making their way down from the track now, only a couple of hundred metres from the entrance to the lighthouse.

'Maggie!' she called, hoping the wind wouldn't whip her words in the wrong direction. Her sister paused, looking back.

'Look, I'm sorry that whatever happened, happened. But my dad really loved you and missed you. I've seen the letter he sent you, I know he was reaching out to you while he was still alive. If anything, it looks like sending me was a last resort! He didn't open up easily and there is no way he would have left me that letter if he didn't really want to connect with you somehow ... '

Maggie had paused on the path. She was looking down at her boots, listening.

'I don't know about Paris,' Clara rattled on. 'I don't know

about any of it, but I just hope you're OK. I don't know what happens in someone's childhood to make them want to live out the rest of their days entirely alone in the middle of nowhere. I don't know why anyone would reject a dad like ours. I don't know why he and your mum broke up.

'I just came here because you don't have a father any more and you deserved to hear that from family. I have some stuff my father left me for you – photos and bits like that, which mean nothing to me but might be worth something to you.'

Clara was almost shouting now, determined to be heard over the wind, emboldened by the fact that Maggie was still standing, listening.

'It's so beautiful here I can't believe it's even real, and I know I'm not as old or as wise about the outdoors as you, but I can see that it's also bloody lonely. And I just want you to know that you don't have to be. You have a sister now – I know it's only me and not anyone more impressive. But it's not no one either.

'I've never known anyone like you. You're amazing. And I wish I could have got to know you better. I just want you to know that. And I'm sorry if it made you uncomfortable. Or sad. Or angry. I'm not even sure which. I'm just sorry about *all* of it. Especially the bit about how our dad's gone ... because ... well, because he was amazing too ... and I miss him every day ... and I know how much he must have missed you.'

Clara felt light-headed. When she was eleven, she had broken her arm falling from her bicycle, and had had to wear a cast for an entire, bored summer. She spent hours trying to slide plastic rulers, twigs and combs into it to itch her arm. She was convinced her arm was shrinking inside the plaster as she gradually found ways to scratch the spots she needed to. For days after the cast was removed, her arm felt disproportionally light: she would reach for door handles only to see her hand go flying two inches too high. She would lift her hand to push hair behind her ear and find it going whizzing behind her head. But it wasn't the arm that had become lighter, it was that she had become used to the extra weight.

And that was how she felt now. A weight she had not realised she had been carrying was lifted. The things she had not dared say for as long as she'd been on the island – for fear of letting down her father, for fear of upsetting her sister, and for fear of her life – were out. That same lightness, that same sense that she might now misjudge things and slip out of control, were beating in her chest as she stood there, breathless, looking at her sister.

Maggie was still looking at her boots. Slowly, she lifted her head to Clara, her eyes clear. She said one sentence.

'You made me a promise.'

There was nothing Clara could say. She had broken that promise, knowingly, and now all she could do was to nod back.

They finished the steps to the lighthouse, and walked in silence to the door Clara had entered with Arve a few days before. This time, it was shut and locked. And pinned to it, in a plastic waterproof folder, was a note.

Maggie,
I have had to return to the mainland, my sister is sick. I may be gone for weeks.
You know where the key is, and your sister's bag is in the lobby.
Please, let yourselves in if you need the bag, or access to the Wi-Fi.
With all best wishes, Signe

Slowly, Clara moved her hand to her mouth, realising that her earlier worries about what awaited her at home were now inconsequential: there was no way off the island.

# Chapter 21

The wind was growing stronger now, making Clara wonder if it might be possible to be blown off the path. Was it the breeze that was making her wonder this, or the fact that she felt as if she'd been winded by Signe's note? As Maggie stood, staring down at it, gnawing at the side of her mouth, Clara also wondered if her sister might just leave her there, at the lighthouse, indefinitely. Instead, she had said quietly, 'It looks as if you're going to have to come back. You'll never last out here alone.' And then, grabbing the note from the door, 'And I couldn't do that to my ... to you.'

Sometimes, on occasional darker days that followed, Clara wondered if she had really heard that, or if the wind coming off Hestøy had twisted Maggie's voice like it did the wild grasses beside the path. But on most days, and the longer their gentle truce lasted, she became sure. She had been so close to saying *sister*, hadn't she?

Maggie headed down to the boat house, rummaged around inside for a while, and returned with the keys – an old-fashioned iron one and a more modern electric fob. After a couple of beeps and a twist of the metal, they were inside the lighthouse.

Clara followed Maggie inside as she flicked on lights and looked around, before walking confidently into a small, windowless office at the rear of the tower. She turned on the computer, logged on to an email account Clara had never even known she had, and then offered Clara the chance to do the same.

'I've emailed Signe wishing her all the best, offering to keep an eye on things here. She has stopped over on the mainland before; she knows that I know where most things are here. I'm going to get some bits from the kitchen if you want to do whatever you need to on the computer now.'

Clara logged on to the government website, found the verified travel documents that she needed, and then realised that she didn't really need them now: after all, she couldn't leave the island. Unless she swam off it. She printed the documents off anyway, her heart fluttering with anxiety at the thought that she seemed to have replaced one cage for another. But there was also a small grain of something else: a speck of ambition reminding her that she had wanted this adventure, this time with Maggie. And that this was a chance to truly turn it into something without entirely burning her bridges at home.

She had a week here, maybe two, she reckoned, as she sat at the computer. She tried to work out what admin she needed to do, so that she didn't have to do the walk back here again. She followed the links on the government website and realised that she could apply for a new passport right now. Luckily, the bright whitewash of the walls in the lighthouse made a perfect backdrop and she managed to take a new passport photo with her now semi-charged phone.

The website indicated that she would need a second party

to verify her identity and she noted with relief that that person couldn't be someone she lived with. Simon could be left out of the process. She realised that she had the perfect candidate in Mr Tandy, so she quickly emailed Audrey at his office to explain the situation, and that they would be required to tick whatever boxes were needed. She also thanked Audrey profusely for everything she had done so far, letting her know that yes, she had met her sister, and yes they were spending some time staying together in Northern Norway. To admit the time together was somewhat enforced, and that neither of them seemed to be getting much out of it, felt too close to admitting to her father that she had failed, so she kept the details chirpy and scenic. She signed off by promising to let Audrey know when she was back, and sending all her best to Mr Tandy. She felt a stab of guilt that it was Audrey whom she was writing to in the most depth, but she didn't feel quite up to any probing that a reply to Nikita might prompt, and she wasn't sure if her mother wanted to know much about the trip at all.

So she took a couple of photographs from the window of the room she was in, marvelling at how blasé she had already become about the views. Once compressed onto her small phone screen they were outrageously beautiful, and exactly what she needed to send to a couple of friends, reassuring them that she was having a fantastic time and that she was looking forward to seeing them when she was back. Nikita got one too, of course. But it was the friends who had started a slow creep to the edges of her life with whom she was hoping to reconnect. If she could blame her absence in their lives for so long on the death of her father, on the trip itself, then perhaps she would be accepted more readily back into friendships that she had started to let wither as Simon had come to dominate her emotional landscape. She kept things chatty, she talked about how much she was looking forward to being in touch when she was back, she attached the photos. And she hoped for the best.

To Nikita, she stressed the patchiness of the Wi-Fi, and made sure to attach the photos in the smallest possible size. She thanked her again for looking after the suitcase of belongings she had hastily delivered to her the day that she had left for the Arctic. And she promised that she would let her know how she was getting along in more detail soon. What she didn't clarify was whether she meant how she was getting along with regards to Simon or Maggie. Did it even matter? They were becoming part of the same problem, after all.

Finally, her mother. The woman she had spent a lifetime trying to escape and was now aching for a little. When she had been planning the trip, she imagined herself radiating with smugness as she told her mother she had found another, more meaningful family connection. From this side of the trip she had a little less swagger, but she wasn't prepared to lose face quite yet. So she sent some snaps, used the word 'we' twice as much as in any of her other correspondence and kept things brief. Most of all, she made no mention of her larger problems: her joblessness, her potential homelessness, and the churning well of anxiety about what Simon was going to do next – if indeed anything.

She was done. But her fingers hovered, wondering if sending some sort of holding email to Simon was a good idea – would it placate or enrage? She had lost all sort of perspective from where she was. She stared at the screen, before deciding that if she didn't know what to write she shouldn't write anything at all. Instead, she googled *geitrams* and discovered that it was willowherb, a word she had heard many times, and had no idea she could or would ever eat.

Just as she was about to log off, there was the soft ping of a new message in her inbox. It was terse. The tone he adopted when there was going to be no arguing. The decision was made.

Paid those bills from your account. Assumed you would want me to as they were your responsibility and you never told me otherwise.

Her heart was hammering in her chest as she made a mental note to see how much her phone had charged and to check her bank account. She opened her suitcase and filtered through it, looking for essentials to take back to Maggie's house. She found the wallet of documents from Tandy, Nitt & Co, a couple of novels and her Mooncup, which she had a feeling she would be needing soon, and packed as much as she could into her rucksack. She felt as if she had done as much as she could to keep the real world at bay a little longer so she headed down to the kitchen to find Maggie, who was busy making them dinner.

They ate at a small table by the window, looking down at the infinite expanse of sea below. The height of the lighthouse made Clara feel even further away from everything she had ever known than she did at Maggie's house, as if she were about to spin out from the earth's orbit altogether.

She thanked Maggie profusely for the meal, yet again. Her sister was certainly more polite than Simon, and obligingly answered all the questions Clara asked her about how she had made the simple dinner. But not even an optimist like Clara could have called her responses enthusiastic. They washed and dried the dishes largely in silence, apprehension about the return across the island growing as Clara braced herself for the next week or so. They walked until late, safe in the seemingly never-ending sunset, until they finally reached what Clara didn't yet know was going to be home for the next few months.

It was only when she woke with a start in the middle of the night that Clara remembered she had not checked her bank balance. Indeed, her phone was now on the other side of the island.

# Chapter 22

Clara still thought it might just be a matter of a couple of weeks, and she found it hard to shrug off her desperation to make every second on the island count. Maggie was an attentive host and a kind older sister, even if she continued to resist using that term. She rubbed antiseptic ointment onto Clara's feet until they were entirely healed, the new skin gleaming like fresh peach. And she fed and looked after Clara with a tenderness she had not known from anyone besides her father. Without a second thought, Maggie included her in the rhythm of the house, getting her to help with the tasks that kept her small existence going, as well as introducing her to the pleasures that seemed to make this lonely existence a positive choice for her. She even shared the secrets of the kitchen far more easily than Clara had ever imagined she would after her clipped responses to dinner at the lighthouse.

There was a large larder to the side of the kitchen, filled with huge sacks of flour which had been delivered to the lighthouse by arrangement with Signe. There were also canned goods and plenty of frozen dairy staples. But most of what they ate came from the island: as summer progressed, Maggie took Clara out to the spots she had mentioned on that first walk and showed her where to find wild asparagus in the shady perimeter of the forest, where the wild mushrooms grew and where the berries sprang up on the marshy land approaching the trees.

There were blueberries, juniper berries and fresh Nordic vanilla. Maggie's fingers riffled through the greens at the edges of the woods with fingers as confident as Clara's were sifting through her make-up drawer for exactly the right colour lipstick. Later, at home, Maggie had shown Clara what to look for in the future, producing illustrations of the lifecycle of blackberries and strawberries for her to study and even copy. She explained how the wide white petals of the strawberry flower around its buttery-yellow centre would soon fall away, leaving the vivid-green hull to slowly grow into a strawberry. And how the scraggier white of blackberry petals would make a similar transformation, the berry emerging hard and yellow before becoming red – still too sour! – and finally a luscious blackish blue. But it was the exoticism of the cloudberry which fascinated Clara above all others, unlike anything she had seen in the pick-your-own fields of childhood trips in the West Country.

The berries seemed to ripen in reverse, starting a more pedestrian red before letting the sun turn them a jewel-like orange. Maggie had shown her early on where her favourite patch to collect them was: on some marshy grass in the valley behind the forest. Every time they visited the trees, the sisters would peek back there, checking on their progress several times a week, watching, waiting as the sun's heat filled the segments with juice and the petals fell away.

*Just a couple more weeks*, Maggie had told her more than once. *Just a couple more weeks.* Each time she returned from the lighthouse there had been further news from Signe to say that she wasn't returning just yet – complications at the hospital, some bookings for the lighthouse cancelled, catching up with family while she had the chance on the mainland. And each time Maggie had replied on their behalf, saying that that was no problem, that all was well here. Clara didn't know how to interpret this – affronted at her ongoing imprisonment or delighted at her sister's willingness to spend more time together. After all, she was behaving like a woman who didn't mind her sister being around, but she was also behaving as if Clara was anyone but a sister.

Either way, Clara was still not sure how long she had left on the island, and had come to see the cloudberries as a sort of talisman. She barely dared hope that Signe wasn't back until she had had the chance to taste a ripe cloudberry, but the months seemed to be passing faster now, and that small coil of panic in her gut when she realised that her leaving the island was entirely out of her hands was tightening now. Thus far, the only manageable way of loosening that coil had been to focus on letting her time on the island – and her time with Maggie – soothe rather than panic her. And she had surprised herself by finding that easy.

They ate well over the summer, with Maggie sharing her fresh sourdough every morning, as well as the variety of jams she had made from last year's berries. Lunch had generally been salad and vegetables, often foraged or sometimes home-grown, and dinner mostly fish and produce from the garden. Clara never felt hungry, no longer craving the beige biscuits and snacks she normally relied on to surf from meal to meal, a habit which had been especially pronounced in recent months while she navigated the swollen-hearted grief she still felt over her father. Each meal that Maggie produced looked like the sort of thing you might pay £38 for in a chic Kensington spa, but seemed not to have cost Maggie more than mere pennies, and not a single one left Clara dreaming of sugary treats.

Despite there being no one else on the island and no Wi-Fi or even phone reception at the house, Maggie seemed to be consistently busy. As well as the time she spent showing Clara the island, she tended to the garden, prepared meals, and took care of the rainwater filter and solar panels which were providing the house with both fresh usable water and electricity, making it truly independent in a way that the lighthouse wasn't. She would also disappear on walks for an hour or two at a time, referring to them as 'her' walks – making it clear that Clara would not be invited. At first, Clara felt bereft when Maggie left for these missions, but slowly she gathered the confidence to make trips of her own – to parts of the island she dared to hike only after checking them out from a distance on earlier expeditions with her sister.

She made it round the headland of the island, following a faint path she was sure had been made by Maggie's boots a few days before. She saw smaller coves with pristine sand which reminded her of Cornish summer holidays – surfers, sandcastles and ice lollies were all long-ago memories now. Picture-perfect pines framed these beaches which were otherwise inaccessible, surrounded by steep, jagged rock. She roamed the marshland around the forest, checking up on the berries but never quite daring to enter the dense woodland alone. Maggie, more experienced at keeping her bearings and following trails, would lead them into the woodland without a backwards glance, but Clara found the prospect of doing it solo utterly terrifying.

Most terrifying of all was the maelstrom, that mass of water at the far side of the island which would, twice a day, turn into a seething cauldron as two tides passed both in and out between Måsholmen and the island next door. The distance between the two land masses was about four hundred metres, but when the maelstrom began it seemed infinite. As the two channels passed each other, fighting for space in the sea, Clara would watch as hundreds of tiny whirlpools would form, each one sucking down into the sea in the fight for space as the water pressure rose. The water seemed both frightening but more alive than ever at these times, and Clara often found herself walking to the edge of the island to see it. Fish would occasionally spring from the churn as the water whitened, the roar of the water increasing until she felt sure the edge of the one of the islands would move, pushed away by the force. She saw herself in that churn, as she fought within to find space to grieve while determinedly forging a sisterhood, as she fought to stay on the island, safe from Simon, while suffocating under the pressure of knowing that she couldn't stay for ever, that these things had to be confronted at some point. And that they would have to be done without the support of her father, and perhaps even done without the love of her sister. The channels swirled, the pressure mounted.

When she could calm her nerves for long enough to truly consider her position, she could see that in Simon, she had chosen a home in haste because she had never really known the true warmth of one growing up. She thought about Nikita's family, the chatter around the kitchen table, the familiar ease with which the adult children were welcome to visit, and cherished it. She had tried to recreate the sort of ease and comfort she imagined a 'proper' home had with Simon, but just as in her own childhood, something had always been off. Back then, as she scurried around the flat trying to check for anything that might set him off when she knew Simon was on his way home, she had told herself it was her. She was the constant after all. Holding her mum back, holding Simon back. It was only in the sanctuary of her dad's place that she felt at rest, and now, as her memories of him started to sit differently, she wondered if even that had been true. Because some days on those island walks, that sense that *she* was the problem, the common denominator, was creeping back. The elation of the early days on the island, the dizziness that Erik had prompted in her on the train, the relief of knowing that she was physically safe once she reached Måsholmen, was slowly fading as she repeatedly hit the emotional granite of Maggie's polite but undeniably formal sisterliness. Again, she told herself that as *she* was the constant, it made sense that *she* should be the one to squeeze and adapt herself, liquid under pressure, until she could better fit into these people's lives: Maggie, her mum, Simon. Perhaps, she told herself on some of those endless nights, it hadn't been that bad. Perhaps she could just go back to the flat when all this was over, and fit around him once again.

Liquid under pressure.

The mornings that she woke with a start, remembering his palm around her neck, were getting fewer after all.

Occasionally there would be a flicker deep inside, reminding her that simply turning her phone off and leaving it at the lighthouse was not going to solve any of the problems that lay waiting on the other side of that screen. In almost every other way, these last couple of months following that return from the lighthouse had been the best few months of her life, hadn't they?

On other days the water would be clearer, her emotions less frothy. Clara would just sit staring at the sunset, the enormous orange sun a dropped ice lolly melting into the horizon, and sob. Sometimes she felt the tears incoming before she had left the house, a tide as unstoppable as the ones she would watch from the house every day. She would sense the heaviness she carried in her heart daily becoming a swell, a thousand pebbles weighing on her chest, and would have to grab her coat and boots, desperate to get outside in time, to find a vantage point that might console her when the tears came. Other times she would simply be walking, examining the plant life, jotting down a note about something she'd like to ask Maggie later, scribbling the outline of a leaf she might like to draw in more detail, lost in wonder at the island, when she would feel grief wash over her, shocking in its speed: a cold wave catching her unawares. More than once she had instinctively thought about how she must text her dad, how cheering it would be for him to know that she could find wild garlic, or her own potatoes – before she would remember that her text would have no reader, and she would find herself bent double with tears, as if she'd taken a blow to the gut. She wondered if Maggie knew she was doing this, if she saw the glassy gleam in her eyes when she returned home, hanging her jacket up with a breezy smile. Perhaps she was doing the same thing elsewhere on the island.

Back at home, prior to the constant tugging of grief at her sleeve, Clara only ever found bouts of crying like this crept up on her a day or two before her period. Then, they would be for no reason at all, or at least no reason beyond her realising what day of her cycle it was – usually too late for it to be any consolation. But here, the inexplicable bouts seemed to ease. Her cycle seemed to enjoy the diet, or the air, or the sleep that she was getting, and she began to feel a greater sense of ease in her body. She had no idea about her weight and she had little idea what she looked like. The gel pedicure that she had had 'so her sister thought the best of her' had long peeled off, and she had no razor and no inclination to use one.

Slowly, a sense of her body being there to serve her, or at least to work alongside her instead of merely existing for the enjoyment of others, had crept in. Perhaps it was the fresh air, the good food, the release from the endless scroll and check impulse that her phone had held over her. Or perhaps it was simply that she felt full ownership over her body again. It no longer tried to rest, semi-coiled in readiness for the next rage, the next threat. It knew it could lie for a whole night, untouched, and was responding to that by growing stronger, clearing the space for Clara to consider what she actually wanted from it. Or maybe it was nothing to do with Simon, she sometimes told herself: everything seemed so much easier with no one around to see her, no one's gaze on the commuter train to be monitoring, no social media to be feeding. No wonder Maggie seemed so self-assured, she found herself thinking: solitude was addictive if you looked at it from this perspective.

But no matter how liberating her time on Måsholmen was, Clara could now admit to herself that she wished she could speak to her mother. After a while, the sisters began walking together to the lighthouse every couple of weeks and Clara spent a little while catching up on her emails, updating pals on what a wonderful time she was having, how it was the year out she had always longed to take, how treasured this time bonding with her sister had been. She glossed over the details, things that would only make people worry, before logging off with a flourish and heading back along the increasingly easy-to-manage path to Maggie's house.

But each time she did this, she also knew that she was avoiding Simon. She would scan her emails quickly, checking for anything from him. Once or twice there was a late-night rant, telling her how much he missed her, talking about all the things they would do once she was *home*. Other times, there would be ultimatums. The times of day or night that the emails were sent were often revealing – the melancholy of a night in drinking alone, the remorse of a hungover mind trying to make amends for words sent in anger. Her blood would chill when she read these, unable to place them in any real context while so far from him. A threat, or a moment of anger that would be forgotten

215

by morning? So she would just focus on how far she was from him physically, log out, push all thoughts of him to the back of her mind and return to what she kept telling herself was what she had been sent to do. What she was supposed to be doing. What she was enjoying.

It was during the evenings that Clara felt she had been getting closest to the life she was telling friends and family she was living. Without darkness properly falling during the summer months, she and Maggie had come to rely on rituals to indicate the time of day. In the late afternoon, Maggie would start the stretch and fold of her bread, turning it slowly every half hour or so, preparing it for its night alone, rising as they slept. And in the absence of a TV in the house – which Clara would usually turn on the minute she made it home from work, or college for the years before that – she had taken it upon herself to 'educate' Maggie on British TV. She would spend evening after evening telling her the story of another UK soap opera or reality show. At first Maggie had feigned a sort of professorial distance, displaying a reluctant curiosity that she tried to maintain was merely to indulge Clara. But as Clara's stories became ever more intricate, sometimes even requiring pen and paper for a quick map of Albert Square or Platt family tree, she became convinced Maggie was enjoying it.

As she sat and listened, a small smile on her lips, Maggie would knit. It turned out that the room in which Clara was sleeping was a sort of studio, where she both designed and knitted intricate colour-work items, the sort of traditional Fair Isle or Scandinavian items that Clara had only ever seen before on royalty or in period dramas. But the clothes Maggie produced did not look like costumes or luxuries – here, in context, they seemed to fit entirely with the environment on the island. She created jumpers, cardigans, hats, gloves and blankets, emerging from both circular needles and traditional wooden ones. As they sat and chatted – always about popular culture or life on the island, never about themselves – fine lacy shawls would emerge from thin, candy-floss fibres and chunky fishermen's sweaters would appear from thick balls of yarn as large as Clara's head. Inch by inch, they would work their way down Maggie's lap, shapes revealing themselves like Renaissance statues stepping out from Carrara slabs.

'How on earth did you know how to begin?' asked Clara.

'The appeal of knitting – apart from being able to clothe yourself – is that there are only really about three stitches. You just have to follow the pattern ... '

Maggie made it sound so simple, so doable. As ever.

'It might feel like a leap of faith the first time,' she continued. 'But the patterns are so reliable. You just follow them, believe in the process and it grows.'

'If only more of life were that simple.'

'Well, now you know why I love it.' That small smile again. A tiny admission that she needed her life small, reliable, and that within that she could be herself. Again, Clara's admiration for her sister grew.

In time, Maggie showed Clara the basic stitches, helping her to loop the yarn around the needles, starting her off on tiny toddler-sized socks so that she could see the shapes forming quicker, then letting her loose on larger items. She radiated the same patience that she had with sourdough, wild-asparagus hunting or fishing for cod, while Clara marvelled that someone who had chosen to cut herself off from her family could be such a generous and natural host.

Maggie explained she had been taught to knit by the mother of the same boyfriend who had led her to Norway, and once she had picked up a few basic stitches she had just carried on. She bought wool in bulk whenever she hit the mainland, or asked for orders to be delivered with Signe's goods from Hestøy.

After once gifting an immaculate patterned sweater to Signe by way of thanks for a favour, Maggie had ended up being asked by some guests at the lighthouse to make a pair of gloves and matching hat. After this happened a few times, she had started to build a slow, small business selling items to gift shops on Hestøy and even taking commissions for larger and more intricate work from wealthier guests at the lighthouse.

Sometimes Maggie reminded Clara of Nikita's mother, a keen dressmaker. The sewing machine was noisier but the peaceful look of absorption was the same. Clara felt a gentle delight in the task that she had not experienced since childhood jigsaw puzzles, and even then they had seemed like penance on a rainy holiday day. It seemed strange to Clara that Nikita had not asked more about how she was or how long she was staying. Perhaps she had simply taken Clara at her word, believing that she had chosen to stay this long, that she was sorting everything out, reconciling herself with her father's past. Or perhaps she too was experiencing that sense of absorption in her task, busy making her film, thinking little of her friend in the Arctic. As time seemed to slide away, it felt as if it mattered less.

# Chapter 23

And time *was* sliding away. Midsummer came and went, but not without Maggie insisting on a small celebration. They hunted for the first of the berries, found wild asparagus and decided to stay up all night and watch the sun. Maggie even caught fish that morning before making a frothy batter, digging up fresh potatoes and frying the lot.

'Fish and chips for my English guest,' she said as she put the dishes on a table decorated with flowers from the other side of the island. Pinks, yellows, corals, dancing in a vase for Clara on their little holiday. After they had eaten, they went to the highest point on the island – a climb Clara would never have undertaken just a couple of months before – and sat to watch the eternal sunshine.

They perched on a flat ledge of rock, even higher than the lighthouse, peering down at the sea, waves now toylike below them. The preceding days had been breezy, but that night there was barely a breath of wind. Where Clara's hair had whirled around her face for a couple of her recent island walks, today the air was still. She pulled at her T-shirt where it was sticking to her back after the clammy hike up and pushed back the hair clinging to her face. Maggie, as ever, was more suitably dressed, her hair in two neat French plaits leading from the side of her face. Clara had put some Scotch into a flask, and they took it in turns to sip as they watched the light shift and shimmer around them.

They were surrounded by sky: if it had been an overcast night, Clara was sure that they would have been sitting in the clouds themselves. There was no direction in which the view was not breathtaking, and the height they were at gave the impression they were on the very edge of the world, that just an inch forward might see them not only heading over the edge of the mountain, but tumbling off the curve of the planet.

This was the night that Clara came closest to admitting to Maggie how terrified she was by what a mess she had left behind her, and how she was increasingly sure that the situation was only worsening the longer that she stayed on the island. For the few days preceding it, she increasingly found herself rehearsing lines, planning strategies to open the conversation, and running through all the ways that Maggie might respond.

Clara felt torn between not wanting to burden Maggie, not wanting to make her feel that she planned to stay, hiding from her reality for ever, and thinking, why not? After all, wasn't Maggie effectively doing the same? Wouldn't this confidence, admitting that she too had secrets, bring them closer? But just as Clara had planned one set of lines, she found herself rewriting, once again trying to fit herself around the quicksilver moods of her infinitely unknowable sister.

She decided that confiding in her would be the best way in, a way of building some solidarity away from the umbrella of their father's expectations. Not asking for help, not asking for details of her sister's experiences, but letting this dreadful secret out before it gnawed away at her any further. And this, she decided, this admission that she wasn't just a flibbertigibbet with no life experience, would also be the key to unlocking a part to Maggie which had so far led to her resisting attempts to be a true sister.

As they sat there taking in the midnight sun, Clara noted that she had only ever known that sense of being millimetres from not just a precipice but an entirely alternate life only once or twice before. In the seconds at the end of a great date, when she had nudged her head that imperceptible sliver of space forward – enough that someone feeling the same might sense that the door was open for a kiss, but never so far that someone who wasn't could reject her. Those small breaths between two potential lives, when both can exist for a moment, possibilities dancing together, until fate or choice, or something between the two nudges one out of reach, and the course of one's life is rerouted.

That sense had been rendered Hollywood-spectacular here on that peak as the midnight sun blazed down on the two of them. A physical push from one sister, and the other would be dead, Clara had no doubt of it. Had she just removed herself from one source of jeopardy and been living under another all this time? After all, this was Maggie's land. These paths had been built by her hand and worn by her feet. If Clara were to 'fall', who wouldn't believe it had been her own clumsy fault? Was she right to find this time with Maggie threaded through with these occasional moments of fear? Or was her mind addled by years of living in the shadow of someone she was never quite sure wouldn't hurt her? She tried to force such a thought as far down as she could push it, to focus on the peace she might yet find that night. She had been telling herself for weeks that Midsummer would be the night she would try again, to open up herself, and to see if she could finally get Maggie to open up in response. The year would pivot to its second half after this;

she might be only days from heading home. And she wanted that moment, that perfect moment she had come here for. The moment that would be the balm on her sad soul, enabling to her to face whatever life was waiting for her when she returned.

But as midnight came, and they sat there in silence, the majesty of the sky seemed ... uninterruptible. And a few minutes later, the best that Clara found she could manage was, 'It's a lot warmer here that I imagined it would be.'

'You know it's the middle of summer, right?' said Maggie, passing her the flask. 'It is literally, this hour, the middle of summer.'

'I know, I just mean ... it *is* also the Arctic.'

'Well, I guess we shouldn't make assumptions about things,' said Maggie.

*You* shouldn't make assumptions about things, Clara felt sure she meant.

'But I do know what you mean,' said Maggie. 'Things often aren't what they look like up here. On the one hand some of the bays look like they could be in Barbados ... '

'I know, right? That white sand is outrageous!'

'On the other hand there is the Gulf Stream – that water down there is warmed in Mexico and has made its way straight up and over here. There are spots further south which don't get a whisper of it, and you can feel it. So yes, it is a lot colder than Barbados here, but it's also a lot warmer than a lot of people anticipate.'

'Do you think people are like that?'

'What do you mean? '

'Well, deceptive in both directions I suppose.' Clara swallowed, her mouth suddenly dry. 'Like Dad?'

Why was she talking about her father when she had meant to talk about her boyfriend?

222

'Clara ... '

'It's just that sometimes I feel that yeah, you obviously didn't know Dad like I knew him. But also – maybe there were things about him that you know and I never did. It's like, I only saw Barbados and you only got ice water.'

'Clara – it's fine. Please. As you can see, I am doing very well with ice water.'

*But are you?* she wanted to ask. At that moment a bank of clouds came from behind them and the safety of the sunshine maintaining the sense of a perfect moment was gone. Clara thought of Maggie, so often sitting on the rocks above the bay or in her kayak on a calm morning, fishing rod in hand, collecting food for them. Perhaps she was doing well, perhaps she needed none of this.

And just as Clara drew breath to press on with the discussion, Maggie said it was time to head back, so, once again, the door closed on the conversation.

# Chapter 24

They made their way back to the house largely in silence and as Clara's head touched her pillow, she tasted a bitterness at how the evening had unfolded. It was no longer that she wanted to talk about the past because she wanted to sell the idea of a perfect father to Maggie, or even that she had any faith in how sharing her own confidences would turn her mood around. It was that the longer she stayed, learning to trust her sister, the more she began to suspect that perhaps there was a side to Ben that she had never known about. Could she, in Simon, have chosen a man just like her father after all – only without ever realising what that had really meant?

Perhaps the ice water of her father had been there all along and she had just been too young, too naive to spot it. Her eyes were dry with tiredness. She lifted her arm, bent at the elbow, to cover them, and as sleep crept in, she promised herself she would try again. She needed a new deadline to keep herself focused. When the cloudberries ripened, she told herself. When the cloudberries ripened.

As summer itself ripened, Clara kept checking on the few cloudberry patches that she knew. She would walk over every week or so when Maggie was either busy or on one of her own walks. She began to see it as her own special project, watching them perform this strange reverse colour change. At first they were perfect white flowers low on the ground, sitting atop longer stalks and reddish leaves, then they became the sort of red that a child might choose to paint with, and a fat, fleshy shape that one might draw. In time, they slowly began to fade, at last ending up as beaming orange as the midnight sun itself.

The morning that Clara decided to pick them, Maggie left for one of her walks with a face sterner than Clara had seen for weeks. It was blustery as she headed out, the door slamming behind her, but Clara had at last started to find it easier to accept that some days, her sister simply wasn't chatty. She watched Maggie set off for the lighthouse with an empty rucksack, having said she needed to collect some more flour and various other bits from the storeroom, as well as emailing some clients about the current lack of a postal service on the island. She warned that she might be some time. Clara darted out of the door as soon as she was sure Maggie was far enough down the path, and headed to the forest straight away. Well, not quite to the forest, but to the marshy land just before it, where she knew the best of the cloudberries would be.

She half ran as she scrambled down the hillside to the valley, having become accustomed to the way that the various walks around the island made her heart hammer with the effort. It seemed impossible that she had once found this landscape daunting, that she had doubted her body's ability to scamper across it as nimbly as Maggie did. How proud her father would be! And how different it was to the punitive sort of exercise that Simon had always done: intense, long-distance cycle rides, gym trips defined by a grim determination, rain-sodden runs which seemed more like an atonement for indulgence than a pleasure in themselves.

Then she saw them, cloudberries as plump and golden as she had dreamed. She pulled off her sweatshirt, tying one end shut to create a makeshift bag, and immediately started picking, unable to resist taking a bite or two as she went. They were ready.

They weren't as sweet – or perhaps simply as familiar – as the strawberries she had tasted earlier in the summer. They were exotic, sharper than any other berry she had tasted, but with a creaminess she had not been expecting. They tasted as if they had already been mixed with yoghurt, or blanched into a sort of opacity. They were immediately the most delicious and the most unusual taste she had ever known, and she wanted to talk about them with everyone she had ever shared a good meal with. Images of licking the spoon as she baked with Nikita, of sharing fish and chips with a pre-Simon boyfriend, of her dad popping that biscuit in his mouth as they sat in the Place des Vosges all flashed past her mind's eye as she plucked, hungrily, busily, as if she might one day be able to share this taste with them all.

Once Clara had collected as many berries as she thought were properly ripe, she sat and took a sip of water, looking towards the forest. She longed to head into the trees and stretch her independence on the island even further, but her legs were tired. She decided to ask Maggie to take her again, to show her some landmarks to keep her on track, and then she headed home.

Maggie was still not back when she got there, so she busied herself putting the berries into a tinted glass bowl on the main table, making sure that they were sitting just so the light from the garden window hit them. They gleamed like jewels, leaving

Clara longing for enough reception to post a perfect image online, reassuring people that she was having a deeply content but also slightly exotic summer. Instead, she paced anxiously, running through her lines again, all those ways to start the conversation with Maggie about each of their pasts. She was putting away the washing up when the front door opened and Maggie finally reappeared. Her hair was wild and her eyes looked bloodshot. It was impossible to tell if wind or tears were the culprit.

'Hi!' said Clara, hopefully.

'Hey there.'

'All OK?'

'Well there's good news and there's bad news,' replied Maggie.

'OK ... '

'There was an email from Signe when I checked. She has to stay away for longer, but she is very aware of the position she has left us in here.'

'Oh, right.' Panic was bubbling in Clara's veins.

'She has offered to send the boat back for us – so that you can leave, and that mail can be collected, some more supplies ordered and so on. She was worried as she knows you never intended to be here for this long, and she had remembered that I was due on the mainland for a short while too.'

'It's been no trouble. I've enjoyed it. I hope you didn't say—'

'So I told her to send it in a couple of weeks. I have some projects I can finish for clients and then mail over, and you can book flights, make plans and so on.'

'Oh, right,' Clara said again, her voice small.

The world she had come to rely on was suddenly slipping out of her grasp, glass in soapy wet hands.

'I hope that suits you.' Maggie was not looking her in the eye. Clara couldn't work out what the problem was.

'Yes, of course, whatever suits you really.' Why was she replying in similarly formal tones? Hadn't they been close for these last few months? 'Thank you for putting up with me for this long.'

But Maggie offered no smile in return. She started to unpack her bag slowly onto the kitchen counter, her eyes slightly glazed.

'Have you eaten?' she asked after a while. 'I think I am going to have an early night.'

'No, but I can make myself something. I have had rather a lot of cloudberries today though ... ' She dipped her head, trying to catch Maggie's lowered gaze. Nothing.

'Well done you,' she said softly, nodding at the bowl of fruit. 'I'm delighted that you found them, and so many.'

'And I'm thrilled that you're proud of me.' Clara grinned, aware that she must have looked like a daft puppy, longing for reassurance.

Time had caught up with her: she was going to have to face up to her future now, and with every breath the task seemed greater. She wanted to feel believed in, to have someone tell her that it would all turn out fine.

Instead, Maggie was just staring past her, eyes glassy.

'Maggie – are you OK?'

'Yes.' But her slow, ponderous movements suggested otherwise. This was more than just tiredness from the walk.

'It's just ... '

There was a sense that clouds were gathering. Maggie was closing down again, and Clara was still at a total loss as to how to deal with this. Yet again, her eyes were dropped, her guard raised, but this time, there was a lethargy, almost a sadness.

'This is just ... me. It isn't pretty, or charming – like you seem to find so easy – but it's just part of me. Being here helps;

I suppose it's much of the reason why I'm here – it helps me. Until ... well until it doesn't. And now is one of those times.'

'I see. A sort of grief?'

'Yes, but not how you mean. It has been coming since long before you brought your news. And from inside myself looking out, it is something rather more than just, you know, sadness.'

'And you would prefer not to talk about it? Because, well, that is how you seem to deal with things, but also ... I'm always happy to try and help. To talk it through?' Clara felt a fool, throwing out one more hopeful attempt.

'It's rather beyond talking it through, I'm afraid,' said Maggie, eyes as dark as the first day she'd met her. 'But thank you. I know you only ever want to help.'

Once Maggie was in bed, Clara longed for darkness. To have a proper evening. She felt taunted by the daylight, particularly as it was a dreary sort of light, hampered by a froth of half-hearted cloud above. It stayed the same for the following few days. Maggie slept uncharacteristically late, spoke less than usual – even by her taciturn standards – and was visibly struggling to communicate with Clara at all. Clara busied herself with what she could do in the house without needing direction from Maggie. Slowly, she made her way through the bowl of cloudberries, unsure if Maggie had had a single one. Did she even like them? Clara realised that she had no idea.

Maggie's sadness – more than sadness, an absolute emptiness – persisted, and over the next week the weather worsened, as if the sky knew that summer was well and truly on its way out and had given up slightly too early. Winds were getting wilder, and the birds were starting to behave differently, as if the whole island was preparing for the change in seasons and the change in behaviours that it would require.

The anxiety in Clara only grew: a bubble in her throat

which was going to pop if she didn't take some sort of action about her future. So she decided to head to the lighthouse alone one evening, and make some sort of plan for her return. The boat was coming in a week or two; she could no longer pretend that leaving the island was a problem she didn't have to think about yet.

Maggie was by now sleeping for over twelve hours some days, which seemed incomprehensible to Clara in the endless light, and was leaving her lonely for hours on end. Better to be lonely and starting to take control over things, she told herself. So one evening when Maggie headed to bed straight after dinner, Clara took a chunk of bread, a small tin full of berries and a hard-boiled egg, and put them all in her rucksack. Then she took Signe's keys from the smooth wooden hook by the kitchen door, and headed down the path towards the lighthouse.

At first she felt furtive, as if she were up to something she shouldn't have been. But it occurred to her that in her current state, Maggie would probably have barely noticed even if she had told her she was making the trip. Clara had spotted that they were running low on a few household items anyway, and knew that 'taking the initiative' would provide perfect cover if she were challenged.

The walk seemed to be easier than it ever had been, despite the drop in temperature. The balminess of the last couple of trips was gone now, and Clara's legs – in a borrowed pair of her sister's shorts – had fresh thigh muscles visible, like thick rope, each time she took a stride forward. The young woman who had barely dared take a step down this path at all seemed like a distant memory, as the beat of her stride started to help her untangle the knot of thoughts while she picked up pace. Was it renewed fitness that was powering her along, or adrenaline flooding her system as she allowed herself to consider her options for the next few months.

She needed to look up flights back to the UK, and decided to try and book something in the autumn, rather than second-guessing the exact date that the boat might be arriving on Måsholmen. She had no idea if Maggie had actually set a date beyond 'in a couple of weeks' and was yet to pluck up the courage to ask her. A few nights in Trondheim or even Bodø might not be too bad anyway. Should she email Nikita and ask her if she could stay a few days? Her documentary would be nearing completion and Clara couldn't work out if a house guest would be a welcome intrusion or a disaster waiting to happen. Nor could she unpick whether she would be up to talking as much as Nikita did – spending so many months out here, learning to appreciate, if not love, her own company had certainly changed her thirst for chat. Should she try and get some sort of house-sitting arrangement instead? Even if only a week or two, while she got her bearings back in the UK? But how could she advertise that she was looking for something like that without alerting Simon or any of their mutual friends that she wasn't planning to return home? Step after step she turned her options over, examining them from every angle. To return straight 'home' now seemed unthinkable, and to explain the situation and its emotional complexity to her mother from here was equally out of the question.

She berated herself for wasting so much time while she had been on the island, for believing that all that time spent on the garden, at the beach, on the trails, had been self-care, or self-discovery. Hadn't it really been an elaborate set of means to avoid her past rather than a meaningful reach towards her future? Either way, as the lighthouse grew closer, the full enormity of what she had done in leaving the way she had, in using grief to run from so much else, felt clearer than ever to her.

She let herself into the lighthouse quietly, using both the large metal key and the electronic fob that she had seen Maggie use time after time over the last few months. She felt breathless with anxiety, the edges of her hands fizzing in the way they always did when she was at her most nervous. She stood at the large white sink, sipping a huge glass of water and remembering how she and Maggie had eaten there at the window – how much she still hadn't told her. And how much she still had to hear from Maggie. Well Maggie's not here, she told herself, and headed into the office to the computer.

His name was the first she saw when she logged in to her emails. More than once. Her hand hovered as it went to click on the second of the emails from him, this one sent only yesterday.

Babe,

Your passport has arrived!

So lucky I opened the package for you and can keep it safe.

Seems too risky to send it all that way and I have time off due, so will deliver in person.

Time to come and take you home! Let's get things back to normal, babe.

S xxx

It didn't seem possible. Of all the scenarios she had imagined, not a single one of them had involved Simon coming to her. How had she forgotten to give Audrey a change of address when she had asked for her help with the passport application?

Anywhere would have been better than back to the flat. Had it even been possible to change addresses while applying from out here? The whole process was now blurring in her mind, it all seemed too long ago.

She had to get off the island before Simon reached her.

Her fingers trembled as she scrambled for her phone, logged on to her bank account and saw that over £1000 was missing from her account – a substantial portion of the money that Mr Tandy had transferred to her for the purposes of this trip to see Maggie. She had been relying on it to live on while she got herself set up back in the UK without needing Simon, and now she realised that he had taken most of it. It was way more than any household bill might have been; it was his way of keeping her restrained. She still had one thing on her side though: he didn't actually know where she was. She decided to reply quickly, to try and keep things at bay until she could speak to Maggie.

Hi there,

You don't have to go to all that trouble! I have emergency travel documents here, it's fine.

It's very remote where I am, let's just talk when I am back.

I have so much to tell you, so you stay comfortable and I will let you know when I am back. Boat is coming for us soon, just a week or two I think.

C xxx

There. Her telling him she had to wait for the boat would surely imply that there was no way he could get here otherwise? She had a little time. She could still make a proper escape – not just from the island, but from him.

Then, just as she was about to close the application and turn off the computer, the ping of a fresh email.

It's ok baby. I checked your emails too. I know where you are. See you soon xxx

# Chapter 25

Clara walked back through the night, as fast as her legs would carry her. She knew it wouldn't be dark for hours, if at all, and there was no real rush to return – but the only way she could try and temper the adrenaline coursing through her was to push her legs, lungs and heart as far as she could, trying to alchemise panic into exhaustion by whatever means she could.

She knew that she would have to tell Maggie about Simon at some point, but she was also depending on the fact that for as long as the boat wasn't coming to the island, *he* couldn't reach the island. She had time. She had to do things in the right order. She had to hold her nerve.

She got to bed after midnight, and the few hours of sleep that she had were broken, plagued by random snippets of memories and anxieties, the real and the dreaded merging incomprehensibly. Ben dropped in and out of dreams that weren't even dreams, just memories playing on what seemed to be a never-ending loop. He would have a haircut from 2002 during a memory that was only from months before. He would appear, talking to celebrities, politicians and friends of hers she knew he had never met. Then there would be a sensory memory, waking her with the smell of his aftershave which was of course nowhere near here, on this lonely little island.

When she was younger and sleep had not come easily to her, she had been afraid of the dark. Now, it was the endless, all-pervading light that seemed to haunt her, whatever the hour. Despite it never getting properly black, the light crept in from 3 a.m. and was almost blinding by 3.30. Without buildings to block it, it had free rein of the island by 4 a.m. 'Daylight' was brighter than any Clara had known in London.

'You just have to work with it,' Maggie had told her a couple of weeks earlier. 'It's not as if you don't know it's going to be dark again before long.'

It's all very well *knowing* it's going to get dark again in a few months, but it isn't *now*, Clara thought. Her silk eye mask, a gift from Simon which she had never really known what to do with, had been left on her bedside table at home. She remembered unwrapping it, smiling at the colourful illustration of Frida Kahlo with what she hoped looked like gratitude, secretly knowing she would never use it. She had never mentioned Frida Kahlo to him, and she knew the eye mask was from the shop in the station – the one most people reserved for buying a leaving gift for a colleague that they didn't really know. Necklaces with bees on, pineapple-shaped candle sticks and Frida eye masks: just the thing for someone whose soul remained an utter mystery to you, she had thought at the time. Now, she imagined herself wearing it, and finally letting herself have perhaps four unbroken hours of sleep. Instead, she woke sweating, sun pouring in through the gaps between the shutters, her forearm bent across her eyes.

But she knew she would never dare wear a silk eye mask here anyway, not where Maggie would see it. She would find it daft. And she was not interested in beautiful things, unless they were a fern or a gull's egg or something. Clara sighed, tipping her head back on the pillow and letting a finger slide underneath the bottom of the shutter. She flicked it open, resigning herself to no more sleep. Longing for some Wi-Fi, or even a magazine with which to pass the time, she swung her legs round and placed her feet on the floor. She looked out of the window towards the bay and gasped.

A figure was walking towards her. Coming up out of the sea, lumbering. She squinted, realising to her confusion that it was Maggie. Entirely naked, with her long dark hair covering her face, striding out of the water. And yet her manner seemed to suggest that this was entirely normal behaviour.

Clara leaned towards the window, transfixed. So far she had only ever seen Maggie bundled under layers of sensible wool or waterproofs. Even when the days had been endlessly sunny, Maggie had simply worn thinner layers rather than shorter sleeves. It had barely taken more than a day to establish discretion around the bathroom, each waiting to hear the other cross the house to their space before following into the shower. But now, as she dipped her head and flicked her hair back off her face, her entire body was exposed – to the sun, and to Clara.

Where Clara had assumed there was a forgotten, unloved body, she now saw something rather different. Something working entirely within the context of its surroundings, someone entirely comfortable with them. Maggie didn't flinch as she walked barefoot across the beach. She stood tall, unencumbered by the line of a swimming costume. She pulled her hair back into a knot and squeezed the water out of it, before turning to face the sea, the sun warming her back.

The sturdy lack of glamour that Clara had flinched at when she had first met Maggie now seemed rather different. The clearly defined leg muscles, the shiny hair, the warmth to the colour of her skin. She didn't just look beautiful, she looked as if she belonged, everything about her enhanced by her surroundings. Clara couldn't imagine fitting in anywhere as well as Maggie did here – despite the hours she had spent researching careers, the time spent in pubs and clubs laughing at jokes she had never really got, the evenings she had spent online at home trying to work out which make-up look was going to be most 'her' this season. She felt envious, wondering if there was any part of her sister's complete physical confidence that she would, or could, ever have.

'The water's lovely,' Maggie said, almost at the window. Clara blushed and shifted her gaze.

'I don't have a costume. It must be freezing,' she muttered, somehow ashamed to have been caught looking.

'The fish don't care if you're wearing a bikini,' said Maggie. 'And the seals are friendly.'

'I can barely swim anyway.'

'Don't swim then. Just let the water hold you. Look at the sky. You never know, you might like it.'

Clara's gaze followed as Maggie walked around the front of the house and through the front door, flicked a switch on the kettle and reached for a jar.

'Coffee first?'

'I'm not sure.' Clara was standing at the door of the room in which she had been sleeping, barefoot and in a long T-shirt, feeling like a child.

'About the coffee or the swim?' Maggie grinned. Not for the first time, Clara saw the flicker of her father's face in her. She didn't know if she wanted to cry or hug her.

'About anything, it seems.' If only Maggie knew how much she wasn't sure about.

'Well, in that case I recommend a swim then a coffee. Go on, you get out there. Your mug will be waiting for you. I promise I won't look, but I can't promise the puffins won't.'

There was something in the free and easy mood she had never seen Maggie in before that suddenly made Clara want to do it. This giddy, almost silly side of her sister was new and it threw her off guard. The tightness she had been carrying in her chest for the last few weeks on the island loosened a little at seeing her like this. If this lightness was what swimming could elicit, then she was up for it.

'OK then, I will,' said Clara. And she headed towards the front door, which Maggie held open for her, calling 'good luck!' after her as she walked towards the sea.

The tide was out, and the sun was as unrelenting as it had been when she'd woken up. She walked away from the house and down to the sand, taking off the T-shirt Maggie had lent her to sleep in and scooping a handful of sand over it to stop it from blowing away. She didn't dare to take off her pants though, and just kept walking, lest Maggie were watching her from the window.

The sand was warm and soft under her feet. Not baking hot like the Mediterranean beaches that had made her cry to stand on as a child, but a gentle warmth – like expensive underfloor heating in a smart hotel room, she thought, just as the first dappled waves hit her toes. She gasped at the cold.

It seemed incongruous that the water could be so bitter when the sun was so bright. But despite the shimmer of the sand and the neon stripes of green and blue as she looked beyond it, the water was still fresh from the Arctic. Of course it was.

She kept walking, the water lapping at her ankles, then up her legs as she walked slowly towards deeper water. Clara was now familiar with the beach at both high tide and low, but she hadn't realised how far the water would remain shallow at low tide, and how long it would take to reach deeper sea. A sea which might be able to hold her.

She kept going, trying to breathe out as hard as she could to stop herself from panicking as the tiny electric shocks of cold nipped higher and higher up her legs. She went into a sort of trance as she breathed, step after step, trying to keep herself calm, trying to keep slowly moving towards the horizon.

There was a catharsis in those jolts of cold, the sea reflecting the panic that had been growing in her, unanswered and entirely ignored.

And as Clara lay in the sea, the liquid gold of much-missed sunshine pouring onto her chest – she knew that something had shifted in Maggie too. A lightness was back in her gait, a clarity to her voice where it had seemed deeper, foggier for weeks now. Clara swam parallel to the shore, first looking out towards the lighthouse and then back towards Maggie's home, and she accepted that her time here was coming to an end and she could no longer avoid what was coming next.

It was Ben's birthday in ten days – 16 September – and only a few days after that she would be leaving the island. For the first time, she felt that she might be up to the task ahead. Simon had now done something unforgivable: he had taken her father's money, her legacy, the money that was supposed to be for her to find her sister. All those nights wondering if she was imagining him bending her to his will. All those times she wondered if he had checked her phone when she'd left the room to make a cup of tea. All those comments from Nikita, checking if she wanted to talk about things, if she was OK. She had brushed it all away for so long, but now she could see – in her own sister – that brushing things away was never going to work for her. An island retreat had been a haven for her, but it could never be a long-term solution. And finally, as she felt the sun's warmth on her chest and heard the gentle lapping of the water in her ears, she felt that she had changed enough to face it all. She had come here looking for her sister, but the real discovery had been herself. Perhaps her dad had known what he was doing after all.

But the rest of her time here was going to be a tussle between making the best of Maggie's renewed happiness and doing what she could to plan for her return. She would have to get in touch with Audrey again to seek proper legal advice about the money, the account, the passport. The whole bloody mess. But she could do it: it would be mortifying, but it would be better than running away for ever.

The final remaining task she had to do on the island was to present Maggie with the packet of memorabilia she had been sent to give her. So far she had not mentioned it, for fear of creating an unbearable tension on an island inhabited by only two people. And she had only looked at it once, back in England, not daring to even open it here on Måsholmen in case Maggie caught her prying. But she was done with fearing tension: seeking to avoid it had only ever yielded more. Yes, the conversation had to be had, and now that her way off the island was set in stone, she could make a grander gesture than she might have dared to earlier in the summer.

She would collect more cloudberries, maybe even try to make a cake to celebrate their father's birthday, and they would look together at the envelope of memories that Maggie had been left. Yes, that would be the kind thing to do. Closure for everyone.

Clara rolled off her back, dipped her head underwater, and swam back to the beach, finally certain about what the next steps in her life should be. At last, a future as clear as this Gulf Stream water.

PART THREE: AUTUMN

# Chapter 26

By mid-September the island had made its full transition to autumn. Over summer, the yellows and oranges on Måsholmen had been lichen splotches on the rocks, reminding Clara of discarded chewing gum on Tooting High Road as she sat watching her sister fishing. Or the soft, salty innards scooped out of sea urchins and eaten with their toes in the water, which reminded her of nothing she had ever tasted before. Now it was the trees around her that were turning. The lushness of summer now lost to the fiery reds and oranges of autumn, trees licked with flame.

She tried to tuck away these moments, sitting enjoying the apparently infinite bounty of the island and the indulgent care of her sister, to keep them somewhere safely in her memory bank. For surely one day, when all of this was over, she would never believe she had made it. And with no father to report back to, to sit at the kitchen table over macaroni cheese, describing every moment, every bite, every emotion, she was worried that it would all just fade away, warping like a photograph facing the sun. Even now, as yellows and oranges started to appear at the edges of the trees, things seemed to be shifting around her. Summer had turned its back on Clara and she was trying to relish the sheer gorgeousness of autumn while longing to get safely off the island before Simon arrived.

She waited to hear back from Audrey, who she had emailed for advice, while making an interim plan to spend some time in Trondheim on her way back, hoping to create a sort of buffer between her two worlds. It felt easier to focus on her future now that she had realised so viscerally that it was hurtling towards her anyway. So she tried to work out how she was going to reroute her professional life as thoroughly as her mindset had been rerouted by her time on the island. She knew her current career was at a dead end, and she wasn't even sure if she would be able to remain anywhere near London. Sure, her mother was there, but the more time she spent elsewhere, the more of her childhood in the south-west she remembered, the greater her longing to return there felt. The last few times they had been over to the lighthouse, she had quickly scanned online for possible job openings in Bath or Bristol. But she had come to find the internet utterly overwhelming after living so long without ready access to a screen. And now she had the added terror of wondering how much of her online life Simon had found a way to access. These days, an hours-long walk to check an email sharpened the mind in a way that a casual thumb swipe watching Netflix never could. Now, the volume of information littering the page, the pop-up ads, the unnatural brightness of the screen and the colours all felt like an assault on the senses, and left her trekking back to Maggie's house more convinced than ever that she could never have a screen-based job again.

And despite the volume of things she was going to have to deal with in what she was now thinking of as her new life, there were also things here on the island that she was starting to look forward to leaving behind. The self-composting loo was fine, but as the weather got colder she longed to walk barefoot into the metro-tiled splendour of her mother's London bathroom, feeling her soles warmed by the underfloor heating, and her shoulders pummelled by the strength of her shower. Obviously the miraculous independence of water gathered entirely naturally had its charms, but so, Clara thought, did urban plumbing.

Above all, what was occupying the greatest emotional energy during her walks, her time in the garden or even those last few seconds before she gave in to sleep, was her plan to hand over the packet of mementoes to Maggie, and what this would mean for any further clarity she might get on her father's past – and her sister's choices. A few nights before the anniversary of Ben's birthday she stayed up until long after she knew Maggie would be asleep. She had waved her notebook at Maggie as she headed to bed, muttering something nebulous about 'journaling'. After half an hour making lists of jobs she thought she might be able to do, or might consider retraining for (park ranger, surf-school instructor, forest-school teacher), she admitted to herself that it was art school she should pursue if she really wanted to make her heart sing. Then she quietly took the envelope she had been given by Audrey and shook the contents out onto her bed.

She remembered some of the bits and pieces from the first time she had come across them: the beer mat, the ticket stubs, the hospital wristband. And the thin, elongated pieces of paper were still there. Was this what printer paper looked like twenty-five years ago, she wondered.

Now that she knew that Stéphanie was French, that sharpness of tone in her own mother whenever had she expressed her teenage longing to visit Paris made much more sense. Jackie, who had grown up in Ramsgate, seemed to have spent her entire life trying to improve her circumstances – and by default, those of Ben and Clara. Parents' evenings at school had been huge sources of tension, a chance for Jackie to not just hear how Clara was doing but to gauge how she herself was doing in comparison to her peers.

'I see the Ballards have had their lawn replaced with AstroTurf.'

'Sally's mum is looking plumper, isn't she?'

'Of course you can go to the cinema with Rob – his dad's quite the bigwig at the council you know.'

How she slotted into the social fabric of her world, whether she was woven close to those she should be, and what this might all mean – these were the matters that preoccupied her mother, while Ben buried his head in textbooks or newspapers. Now, as Clara held the photograph of a beguiling young French woman and thought about her father leaving that marriage behind him, it made perfect sense that her mother had always been looking over her shoulder. How could she not have seen her mother's more sharp-elbowed moments, which she had always found so mortifying, as the anxiety that they were? She knew how stifling it could be to feel the perceived charm or glamour of an ex-lover cast a shadow over your own romance. She knew how corrosive it was to feel diminished by indifference despite your better judgement. To have been competing with a charismatic French woman with eyes as pale as the sea on a white-sand beach must have been agony for a woman with as fragile a sense of self as Jackie. Clara had always seen pushiness. Now, she saw fear.

Consequently, what had seemed like cruel indifference when Clara had announced her departure for Norway now seemed more like apprehension. Her mother must have known how much this trip would have meant to her, and she might even have felt relief at no longer having to keep Maggie's existence to herself – but she must also have been worried for Clara, heading out to meet a woman whom she clearly perceived as an adversary's daughter. And at the behest of a man she had left years ago. The potential for emotional shrapnel was immense. Of course it was.

Now that she was sitting here, so far away, Clara marvelled at the fact that Jackie had let her come at all. She couldn't have stopped her, but her acceptance had been uncharacteristic. She must have known that there were loose ends to tie up; she must have known it was for the best to open those doors left closed all this time. So, Clara told herself, it was time to get that done. She tidied the bits and pieces into small bundles – photographs, documentation, memorabilia – and placed them gently back into the envelope before sliding it under her sofa bed. The next morning, she put her plan into motion.

# Chapter 27

It was the day before her father's birthday, two days before the boat was due to take the sisters off the island, and as soon as Maggie left, Clara set about baking him a birthday cake. She had long been paying attention to Maggie's baking, even enjoying some lessons in Signe-style cinnamon swirls, so she knew where the relevant pans were when she sprang into action. She made a batch of them in order to disguise the baking smell in the kitchen, while also making a small 'birthday' cake in a loaf tin. The previous week she had found some candles in the kitchen at the lighthouse, under the guise of looking for evaporated milk, as well as a cardboard box in which she hid the cake in 'her' room before Maggie returned. For the rest of the afternoon, Clara was jiggling with anticipation, trying to disguise it as excitement about the journey. She had very little to pack, having borrowed so much of Maggie's clothing while she'd been on Måsholmen, and purported to be making important lists of things not to forget, or to check when they got back to the lighthouse in thirty-six hours' time.

Time was dragging. She was jittery with nerves about leaving the island. She didn't want to hurry her time there, but she was desperate to get away before Simon attempted the journey, and of course she wanted to get on with the business of celebrating her dad's birthday with Maggie. Mercifully, dusk now fell far earlier than it had only a couple of weeks ago, the seasons changing at an alarming rate. It created the impression, however misleading, that if night was here sooner then surely it would be morning before long. Eventually, after a night spent tossing and turning, finessing her plan and running through key lines in case Maggie was reluctant to celebrate, it was morning. Clara was giddy with excitement but decided not to mention Ben or his birthday until everything was set up exactly as she liked it. Instead, she spent the morning helping Maggie in the garden, bringing in anything that might need to be stored while she was on Hestøy, taking care of a little weeding, and then carefully gathering her few possessions and packing them in her rucksack.

Later, once she had the house to herself, Clara positioned the cake on the table, a line of four pastel-coloured candles running down its spine. She then positioned the envelope next to it, with one photograph of Ben and Stéphanie together sitting on top of it. In the image, the couple were sitting on the square corner table of a bistro, leaning into each other, a candle glowing between them. Ben's hair was longer than Clara had ever seen it, curling when it reached his ears, and Stéphanie's was falling loosely over her shoulders, tousled as if she had just run a hand through it. Whoever had taken the photograph had obviously made them both laugh, as there was an infectiousness to their high spirits as they almost touched noses conspiratorially. How grown-up Clara felt, to be showing Maggie this image of her parents – she felt self-consciously adult, perhaps even a little bit French, to be recognising her father's previous relationship, so long before either of them were even born.

It wasn't far from dusk when Maggie came back. Clara heard her boots stomping outside first, then the thwack of her banging them together to loosen the mud after her walk. It had rained in the night, and the weather had been changeable all day, wind whisking clouds in then out again almost hourly. Maggie had talked ominously about autumn being the most changeable season, and suddenly Clara felt it viscerally.

She touched the cake and envelope, checking everything was perfectly laid out, while Maggie took her boots off at the door. She looked up and smiled at Clara as she hung her coat on the rack and headed into the main living space. There was a streak of mud across her cheek and her hair was wild from the wind outside. She was carrying a small basket with some berries, including cloudberries.

'Wow, it's blowy out there,' she said, scraping her hair back into a fresh ponytail.

'It sounds like it.'

'And it looks like you've been busy in here,' said Maggie as she approached the table, peering at the decorated cake. Clara couldn't reply, anticipation having stolen her voice. 'What's all this then?'

'Well ... now I know you're not mad keen on talking about Dad stuff, and I'm not even sure if you would remember, but it would have been his birthday today. And it's the first one I have ever celebrated without him, so I thought you might not mind that I baked him a sort of cake and ...'

But Clara could see that Maggie was no longer listening. She had reached the table and was now holding the photograph of her parents between thumb and forefinger.

'What is this?' she asked, turning towards her sister. She was standing at her full height now, her hair pushed back. Storm clouds gathering across her face.

'It's a photograph of your parents.' Clara's voice was barely audible.

'Yes, I can see that. But why is a photograph of them on my table, in my home?'

'It was with some stuff Dad left for you. It's his birthday so I—'

'I don't give a SHIT about it being his birthday!' Maggie's hand slammed down on the table. One of the candles slid off the side of the cake, leaving a greasy track in the icing behind it.

'I'm sorry, I just thought you might like to celebrate it … he's our father … and I'm leaving tomorrow and everything. We might not have the chance ever again.'

'Why? HOW do you still not get it? I don't want to talk about him. I don't want to think about him. I don't want anything to do with him in my life.'

'I know that you think that—'

'Excuse me?'

'I know that you think that … '

'Oh, you think I *think* that, do you?'

'Well, yes.'

'Rather than that I *know* that? And that I have known it for over twenty years?'

'I'm sorry, but after having got to know you, I'm just not sure that I buy that. And you can't expect me to understand if you won't talk to me about it.'

Clara's voice was back, and for the first time she felt quite sure of what she wanted to say: it simply wasn't fair to expect her to write off her own father when presented with no good reason.

'You have mistaken me for someone who is obliged to talk about this. *You* came to *me*. Did the journey here not make it clear to you that I wished to be left alone?'

'Yes, I get that, but I'm just not convinced that running away to the middle of nowhere is a valid solution to what seems to be deep trauma.'

Where was this voice coming from? It was as if she were dredging up every popular psychology Instagram post Nikita had ever sent her, *Yes! SO THIS!* typed beneath.

'Oh, you're not convinced?' Maggie's voice was suddenly unnervingly quiet.

'No, not really. I mean obviously it's beautiful here, but year after bloody year, and for what? Just to avoid telling people that you don't really get along with your dad ... '

A button had been pushed. Now Maggie's voice was as cold as the first day Clara had seen her, shot through with that same shard of raw panic. Her face as strained, as it had been that afternoon Clara had arrived, hammering on the front door.

'Do you see this photograph, Clara?'

'Yes.'

'And do you see this woman, my mother?'

'Yes.'

'She's dead, Clara.'

A slow blink, then Maggie looked hard at Clara from beneath those coal-dark lashes.

'She killed herself when I was a teenager. And your father let it happen.'

Clara felt as if someone had thrown a glass of iced water down her back.

'So if you don't mind, I would prefer not to spend the evening discussing what a hero the man was. Because he is the man who suggested boarding school in Paris might work for a grieving child. So he could bugger off back to Bristol and play the merry widower.'

Maggie was sitting at the table now, tapping with a finger on the wood as she said words she wanted to emphasise.

*Paris.*

*Bristol.*

*Merry widower.*

As she stood there trembling, Clara tried to remember if Maggie had ever told her her age. Late thirties? Hadn't she said something about celebrating her fortieth in a couple of years? Clara, at twenty-two, was frantically trying to do the arithmetic ... fifteen years between them. Maggie was a teenager when her mother died.

'Yes, Clara,' came that voice of cool granite. 'Now you can see why I was so reluctant to play host to Jackie's daughter.'

Clara gasped. Maggie had known her mother's name all this time. What had gone *on*? But, like that trek to the house on her very first day here, Clara felt compelled to keep going, putting one foot in front of the other, believing in the task in hand.

'OK, OK, I think I can see where this is going.'

'I somehow doubt it, dear Clara.'

'Fine. So maybe I'll never get it. Maybe I'll never get *you*. But in case you have forgotten, that might be because I *wasn't alive* when all of this happened. And I just don't want to leave this island – to leave you – without trying to at least, you know, find a little peace?'

'No!' Crockery rattled as Maggie's hand hit the tabletop. 'YOU do not get to dictate this. You do not get to come here, unannounced, and decide to "heal" me. This pain is *mine*. And my mother's pain was *hers*. And you are not invited to discuss it, or solve it in any way at all. It's who. We. Are.'

'OK, fine.'

'It is so very far from *fine*,' Maggie muttered. Now she was up, roughly pushing her chair under the table, wiping surfaces, dropping the cake in the bin.

'So you don't want to talk about it. But that envelope is still full of things that Dad wanted you to have. I'll go for a walk or something so you can have a look at it in private. That way, if you don't want any of it, I can take it back – but at least I'll know you've had the choice.'

'Oh, fuck off, Clara. I'm not going to sit here and wallow in the past just because it fits in with your gap-year goals.'

'It's not that—'

'It *is* that. And I'm not your project to finish before going back to living your shiny new life.'

Suddenly the new strength, the new sense of self that Clara had been starting to embrace felt quite overwhelming. Years of being spoken over, spoken past, spoken down to, had been sitting there, kindling for the rage that had now been lit it in her.

'Gap year!? You don't know the first thing about my so-called shiny life.'

'I know it has the space in it to up sticks and leave on an extended holiday when Daddy leaves some cash.'

'You don't know what I was leaving. And you certainly don't have the monopoly on pain. Do you think you're the only one who has ever wanted to just run away rather than deal with feelings too terrifying to say out loud? Do you not think that that might be why I'm here, at the drop of the hat, trying to reach a woman I'd never heard of until a few months ago? Dream on.'

'Right, right, OK. So you've left a shitty flat share and you're not sure whether to carry on travelling until you've truly found yourself. Sounds like a nightmare.'

'How dare you? How dare you make such an assumption? How dare you be so vile to someone who has only tried to extend love towards you? What, you think suffering from depression is a get out clause for being a total fucking bitch? Because it isn't, you know. It just isn't. I might not know you – I haven't been allowed to, let's not forget. But I know enough to call you out on that.'

'Just get the fuck out of my house.'

The accuracy with which she had pelted those final few missiles left Clara feeling as if she had been punched in the solar plexus.

'Fine,' she managed to reply. And with that she spun on her heel and reached for her coat.

# Chapter 28

The wind caught the side of the door as Clara left the house. It slammed behind her with a boom that she would never have dared to inflict on purpose. Her fingers were shaking as she tried to lace up her boots, having hurriedly shoved her feet into them while trying to get out as fast as possible. Her heart was racing, leaving her breath shallow, ragged, desperate.

Hair lashed across her face the second she stood up. She tried to hook the strands caught in her eye with her little finger, pulling it back from her brow. This, and the cold, would have made her eyes water had they not already been filled with tears. Clara stood, facing the sea, and tried to breathe. Something had slammed shut in her with Maggie's final few remarks. Her sister had known all along that Clara and her mother existed, and that Clara needed this project just as much their dad thought Maggie did. She had seen fragility in Clara and she had remained closed, tight as an oyster and let Clara flail. Worst of all, Clara had only just realised that that had been the dynamic all along. She wanted to howl.

She had what meagre possessions she had brought to Maggie's house in the bag on her back, and she was determined to stay away from the house for the night. Lighthouse, woods, wherever – she couldn't stand another minute being patronised, mocked, despised. If she could make it to morning, she would only have the boat crossing left to get through with Maggie, and they would barely be able to talk during that anyway. On landing, they'd be free from each other, and Maggie could go the same way as Simon: a mistake she could work on forgetting about.

Simon. He could yet be on the boat, incoming. Surely not, she told herself. Could he really be that vindictive, that determined? Again, she found the distance between them distorted her memories, flinging images of him at his most loving, most attentive at her – but she could remember him at his most vicious and controlling too.

Clara swallowed, pursing her lips and pushing away the thoughts of him, and the loss of Maggie. She just had to get *off* this island, no matter how much she had come to love it. It turns out it wasn't Maggie, or even Simon, where she had found love and acceptance, it was in the bleak beauty of this island – she told herself loftily – and she was determined to enjoy her last few hours on it.

The path to the lighthouse was familiar now. She could feel her ankles bending and adapting to the familiar bumps and curves of the path. She thought of that young woman who had trodden this path for the first time nearly six months ago, and how much she had learned. There was sourness in knowing that the reason she had come here seemed to be utterly unresolved, and even the genuine joy she had found here seemed tinged with bitterness now as she trudged away from the house alone.

She walked for half an hour or so, letting her breathing right itself as the pace of her hike forced deeper inhales and exhales. What had felt like blind fury at Maggie as she set out was now steadying, becoming something harder, grittier and less fiery than rage. A resentment started to calcify. Maggie could have had all of that extra time with their father but no, she had chosen not to. She had chosen blame, not understanding. She had chosen solitude, not connection. Clara reached a familiar fork in the path: straight ahead, leading to the lighthouse, and a left turn heading steeply upwards before turning down towards the valley and then the forest. Well, Clara thought, she could still choose *too*. She could make unexpected decisions. And if she only had a matter of hours here, she would choose to head into the forest. How bad could it be that she was so often advised to stay out? She thought bitterly of how long she had waited for Maggie to take her into the trees, how much she had wanted to be told she was ready, to be allowed to enter instead of merely playing tourist at the edges.

She had sat quietly waiting to be taken to Paris as a teenager. She had sat quietly waiting for Simon to become the man he had promised her he was. And she had sat quietly waiting to be told she *may* go to the forest. Enough.

Because it wasn't a magic island, and it certainly wasn't Maggie's island. She, Clara Seymour, could go where she wanted, and now she wanted this. Clinging to the steel railings at the side of the path's steepest edge, she felt the nervousness creep at her – spindly fingers of doubt reaching for her hem. She pushed them away, muttering to herself that she could do it, that she had to make the best of the island while she could. Eventually she made it to the end of the railings and the ridge which looked down onto the woods.

She stood there, hands on hips, feeling like an ancient explorer, a Viking princess surveying her land. How she wished she could bottle this feeling, this effervescent sense that there was no time to lose, that she had to be her very best self, and the rewards would be limitless. She turned to look at the sea, the light fading over the water. How well she had come to know this shoreline, she realised. Better than any view other than perhaps the train journey from Bath to London, one she had done countless times before her dad had moved to London. This was a static view though, one she had watched in so many different lights, finding something new each time – the gulls flying at an angle she hadn't noticed before, the tide higher than she had imagined it might be able to creep, the green of the mountainside growing lush and abundant as summer had peaked, then letting in the kaleidoscope of autumn colours.

She turned back, her eyes around the edge of the forest, looking for any clear landmarks she could head for should she lose her bearings. She looked up at the tree line and picked out one fir, slightly inset from the edge, but significantly higher than the others. The very top few feet were bent slightly to one side, as if either the weight of snow or the force of a wind on its spindly upper branches had tugged it down into asymmetry. She was sure she would be able to spot it from a small distance, even once she had entered the forest – particularly as it was so wide at bottom that there was a bit of a clearing around it.

*My lighthouse*, she thought to herself. *My wonky lighthouse.* Having committed its angle and position to memory, she scrambled down from the high ridge, across the marshy land, passing her favourite cloudberry spot and into the forest itself. At last, all alone.

The overhead cover was so thick that she felt a darkness fall almost immediately. There was just enough light for her to see where she was putting her feet, but not much more: her dreams of gently examining ferns or silently watching birdlife immediately seemed unrealistic. Was she the fool that Maggie had taken her for after all? No, she was determined not to be:

surely she had learned *something* on this trip. She looked up, again taking note of where her tall lighthouse tree was from the other angle, then she walked deeper and deeper into the trees.

The smell around her changed as she felt the forest close in around her. This had seemed like a dry, cool place in the summer, somewhere Maggie referred to as a resting spot when the sun was at its highest. But now there was a dampness, a sort of verdant hum all around her. The trees had absorbed the moistness of last week's rain and seemed to be holding it among themselves, creating a steaminess down where there was no light. Incongruously, this autumnal weather seemed almost tropical now she was in the forest, increasingly aware of the busy wildlife: growing, feeding, bustling. She felt like a newcomer in a busy, unfamiliar city: a wide-eyed traveller, getting off the bus at a teeming Port Authority Bus Terminal, overwhelmed by the crowds and how oblivious they were to her.

She decided to walk a little further, until she found a log to sit on and enjoy the forest and its private beauty. Twigs snapped and crackled underfoot as she went, brushing branches and fronds gently from her face, occasionally peering around a tree trunk to check that a path beyond was clear, keen to leave the place as untouched as possible.

It seemed as if the canopy above was getting thicker: the light was certainly fading fast. When Clara looked up she realised that it was not the coverage but the sky that was darkening. Of course, the axis had turned and the island was heading fast towards winter. It would be a swift dusk before long – she should get what she needed from her bag now while she could still peer into it, so she unhooked it from her left shoulder and swung it down onto the forest floor.

Crouching, silently, she suddenly felt intensely vulnerable. Her fear was of nothing specific; in fact, that was the problem – she had no idea what might be out there, who came to life in the dark, or what they might want from her. She listened to the rustle of the leaves. Would she know if something was approaching her? Some*one*? And if they meant any harm? Or what to do if they did? Could Simon even have made it to the island alone? She pushed her hand down into the side pocket of her rucksack, urgent fingers feeling for the slim torch she had had in there all summer. Pushing past rolled-up socks, a biro, a lighter, she finally found the torch and yanked it out.

She fiddled with the handle, pushing the button back and forth, unsure which way was on and which way was off. Memories of her hopelessness on school camping trips tiptoed across the back of her mind. Sausages slipping sadly off inexpertly chosen sticks into campfires; evenings spent jumping in the dark at any sound made by nearby campers, tents drooping with condensation at dawn after being inadequately set up. How hard it had been to love nature back then, when nature had seemed hellbent on not loving her back.

She pressed the button one final, glum, time, but the truth was unavoidable: the battery was dead. It probably had been for some time, after being rammed into her back with the button pushed to 'on' for weeks on end. She shook it just in case. Nothing. A rookie mistake – but one she would never make again, Clara told herself, determined to keep up the spin that her trip was a triumph.

Her phone was in the other side pocket, but she knew it would be just as useless. It had gone untouched for weeks in the absence of any reception at Maggie's. She had planned to charge it a little for the journey at the lighthouse the following morning. Clara pictured it sitting on the desk in Signe's office while she and Maggie checked heat and light fittings, readying the lighthouse for their departure to Hestøy. She could see herself sitting on the boat, huddled up to Maggie, waving at the island, heart swelling with pride at what a wonderful job of it she had made for everyone.

These luxuries seemed rather out of reach now; she was crouching on the forest floor beneath a darkening sky, desperate for a pee and hoping that that ache in her lower back was PMT and not a kidney infection from the damp. Get a grip, she told herself, you've been in here less than an hour. *Yes, but you've still been thrown out by your sister though, you idiot*, came back the internal rebuke.

The trees rustled in the wind: Clara tried to tell herself it was the forest reassuring her, reminding her she was protected, but she simply didn't feel it. However she tried to twist it, deep down she *did* feel like everything Maggie had thought of her: an indulged little fool. A silly girl who had had a tantrum when things did not work out how she had planned and had stomped off to the woods. It was a folly.

She stood up, wriggling her arms into the straps of her rucksack, shaking it onto her back. Then came a sudden movement, a flicker, just at the very edge of her eyeline. A flash of blue-green light, as if someone in the near distance had tapped on a mobile phone. Clara whipped her head from one side and then to the other, as fast as she could, trying to catch where it might have come from. Nothing. No one?

She carried on walking a little, wondering at how textured the ground beneath her feet was. Soft moss, a scattering of autumn leaves, various twigs and roots. Each step was different, and strangely noisy. Sometimes a softness would give way to a crack beneath it, sometimes she'd hit a larger, unyielding branch, sometimes she'd feel her foot almost disappear into the damp moss underfoot. The light was almost gone now and without her torch she was reluctant to go any deeper, especially as she felt her mission had been accomplished. Whatever Maggie thought of her, she *had* made it to the forest, and even better, she had ended up doing it on her own terms. The trouble was, she wasn't quite sure what to do now. Stay here in some sort of defiant final gesture or turn around and return to the safety and solitude of the lighthouse?

Looking up, she found her Lighthouse Fir pretty quickly. But as she shifted her gaze back down to her feet, she felt another one of those flashes, somewhere just out of sight. She swivelled, trying to catch it this time. Again, nothing. Again, she walked. But after a few minutes she could no longer see the tree she was aiming for. The trees seemed to be thicker here; there was no longer any sense of where the light at the edge of the forest might be. Had she just been walking further into the forest, or was it just that there no longer was any light at its edge?

Clara took a few more paces, trying to use tree trunks to orientate herself. She would look up, trying to spot the tree she was aiming for every ten steps. But the light, the trees and the constant hum of invisible activity around her only served to disorientate her further. She kept going. Ten paces, a look up. Ten paces, a look up. Another ten. Another look.

It wasn't working. She had now completely lost her bearings, and as she had dreaded, the sky above the trees was entirely dark. A hopelessness crept up on her, a despair, a vapour working its way through the trees at knee height before rising and engulfing everything. After the dejection came exhaustion. She had lost track of how long she had been walking, changing her mind between leaving and trying to find a space where she felt safe enough to stay. Slowly, her legs brought her to a halt. Above all, she needed to pee, having necked her huge cup of coffee just before leaving the house. It had been done without elan, leaving a mortifying splash on one eyebrow as she had tried to drink with self-righteousness, but she had been glad of the warm caffeine inside her at the start of the walk. But now, she needed to get rid of it. And at least it would give her time to think.

She wearily took the bag off, pulled her leggings down and squatted in the dark, trying not to wonder if it was unwise to do so. The relief was immense, and she felt immediately cheered, a little braver. She was in the wild, alone, doing this! The Clara who had hidden a wrapped tampon in the inside of her sleeve when she walked to the bathroom, even in front of friends, was perhaps long gone after all.

She stood up, pulling at her leggings with one hand, only to lose her footing a little as the leggings failed to unfurl neatly over her upper thighs. Her ankle twisted slightly as she stumbled, trying to avoid falling in her own urine. She landed just to the left of it with a soft thud, glad at least that absolutely no one knew where she was or what she was doing. The ground was damp, but not as sodden as she had feared it might be. And she wasn't in any real pain. In the dark she suspected that there was mud and moss on her hip, and tried to brush it away as best she could. She righted herself, pulled her jumper back down over her hips and straightened her jacket. Smoothing the jumper pulled at a small thread of sadness: it was a classic Marius sweater, made for her by her sister only last month as they prepared for autumn.

'You should have something to commemorate your trip,' Maggie had said, her voice betraying as little emotion as ever while she drew the tape measure around Clara's chest, and then from the tip of one shoulder to the other.

'Yes, but what a thing to own!' replied Clara, her own voice bubbling with as much emotion as always, despite her constant attempts not to overwhelm Maggie. And as night after night passed, Maggie's fingers curling and pulling on the yarn and

266

the needles, Clara found it impossible not to see the gesture as one of love. Surely she couldn't be reading the situation *that* wrong, she wondered, as her hand ran along the ribbed edge of the jumper.

Just as she was losing herself in melancholy, Clara looked up, realising she had to make a move before she was dangerously lost. The light was now entirely different yet again. Had so much time passed that morning was already coming? Surely not: this wasn't like any other dawn she had known on the island, not even the eerie 1 a.m. dawns that had unsettled her so much back in June. But then again, that flash, a flicker somewhere in the woods. An unnatural neon tinge to it. Clara readied herself, determined to find her way out of the trees, even if she ended up in a different spot on the island.

She kept walking, realising after a few minutes that the bursts of light were not what was lighting her way. Still, she could not work out what they were or where they were coming from. Then, suddenly, the trees thinned, and yes, up above was her Lighthouse Fir.

As she stared up to the space where the trees gave way to sky, it became clear what had been illuminating her path. It wasn't dawn, it wasn't an unnatural light, it was quite the opposite of both: above her, the Northern Lights were dancing, filling the entire sky with their glow. Adrenaline flooded her body – this was a treat she had never dared dream she might see before leaving the island! She had had no idea they might make an appearance this early in the year. And now they were here, glimmering exactly when she needed them.

She reached her hands out in front of her, determined not to fall again onto her already damp behind. After another hundred metres or so, the trees parted and she found herself free from them, standing in grass, looking up with tears in her eyes. Childhood memories of the Northern Lights flooded her mind: her dad reading her *The Snowman* as she sat curled in his lap in her radiator-warm pyjamas, or the hours she spent poring over *All About Night*, a book about what goes on at night in different places all over the world, from New York office blocks peopled by tired cleaners to the wide-eyed tarsier monkeys of the Savannah. Then there had been her teenage years reading *Northern Lights* itself, lost in Lyra's adventures as a means of escape from the clatter of domesticity and the increasing arguments between her parents as their marriage started to fragment and eventually fail.

All of those hours, letting herself explore the world via her imagination, had led her to believe that the lights themselves might not actually be real, that they were somehow beyond the gaze of mortals. And yet here she was, on an adventure of her own, that she had undertaken despite grief, and fear, and inexperience, and the lights had danced off the page just for her.

She smiled at the sky, marvelling at the greens and ambers as the waves passed above her. It was as if someone way above was wafting a length of fabric, a curtain or a towel, its hem glowing with ripples of light from the bottom up. She could sense the electricity in the air, knowing from those hours reading on her tummy, knees bent, ankles up high, that these lights were caused by solar winds hitting magnetic fields.

It wasn't just the lights themselves that were putting on a show: the night winds had blown away the earlier clouds, leaving the sky a crisp, clear background for a confetti-throw of stars as far as she could see. Each tiny one was a perfect individual, seen for the first time in Clara's life. The absolute lack of any electric light meant that she could pick out each individual star, the showy pale-yellow lights, the white-gold pinpricks and the glowing ice-blue diamonds.

'"Clara" means bright, or clear,' she recalled her father explaining as they wandered down a west-country lane, gazing at the stars. It was eight or nine Septembers ago, the evening of a pub supper outside of Bath to celebrate his birthday. She had been miserable that evening, feeling wretched about school, uncomfortable in her newly adolescent body and increasingly aware that all was not well between her parents. 'We chose it because we wanted you to shine,' he told her as he hugged her tight.

At the time, his comment had felt like unbearable pressure to *be* a star. She had interpreted his encouragement as an instruction to find fame or at least a showiness that had never felt within her grasp. Now, as she looked at the infinite variety among these stars, she realised he had only meant to let her know she had a *right* to shine. There were so many ways to be lit from within, and she had spent so long trying only one or two. The crushing desperation to do something creative, followed by the grim realisation that she might never make it. The shaky pride she felt at seeing Nikita use the skills she had learned, while she felt anything she had accomplished wither and fall away. The parent-pleasing attempt at pragmatism that her job in property had been intended to be. And her desperate efforts to be the career-friendly partner for whom Simon seemed to yearn.

Now, it seemed obvious that there was a galaxy of Claras she could be, and she didn't even need to pick one right now. And, even better, perhaps it didn't matter if Maggie wanted to love her back or not; perhaps simply knowing that she was there, that they existed under the same stars, was going to be enough.

Clara had been slowly hiking back up to the ridge, and now she was approaching the point where the path headed back down the mountainside and on to the lighthouse. As she reached the turning, she cast her eyes in the direction of Maggie's house. It was around the curve now, just out of sight. It was here, she realised, that she had stood that first evening on the island, despairing about whether she would ever make it, if the house was ever going to reveal itself.

She wondered if Maggie could see the aurora too. Did she look out for them? Did she care? Or was she as closed, as apparently nonchalant about them as she was about so much else? And if she was watching them, was she wondering if Clara was too, if they were staring up at the same sky?

How little they had talked, how much pain Maggie must have been holding in. The lights themselves seemed to be casting a different filter on the sisters' relationship. There seemed to be a pause, then a fresh ripple of lights. Clara was halted on the ridge, transfixed by the show even if the cold was starting to nip at her. She longed to be able to tell her father she had seen this, that she had made it, and she was beginning to see why she had been given the name she had.

He couldn't have been a bad person, she was sure of it. But here, with the Arctic sky giving her – literally – a sense of perspective, she allowed herself to admit that he might not always have been as open-hearted, as ready to love, as he had been with her. Could it have been that he learned lessons with Maggie of which she had been the beneficiary? Was that one of the missing pieces to the jigsaw of their lives? Was that what she should have acknowledged to Maggie, instead of merely expecting celebrating their father to staunch the grief *she* still felt?

Instead of heading west towards the lighthouse, she was seized by the realisation that she had to find Maggie and apologise to her, to let her know that she understood now, and that she was sorry she had tried to force a past, to force a father on her that she simply hadn't known. Above all, she wanted to stand there with her and stare up at the lights, sharing the beauty of the island with the person who had opened it up to her. She had to admit that she had intruded on Maggie's life before she left the island, instead of just presenting excuses.

The path was lit well enough by the sky now, making it just about safe to take the steep sections of the path, using the steel chains for support. She measured her pace every few steps, as she had done in the forest but for the opposite reason. Now, instead of not being able to see, she was overwhelmed by there being too much to see. Her heart danced as ripple after ripple after ripple of the green light, followed by an almost cartoonish pink, and then something more blue, moved above her.

How small her problems seemed when nature could throw exhibitions like this for her. How much hope she felt when there were sights like this to raise the spirits and lift the soul. She gave a whoop of joy at having seized something wonderful from an evening that seemed so utterly lost. Snatching an extra glance up at the sky in case the view wasn't as good when she began her descent, she reached for the steel railing as the path headed downhill.

It was only as she felt her body fall several feet that she realised she had missed it entirely.

The plummet felt not dissimilar to the core-shaking impact of early grief. Airlessness, then a thump which left her winded.

Her ankle, already weakened by the earlier stumble, twisted fully as she hit the ground, and her leggings were ripped where the rock had gouged into her thigh. She tried to steady her breathing, not to panic. Her rucksack had stopped her head from taking an even more enormous blow, but she nevertheless seemed to have been hit, and to have a sort of whiplash from the suddenness of the fall.

She reached for her thigh and felt her hand damp with

blood. Her leggings were macerating in it, the insufficient fabric having provided no protection. She did not know what the best course of action was. Why had she never paid attention all those times that her dad had tried to instil a bit of mountain-awareness in her?

Should she try and right herself? Should she cry for help even though no one was there to hear her? Or should she try and drink something? A hot drink ... a sugary tea. That was what she was supposed to have. Wasn't it?

After a minute longer, the option to make any sensible decisions was taken from her, as she started to drift in and out of consciousness, feeling pain rippling through her body like the lights above. Memories came in waves, a tide of grief, the likes of which she hadn't experienced for months, then flashes of the joy, the hope, the optimism she had felt only an hour or so ago. As each emotion dialled up or down, she felt tiredness intensify, until at last she knew she could not fight it. She tried to pull her jumper closer for warmth, her fingers burrowing into the stitches Maggie had sown for her.

The cold felt sharper now, then suddenly, a deep, molten-honey warmth.

# Chapter 29

Clara came to to the sound of her name being called. It was Maggie's voice, but not as she had ever heard it before. There was a desperation to it, rasping to be heard against the wind of the storm. She pushed her hair – wet with rain – from her face, and realised that her clothes were almost sodden through. She sat up and felt for her thigh. The cut was still there but the pain was duller now, radiating across her leg.

She rolled onto all fours, and tried to crawl along the path in the direction of the shouting.

'Clara! I can see you! The path is up here!'

She looked up and thought she could spot the ochre of Maggie's jacket against the edge of mountain. The area where she had fallen was several metres below the path, scrubby with grass, with rock poking through the mud; she'd have to crawl across it to rejoin Maggie higher up. She began to pull herself on her hands and knees diagonally towards her sister, her backpack now slipping, her hands reaching for tufts of grass to grab as she began hauling herself up and around the curve of the mountain to meet the path.

'Keep going, Clara!'

Maggie's voice was clearer now, and still there was an urgency to it that was entirely unfamiliar. Gone was the granite wall of self-composure, and – to Clara's relief – gone was the glassy edge of cruelty that she had heard in it in those moments before she left the house.

'I'm coming! I'm trying!' she shouted back, unsure if her voice had been carried away by the wind. She kept going, tearing up at the sight of her sister waiting for her, arms waving, beckoning her against the noise of the storm.

Eventually she made it, pulling herself up the final few metres onto the path with the help of the steel chain she had missed earlier, now hanging perilously from the metal rod that had been holding it up. Her head was hammering with pain now, but she had made it.

The sisters embraced, Maggie shouting into Clara's ear that she had headed out to find her, to tell her to come in to chat, then spotted her moments before her fall.

'I'm so sorry,' she said, her mouth close to her ear as they held each other against the wind.

'It's OK, it's OK,' said Clara, floppy-limbed with relief as much as tiredness or pain. 'There is a lot I haven't told you too. I can see that now, I can see it.'

'Come on, let's head back,' replied Maggie. 'The storm is picking up.'

It seemed like days now since she had left the house, but it had only been a matter of hours. Each pull forward had felt infinite; Clara's clothes were covered in mud and blood, and she was desperate not just for the comfort of the house, but to bathe in the warmth of her sister's forgiveness. She reached out her hand for Maggie, who took it with a smile.

As she turned to face the path and begin the walk back, her rucksack, already loose from the fall, slid off her left shoulder and swung round to her side. As it did so, it slammed into Maggie's right side, knocking her off balance a little.

It only looked like a little stumble.

'I'm so sorry!' said Clara, yanking the bag back around and tightening the strap. She reached out to Maggie to help her up, and as she did so, she saw a look of blind panic across her face.

'What's happened?'

'My leg.'

And that's when she saw it. It had only been a small misstep, but Maggie had caught her shin on one of the hooks that had been holding the metal chains. It took Clara a second to understand what had happened. At first she saw the gouge of flesh on Maggie's leg and thought it was a slug sitting on her shin. Livid with blood, with flesh peeling back, the wound made her feel light-headed once she fully absorbed what she was looking at.

Maggie was silent, staring at her helplessly.

'It's OK,' she said. 'I'm here.'

She took her rucksack off and dug around inside until she found a long-sleeved T-shirt which she yanked out and turned into a makeshift tourniquet just below Maggie's knee. It was already dirty, and now it was stiffening with rainwater, but Clara hoped that it would at least staunch some of the bleeding.

'I've got you, Maggie,' she said, kicking the metal hook as far as she could, and slinging her bag back on. 'Let's get home.'

# Chapter 30

Maggie's limp was heavy, and the path was not really wide enough for the two of them, so the walk took well over an hour. Clara was still in pain herself, and felt as if a terrible sleepiness was only moments away for the whole of the walk back. All she could think of to stay focused, and to maintain Maggie's focus, was to keep talking. Eventually, the wind subsided a little, meaning they could stop shouting at each other, but it was still far from the eerie silence that Clara remembered from the first time she had made this trip.

'Did you see the lights, Maggie?'

'Yes.' Her voice was weak, her strength clearly fading.

'They were magnificent. I never imagined I would be here long enough to see them. They were like nothing I had ever imagined.'

'Yes ... '

Clara wasn't sure if she was listening, if she was even able to. So on she babbled. Talking about how she had visited the forest, how she had had a fleeting moment of thinking she could spend the night there, how she had headed to the lighthouse instead.

'The thing is, I was still nervous that Simon would have

made it to the island ... ' she said, still unsure if Maggie was listening. She realised Maggie had no idea who Simon was, and in the absence of her responding, or even asking who he was, she felt a grim sort of freedom to carry on. So she told Maggie about her boyfriend, how he had made a slow, inexorable shift from friend to one of those boyfriends who was really clear about what he wanted, to someone who seemed to be controlling how she lived her life – hour to hour, even from the other end of the continent.

For the first time, she heard herself say out loud sentences that she hadn't been sure she even dared to believe.

'I don't know what he is capable of really. I mean, I don't know what he might do next.'

'The trouble is ... when it began I thought it was just because he really loved me.'

'The only thing I really know now is that I can't carry on like this. I won't.'

And as she finished say that last sentence, she rubbed Maggie's hand, draped over her shoulder as she helped her walk.

'Don't worry, I wasn't planning to stay for ever. I *was* going to go back. I'll only stay until you don't need me any more.'

Softly, through lips that were dry, and breath that was rough with the effort of continuing to walk through the pain, came the answer.

'Thank you. I do need you. I do.'

The words she had imagined hearing for so long. But instead of just grinning and giving her sister a hug, Clara realised she really *was* needed – not just emotionally but practically. It was time to step up or lose everything she had come here for.

By the time they got back to the house Clara felt woozy with tiredness and ached all over from her fall, but Maggie's needs were clearly significantly greater. Clara got her to lie on the sofa with her leg up, while she created a mountain of coats to keep it raised. Maggie was barely conscious now, having lost a huge amount of blood – her sock and walking shoe were sticky with it, and her jeans ripped roughly where her leg had hit the spiked hook. Clara managed to find painkillers in her sodden rucksack and held Maggie's neck as she took some, followed by hot coffee.

She tried her hardest to clean the wound, but it still made her stomach lurch every time she looked at it. It was full of grit, mud and shreds of fibre from her torn jeans. The fold of skin flapping above the wound itself was now grey and lifeless – looking more like a movie prosthetic than anything she could quantify as real. She tried to mop at the gash, carefully pouring cooled boiled water over it to clean it, but terrified of encouraging the bleeding. It was obvious how much strength Maggie had lost, but Clara was at a loss as to how to help. There were no snacks or biscuits, the sort of thing that might give her a quick sugar hit. When she had tossed a handful of sodden tissues into the kitchen bin she had seen their father's birthday cake, thrown in there only hours ago. It seemed impossible that it was still the same day.

Eventually Clara managed to get her sister to eat some buttered bread, as well as a mug of milk after the coffee. A little colour returned to her cheeks, but not enough for Clara to feel in any way reassured. There was no chance of getting Maggie into her own bed, so Clara gently washed her face and neck with a warm flannel, combed her hair for her, and helped her change out of the damp top she was wearing and into a soft grey T-shirt. Then, gingerly, she tried to yank the wet jeans down from her hips before giving up, finding the huge steel kitchen scissors and cutting them off with a frown of concentration, softly whispering to her sister what she was doing, that she hoped it would make her more comfortable, that she loved her and was trying to help.

Terrified that she might lose her in the night, Clara changed her own clothes before lighting the open fire in the room and curling up on the rug at her sister's feet.

Time became sloppy, boundary-less in the hours that followed. Once or twice, Clara tried to rouse herself, to check on Maggie, aware that they should be trying to get to the lighthouse in order to meet the boat. But she was woozy, sleeping in fits of a couple of hours, then waking, panicked, to check that Maggie was OK, before realising that the walk was completely beyond her. She was covered in bruises, her own gash was sore to the touch, and she was not sure if she had some sort of concussion or if she was simply emotionally exhausted. From time to time, she managed to make them both some coffee, and she kept loading slices from the loaf of bread with sweet jams from the store cupboard.

Clara wasn't sure how long they existed like this, but by the time she felt well enough to look around the house properly, it was the following evening. Either Arve – and possibly Simon? – had been on the island for hours, or he had assumed the women were not coming and headed back to Hestøy. Clara wasn't sure which was the worse of the two scenarios: that Arve had gone and they were still here without help, or that he had stayed and was not alone. But her thoughts were foggy; she was struggling to plan clearly. Things she had worried about for so long – confiding in Maggie or feeling trusted by her – now seemed like irrelevancies, leaving her both relieved and unmoored. Now, she was preoccupied by whether Maggie's wound was clean enough, by how much food they had and if she was strong enough to either find or make more. As she sat at the kitchen table, with Maggie dozing a few feet away, it all seemed insurmountable, completely overwhelming – everything that Maggie had assumed about her all along.

But the presence of her sister – not doubting her but depending on her – was the spur that Clara needed. Slowly, she tidied the mess of coats and damp clothes from where she had left them on their arrival at the house. She went through their supplies in the larder, finding bits and pieces to keep them going, and slowly, at dawn the following morning, she crept out into the garden – checking the path first to see if anyone was coming their way – and grabbed some handfuls of berries, a few potatoes and whatever else she could find and knew she could cook for them.

These few simple tasks, which had been hypothetical acts of mindfulness while she had been relying on Maggie to run the house, were now what was keeping them alive. But as she stood over the hob, Clara realised that they could not carry on like this much longer. When she had checked on Maggie half an hour earlier, she was sure that her forehead was warmer. Her wound did not seem to be healing, oozing clear liquid instead, and was clearly painful to touch. Maggie had been mostly asleep, whispering thanks and eating, bleary-eyed, when Clara helped her to. But she must have known that the situation was getting desperate.

The weather outside was not helping. Storms seemed to pass through with alarming speed. At one point the house seemed on the verge of taking flight and heading into the sea, but just as Clara despaired of ever being able to leave, the skies would clear. The wind remained though – any walk along that path would feel more dangerous than ever. But it had to be done. Clara's two packets of ibuprofen were long gone. She couldn't find any other painkillers in the house. She had done her best to disinfect the wound but she wasn't sure she had managed it.

And then there was the amount of blood Maggie had lost. If she were going to be the sister she had been trying to persuade Maggie she was, there was no alternative.

She wiped her hands on the towel hanging from the gas-fired stove and knelt beside Maggie, who was still lying on the sofa, leg up, panting slightly.

'I have to go to the lighthouse,' she said softly as she wiped her sister's forehead with a warm damp flannel. Maggie opened her eyes. They were glazed with fever. She gave Clara's hand a little squeeze.

'But what about Simon?'

Clara's stomach lurched. She hadn't had time to even consider whether Maggie had heard her confession as they had walked home – let alone been thinking about it enough to worry for her now.

But what about him?

Had he not done his worst already, fracturing her sense of self, infusing fear and shame into her most basic daily existence, creating a pond of neglect in which she had started to stagnate? And hadn't this grim reality started to shift during her time here? Had she not learned that there were sides to her that she had never explored before, let along cherished? Did the fact that she had kept the two of them alive for the last two days, and was still going, count for nothing? Maybe, even if he was here, she might be the one with the upper hand at last?

'Don't worry. He's my problem and I will deal with it,' Clara replied. 'And I'm sorry, I know you probably don't want to hear about her, but I'm going to call my mum too.'

'It's OK.'

'She can be very ... extra ... but she really means well. And I think she will be able to make calls, get us the right sort of help, if she knows we're in trouble.'

'Clara, it's OK. I know she's not all bad.'

In whispering these reassurances to her sister, Clara realised that she *was* already shifting the shape of her life from what it had been with Simon. She squeezed Maggie's hand back, and set about readying the house for her departure.

Clara sliced bread, laying out buttered slices, leaving cutlery and jars of jam opened ajar beside them. She made two pots of coffee and left them to cool, in case Maggie needed the caffeine but felt too weak to handle hot water. She prepared the pot and stove-top kettle for making a further, hot batch. She boiled water and placed it into two glass bottles, a handful of fresh flannels beside them. And she went into the garden to pick whatever she could, before leaving what she found on the table in the fruit bowl. She wished she had time to head out further and get some berries – especially as she knew that there would be so many more ripe cloudberries today – but she had to leave as soon as she could.

She watched Maggie's breathing as she sat on one of the dining chairs at the table and laced her walking boots. The jagged rise and fall of her chest sent a shiver down Clara's back, prompting a wave of second thoughts. How could she leave someone in this condition? Clammy, burning with fever, eyes unfocused. The alternative was worse, she reminded herself.

'Maggie, I'm going now. There is water just here.' Clara moved the chair she had been sitting on to close to Maggie's splayed arm, a mug of fresh water on it. 'I have to get us help. But I'll come straight back – I'm just going to the lighthouse to send messages. To Mum, to Signe, I have all of the details. Help will come.'

Maggie's hand grabbed her forearm.

'Don't go.'

'I have to. We can't do this alone any more. Winter is going to come fast, and we have barely any supplies left. And … you need help.'

'Please … I don't want to be alone.'

'Maggie, I *have* to. I will be with you though, thinking of you. We have each other now. And my mum will help, I'm sure of it. She used to be a nurse, she can give me advice too.'

'OK, thank you.' Her voice was weaker now.

'I know you won't want to see her or anything, but I have to give her a chance to help us.'

'It's fine,' she whispered. 'I understand. I don't hate her, of course I don't.'

'But I can see why you would!'

'I did, I suppose. I thought she had taken my place.'

Clara leaned forward and hugged her, careful to avoid her leg, which she saw now had a red line creeping up and away from the wound, towards her torso, as if following her veins. She tried not to reveal her shock at how hot Maggie was. She wanted to stay, chatting for ever. But just that quick touch had reminded her how dangerous it would be.

'I'm going to go now, and when I come back I want to hear all about your mum. How much you loved her, and why, and what my dad loved about her. Not just the bad, but all of it. Please?'

'Of course, my little sister.' Maggie was whispering now, her eyes closed. 'I'll wait for you.'

Clara swallowed down tears as she closed the door. *My little sister*. At last, she had heard the words she had longed to for so long. But please, please could they not be the last words she would hear from Maggie.

# Chapter 31

The winds on the path were terrifyingly strong, but Clara now knew the way as well as she knew any, and she also knew that she could not be too long. So she kept her head down and put one foot in front of the other again and again. *Each step brings you closer, each step makes you stronger,* she told herself. Her bag was almost empty this time, just her phone and some water loose in the bottom of it.

Hours later, the clouds parted, wide shards of sunlight shining down, bouncing off the sea as she turned the final corner towards the lighthouse. The first thing she did was to check if the boat was there at the jetty – nothing. No sign of Arve at all. This didn't mean he had not been. Nor that he had not delivered Simon to the island. Where would he be if he were here? she asked herself. He'd be snooping around the lighthouse, she was sure of it. But that was where she needed to be too.

She had to be strategic. She could not let Simon get in the way of getting Maggie the help she needed. So she decided to stay back a little, to watch the area around the lighthouse for a while, to check that there was no one there. After all, if he'd left the area he would most likely take the path this way, in her direction. She knew the lay of the land, she had the vantage point – at last, she had perspective and time.

So she kept focused on the lighthouse gleaming in the sunlight. She breathed in slowly, quietly, and exhaled steadily through pursed lips, trying to keep herself calm, steady. Don't. Fuck. This. Up. Her eyes scanned the two doors she knew the lighthouse had, she checked the jetty area, the steps she had lugged her suitcase up that first day on the island. So far, nothing. Perhaps he hadn't come after all.

Then she spotted the boat on the horizon.

Arve! He had come back for them!

She raised her arm to wave at the boat, before gasping as what she had thought was a shadow flickered behind Arve. No, it wasn't a shadow. There were two men on the boat.

Simon?

She could not tell. She wanted to vomit. She was close enough to the shore now that they would be able to see her, especially since her first instinct on seeing them had been to wave. But had they? Clara stepped back on the path, as if she could melt into the edge of the grassy rock face behind her, invisible until she could see them more clearly. But she knew it wouldn't work. She knew they would be able to see her if they chose to look that way.

Her breath immediately began to fizz with fear. She pressed her fingers into her palms as she watched the slow progress of the RIB to the island. Could she hide? Was it even worth it?

The boldness she had bristled with earlier in the day had evaporated, replaced by visceral memories of Simon's physical presence. His breath on her neck as she lay in bed, curled away from him, pretending to be asleep. The slam of the front door, making the walls shake as he came home, signalling his rage, about what she didn't know. His thumb, pressing into the soft underside of her forearm if she tried to move away from him at a party.

She was frozen to the path, unable to move any closer to the boat while it carved the steady white line through the water, heading for the jetty. Now she saw that Arve had spotted her, and was waving back.

There was no hiding. If that second figure – jeans, navy jacket, mousy hair – was Simon, then she would have to face him. And he would have to do what was needed to save Maggie. Because *she* was the priority, just the other side of the island and in desperate need of help.

So Clara took a breath and began the final stage of the path down towards the jetty. The boat grew closer, close enough that she could see details such as the two bags on board, the spray on Arve's beard and the shape of the white water frothing in its wake.

Finally, as she began to descend the huge stone steps down to the jetty itself, she saw that the second man was perhaps not Simon, but a stranger. She remembered how vulnerable she had felt the last time that she had been on this jetty – utterly alone, effectively lost, and still consumed by grief. Her neck ached with fear, her shoulders stiffened to the boat's arrival.

Then, as it finally reached the jetty, she heard Arve's gravelly voice.

'Clara! We are so glad to see you! We were so deeply concerned when you and Miss Maggie were not here on Thursday. Where is she?'

'She's at the house; she is very ill. She's injured her leg. I think it is infected.'

Clara craned her neck to try and see the second man, now obscured behind Arve as he reached down to the bags on the floor of the boat.

'This is what worried me. It was so unlike her not to keep to her plans, and Signe had heard nothing ... '

'I know.' Clara's mouth was now dry with panic. She barely dared to look any longer. Then, slowly, the man stood up again, and revealed his face.

A total stranger.

'This is Peter.'

'Oh, right ... ' Her legs were jelly, limp with relief.

'He is a doctor friend from Hestøy. Signe asked him if he would come with me today to check on you.'

'Thank you, thank you Arve, thank you so much.'

By now, Clara was sobbing, her relief at Simon not being on the boat completely overwhelming. Arve clambered out, securing the boat and helping Peter out before giving her a huge hug. Her face was pressed into the stiff fabric of the dungarees he was wearing over his bristly jumper, and she took a breath, glad of a moment not to be facing him, to gather herself.

In the moments that followed, Clara shook hands with Peter and filled them in on Maggie's injury and subsequent condition. She explained that she was dipping in and out of consciousness even when she had left the house hours earlier, and that she was not sure how much longer she could last without proper medical help.

'Is there a quicker way to the house?' asked Peter. 'Can't we take the boat round?'

'The maelstrom ... ' said Clara.

'What time is it?' asked Arve, rolling his sleeve back to see his watch.

'Why?' asked Clara.

'We might be able to get the boat round that side of the island in between the whirlpools. The maelstrom only takes place every few hours ... '

'But how will we know?' Clara's voice was desperate.

'I don't have the times, I have never tried to approach the island from that side. No one has for decades.' Arve's brow was creased in thought, trying to assess what was feasible.

'Is it worth trying? I am sure it has been done.' Peter seemed more confident.

Clara felt rigid with terror at the thought of getting in a boat heading towards that swirling mass of water, but she was equally fearful of leaving Maggie for any longer than she had to. She looked at Arve, wide-eyed with dread at what his decision might be.

'We'll get as close as we can,' he said. 'Anything will help, surely.'

'Good call,' said Peter. 'Let's go.'

'Wait,' said Clara. 'Can I just call my mother first? I want to speak to her, I want someone to know what is happening.'

'Quick, Clara. Like you say, we don't have much time.' said Arve, swinging his own bag over his shoulder and turning back towards the boat.

Something Clara had been so reluctant to do for so long now felt like the only thing she could – or should – be doing. So she fished in her rucksack for her phone, waited for it to turn on and find reception in the shadow of the lighthouse, and called the woman she had been tacitly avoiding speaking to for so very long. As she waited, she noticed that the dial tone was different from normal.

'Hello?'

'Mum, it's me.'

'Clara! My god, are you OK? Where are you?'

'I'm OK, I'm still on the island. Maggie is very sick though, we are trying to get her to the mainland.'

'Don't worry. I'm here. Ian arranged tickets the minute I stopped hearing from you. I am in Trondheim.'

'What about—'

'That boy is nowhere near Norway, you can trust me on that.'

'What?'

'Oh, I went round there. I thought it was time to have a chat with him when I heard from Mr Tandy that he had been calling the office trying to find out.'

'Oh my god. Mum, he's taken—'

'I know. Don't worry, just stay safe. He wasn't coming, he never was.'

'Oh, right.' Clara started to feel stupid, as if she had been naive to have spent the last few days in such fear.

'Darling, now's not the time to discuss this ... '

'Are you *sure* he's not coming?'

'Yes, he's had his head turned already, my love.'

A heavy sort of ache hit Clara's heart. Of course that is what had happened. Of course it was.

'Oh.'

'My brave girl. I'm going to see you so soon and we can sort all of this out. You have done the right thing – every single step of the way you have. I wish you knew how proud I am of you. You message me as soon as you're off the island. And let me know how Maggie is, won't you?'

'Yes, of course.' As she said it, she realised that her mum had known Maggie as a young girl, that the care in her voice was based on shared history, shared pain, shared love for the same man.

Arve was waving from the boat.

'Mum, I've got to go.'

'OK. I'm so glad to have heard your voice, and that you're safe.'

It didn't seem fair to let her know that she was about to head towards the greatest danger on the island. 'We will be, Mum, we will be,' was all she could manage.

'I love you,' came the reply. 'You know that, don't you?'

'I do, Mum, I do.'

Moments later the boat pulled away from the island, but instead of following the curve of the land towards the house, it headed in the opposite direction. The sea was choppy and the concentration on Arve's face suggested that he was less than confident about the trip.

'We have to take the long way round the island,' he shouted to Clara over the noise of the engine. She nodded back, to him and to Peter who was listening earnestly from the other side of the boat. 'It's further, but there is too much rock on the near side.'

The boat chugged along, past sheer rock faces that felt so high they might block out the day's remaining light at a moment's notice. Arve had been right though, this north-facing side of the island had far less cragginess fading into the sea than the side Clara had become so familiar with. She understood why she and Maggie had never walked this way – it would have been terrifying. She looked up, seeing what had been her home from an entirely unfamiliar angle. The position of the forest became clear, and after about twenty minutes she realised that they were at the turning point, about to squeeze between the island and the uninhabited land beside it. Through the channel of water she had stood and watched – and watched Maggie watching. Only this time she wasn't going to be a spectator, she was going to be trying to negotiate with the water.

Arve had been checking his watch every few minutes during the approach, and now checked it a final time before solemnly nodding, with half a shrug, towards Peter.

290

'It's going to be tight, but it's now or never.'

Peter nodded in return, but offered no words of reassurance, merely checking his watch too.

At first the boat felt steady, steadier even than it had while on the open water on the edge of the island. Protected by having land on either side, the water was calmer. Clara's instinct was to urge him to hurry up, as the boat had slowed considerably as it approached the channel. But she trusted that Arve knew the best way to negotiate the crossing.

The engine noise was at its lowest now, and the screeching of the wind also fell. The three of them looked at each other, as if to check that the plan was working.

'Nice and steady ... ' muttered Arve. And then the boat started to twist. Clara whipped her head round to see if they had hit something, but no. It was the water itself doing this.

She could see Arve's knuckles, white as he gripped the tiller and tried to resist the swirls, which were starting to nudge the boat further round, as if being rowed by a one-armed oarsman.

'It's OK,' Peter said to her. 'We're nearly through.'

He was right, but Clara had watched this water too often not to know how deceptive it could be as the two streams pushed against each other. She had seen the vortexes and gullies appear from nowhere, and she knew that the moon had been at its fullest just a couple of days ago. Yes, she knew that the boat wouldn't magically be sucked down into one giant whirlpool as in a book of Greek myths or epic adventures, but she could also see the fear on Arve's face, the razor-sharp rock on either side of them, and the increasing height of the waves as the churn headed towards its peak.

Just as she thought this, the boat lurched, spinning almost 360 degrees as swirling water shoved it again. Arve's head swivelled, trying to assess where the biggest whirls were. He gripped the tiller, gave the engine a little more power and tried to guide the boat further from the edge of the channel, but without hitting any of the bigger vortexes now swirling around them.

Clara's stomach dropped as the boat tipped, coming closer than ever to the edge of one of the eddies. Peter was looking at Arve, whose head was still darting around, trying to assess the situation from all angles. Another lurch. Clara reached for the edge of the boat, cold wind blasting her kidneys as her clothes rode up when she stretched. She saw her the muscle in her forearm twist as she grabbed a handle, wrenching to the side as the boat continued to rock unpredictably.

The waves seemed to echo the mountains. Black-blue and flecked with white, each as enormous and uncompromising as the last. The boat tipped Clara and she screamed as she realised it was only her firm grip on the side that had stopped her from flipping over the edge.

'Clara!' shouted Arve. 'Hold on! We have to increase power to get through this last bit. HOLD TIGHT.'

It felt as if she had been holding on for so long, waiting for the worst of it to pass. The endless grief, the torrid nights with Simon, the turbulence of her relationship with her mother, and then her sister. She was exhausted. Freezing cold and exhausted. Her body started to feel both rigid, muscles stiff and inflexible, yet molten to the core. She felt so floppy, sleepiness seizing her. She was done with holding on.

A wall of sea spray hit her, ice water slapping her face like an outstretched palm. She blinked, calling to mind not her shock at the time Simon had done the same, but how alive she had felt at swimming in that same water, at Maggie's suggestion, on one of her happiest days on the island. In that moment, she saw that something had shifted inside. She was no longer carrying around that fear, that apprehension that had dogged her for so long. She was here now, and she knew who she was. Above all, in that moment, she was *needed*. She had too much to fight for to let go now.

'Sorry!' shouted Arve from ahead, as the boat spun on itself one last time.

'It's OK! Keep going!' yelled Clara in return, shaking the seawater from her face and hair.

And suddenly they hit the central channel. The water was as smooth as a lake, and the boat sped up in a way that took Clara's breath away. Frothing water either side of them, they had reached the stream that was moving, fast, towards open water. In seconds, the boat was pushed through the remaining gap between the land and straight out into the sea. Clara was still pushing her hair back from her face when she realised that they had made their final turn, and Maggie's house was within sight.

Moments later, the boat made it round the headland and Clara was scrambling out and running across the beach, yelling at the men to follow her, hoping with all her heart that it wasn't too late.

# EPILOGUE: WINTER

# Chapter 32

'Happy Christmas!'

Maggie sat on the sofa next to her sister, passed her a cup of coffee and gave a polite but cheery wave towards the tablet Clara was holding in front of her.

'And to you Maggie! It's so great to see you looking properly well again!' came the reply from Jackie on the other side of the screen.

'Mum, move the phone so she can see your jumper!' interrupted Clara, at which Jackie shifted to reveal her glorious festive knit.

'You look fantastic, Jackie, you really do,' said Maggie, smiling. Clara felt fizzy at the thrill of the two of them chatting, right in front her.

'Thank you! Now you two enjoy the rest of your day, stay warm, and not too much gløgg!'

Clara rolled her eyes at her mum's clichéd idea of a Scandinavian holiday season, but waved at the screen, wishing her a great Christmas too, before sitting back on the sofa and clinking mugs with her sister. As she looked around the room, a Trondheim rental that they had been in for almost four months

297

now, Clara realised that perhaps Christmas in Norway was the cosiest thing that had ever happened to her, despite her mother's cringeworthy clichés. Maggie had done something clever with coloured glass and tea lights, and her baking had been off the scale once she was up and out of bed again. Outside, the whole city was bedecked in either snow or twinkling lights, and in many cases both. Inside, Clara was experiencing one of the longest periods of contentment she had ever known.

In that first week after their rescue, Clara didn't even want to consider returning to the UK until she knew that Maggie was fully well again. The cellulitis her sister had developed from her wound was serious, and she had spent weeks attached to a drip in hospital to fully recover. By the time Maggie was well enough to be discharged, Clara had decided to stay in the country a little longer, and her mother had taken surprisingly little persuading to stay for a couple more weeks. The time they had spent together – away from the usual backdrop of their long-time fractious relationship – had been transformative.

Jackie had listened intently to how Clara had found herself in the relationship with Simon, and seemed to understand how it had happened. Clara, in turn, had been touched by her attention, and both the advice and practical help she had given her as they had sat on the grey Ikea sofa in the Airbnb, sipping coffee and eating the cinnamon buns that Clara now knew how to make. They had talked through how to extricate herself from the mess, taking advice from Mr Tandy, making plans for an art school application, and having some long chats about how to try and avoid anything similar happening again. Clara was never sure, but sometimes as she waited for the kettle to boil or saw her mum taking her make-up off at night, she wondered if she too had had a bruising relationship in her past. Her readiness to nod in agreement at things Clara had long worried would sound unbelievable, her visible distress at not having spotted any red flags in Simon's behaviour, and of course her rush to the relative safety of marriage to her father all seemed to point in the same direction.

But Clara never asked. If she had learned anything on Måsholmen it had been to let people explain themselves in their own time. Maybe one day her mum would tell her more. Maybe she wouldn't. But she had been listened to, and that was enough for now.

Simon never made it to Norway. Having elected not to contact him any further, Clara never found out why – if it was shame at how he had behaved, a lack of interest once she was no longer there for him to domineer, or if he had simply decided to try and behave a little better himself.

Either way, the result was the same. She now wanted to spend time with her sister, to grieve her father properly and to make plans for the life she truly wanted when she returned to the UK. For Maggie's part, she had admitted that she was not keen to spend a winter on Måsholmen all alone while recuperating, so they had rented an apartment together in Trondheim for six months. Clara found work in a cafe, and Maggie rested, knitted and read. Christmas was the two of them, a mish-mash of Norwegian, English and French customs, punctuated by the long walks that Maggie had never given up and Clara had come to embrace. As she clinked coffee mugs with her sister that morning, Clara couldn't quite believe they had made it this far already.

'She really does look great in the jumper,' said Maggie. 'She deserves it.'

'Do you know, I kind of think she does,' said Clara, putting her slippered feet on the coffee table in front of her, careful not to nudge her framed painting of a bowl of cloudberries she had given Maggie half an hour earlier. 'I used to assume she had had everything put on a plate for her – my dad, a stable job, just moving on so easily when they split, I mean she *thrived*, then finding Ian so fast ... But I guess I can see now that it wasn't always easy. She just wanted me to be happy.'

Maggie reached under the tree and handed her two small gifts, each wrapped neatly in brown parcel paper, tied with red ribbon and decorated with some sprigs from a fir outside.

'These are for you,' she said with a smile.

Clara slowly opened the first one, smiling at her sister. They had long ago agreed not to spend money on new things for each other, so she was bursting with curiosity as to what Maggie might be giving her. She could tell that whatever inside was heavy in her hand, delicate, so she unpeeled the paper carefully. Inside was a perfect dark-green glass sphere, wrapped in new, thick fishing net. It was one of the old-fashioned buoys that had hung outside of Maggie's house.

'Signe sent it for me – well, for you,' said Maggie with a shy smile. 'I wanted you to have something for your desk when you're drawing. A paperweight, to keep things safe, you know, ink while it's drying.'

Clara gasped, remembering exactly where the glass had come from, and thinking at the time how lovely it might feel in her hand.

'Oh, Maggie, thank you! It's beautiful!' It really was.

'Keep going ... ' said Maggie, pointing towards the second gift.

This time, the present was soft, and Clara could tell it was less fragile. But this time, once the gift was visible, she had no idea quite how to react.

It was a small toy animal. A little beanbag puppy, made from the sort of vintage Liberty fabric she recognised from her mother's make-up bag in her childhood bathroom. And she had seen it before, in Maggie's knitting studio, the room she had slept in at Måsholmen. She put the little creature in the palm of her hand, held it out in front of her, her head slightly tilted, and said 'Welcome, little one,' to its small face. She tried to hide the fact that she felt slightly puzzled.

'Your mother gave it to me,' said Maggie, her eyes not quite meeting Clara's.

'Oh, wow,' said Clara. Unaware that the two of them had ever had much of a relationship, she paused, not quite sure how to fill the silence.

'Yeah, I feel like it should be yours now. Even though I hated her when I was a teenager, your mum really *was* kind to me. And you should know that.'

'Was she?'

'She really was.' Maggie's voice was soft now, as hesitant as it had been back on Måsholmen.

'I thought you hated her, that you had just tolerated her for an easy life.'

'Well, I did. She just appeared out of nowhere; it felt like my mum was barely gone. And Dad, well, he just never *talked* to me about any of it. I didn't understand depression like that. I had only seen whispers of it myself back then.

'I thought what I was going through was just grief, and I thought my mum had just abandoned me. Oh god, it was such a mess ...'

Clara stayed silent, as still as she could. Nothing to disturb this unburdening.

'And then your mum just ... popped up ... all neat and smiley and perfect. It was fucking unbearable. Just *exhausting.* And things moved so fast. Boarding school, my dad being back in the UK, god it was grim.'

'It sounds like it,' said Clara quietly. 'I'm so sorry all that happened.'

'Well, it wasn't your fault; you weren't even there yet!'

'No ... but ... '

Clara had longed to hear this explanation for almost a year now. As Maggie explained, it all seemed so obvious, how had they all created so many misunderstandings.

'Honestly, I must have been kind of a handful too. I can't believe your mum was as good to me as she was.'

'I didn't know she had really had anything to do with you ... ' *After all, she never bloody mentioned you*, Clara wanted to add, remembering her fury that day as she had sat in Hampstead Cemetery.

'Well, she didn't at first. But then my dad sent me to boarding school—'

'That must have been tough.'

'Yes, it really was. He said he wanted me to stay connected to France, that he didn't want me to lose sight of that part of me. But I was so angry, I felt utterly bereft.'

'And he got together with my mum so fast.'

'Exactly.'

'It must have seemed like he'd shoved you away to have his fun with her.'

'Well, yes ... '

'If it's any consolation, I am not sure the marriage ever really was like that. These days it seems more as if they both just rushed into it to escape their previous situations.'

Maggie looked at Clara, eyes wary.

'I don't mean escape your mum – I mean escape the pain of her dying. There are so many moments that make more sense now. My mum had this weird grudge about France; my dad never, ever really being able to articulate what happened

302

with his previous marriage. Honestly, he just looked as if he was going to cry, as if he wanted the world to swallow him up whenever I was asking annoying questions. And when I was a teenager I asked even more than I do now. Believe me.'

Maggie smiled. 'I think that's it. I think they were both running from the past. They barely knew each other as far as I understood it; they hadn't had any time to.'

'I think that's it.'

'And,' Maggie swallowed. 'When I see it through that lens, I can see that your mum was never trying to butt in, or replace my mother. She was just trying to be kind. To do the right thing.'

'What do you mean?'

'For years she would write to me at school, telling me what Dad was up to, telling me how much he loved me—'

'I had no idea! I didn't even know she knew you existed until this year. I was so angry that she hadn't told me.'

'All I thought when I read those letters was "Well, why can't he bloody tell me himself," but I think maybe he was ashamed?'

'Yes, he obviously knew he had made some huge mistakes.'

'But your mum persisted. She sent me food, treats, news. For years. And I was an absolute bitch about it, I don't even know if I acknowledged it. It was only a year or so before I left school and did my own thing. I thought I would be relieved, but do you know what, I really missed the letters. When she sent me this, it came with a note saying that the art nouveau fabric made her think of Paris, of me. It felt like, I don't know, like a sort of taunt at the time. Sending a teenager a toy. I didn't know what Liberty was, I didn't know it was meant to be chic.'

Clara felt her image of her mum changing as if new, clear light was shining on her the way that the clouds shifted the views from Måsholmen at certain times of the day.

'You don't mind me telling you all this?' asked Maggie, suddenly bashful, realising how much she had suddenly revealed.

'Of course not, thank you,' Clara felt tears forming.

'Seeing how much faith you have in Dad, it has reminded me of how wonderful he could be, how much love he had to give. I suppose I thought I should share the same about your mum.'

Clara's mind was completely blank. Finally hearing what she had longed to for so long, she realised that she had no appropriate response. She smiled and wiped the corner of her eye.

'I spent a lot of energy on trying to forget it,' continued Maggie, 'but he *loved* Mum, he really did. I suppose he was as destroyed by her death as I was. And he had no idea what to do with me, all my feelings, and how similar they must have been to hers. Maybe afterwards he just wanted to find someone ... easier?'

'My mum is not easy!'

'No, but I bet she doesn't suffer from depression the way that my mum did. And that she is not impossible to help the way that she was.'

Clara nodded. 'I think it's fair to say that my mum is quite clear when she wants help. And yeah, I guess that twenty-five years ago she might have seemed more like an easy, carefree sort.'

'There you go. I bet she's straightforward, like you. Finds it easy to talk. It must have been comforting after living with someone like my mum. Someone like ... me.'

Maggie's voice was softer than ever now.

'Oh, Maggie,' said Clara. '*You've* been a comfort to *me*.'

'And you to me.' Her eyes were paler than ever as she looked up at Clara. 'Thank you for coming all this way.'

# Chapter 33

February winds pulled at Clara's face, and she laughed at the memory of finding October wintry. As Hestøy faded from view behind them, she extended a gloved hand towards Maggie's and gave her a smile.

'We made it,' Clara said with a smile.

'I can't believe I don't even remember leaving.'

'And I don't think I'll ever forget it.'

Clara looked down at her bag, within which were their father's ashes, which they were going to scatter on Måsholmen later that day.

The light as they approached the island was as intense as she had remembered, its fragile beauty making the sea glitter and sky seem endless. Only this time, the land she had only ever seen covered in grass was now a gleaming white snowscape. A year ago she could never have imagined she would find her sister here, much less her sense of self. Today, the island seemed both familiar and entirely new. Change. It was now something she was less afraid of than ever before.

The gentle rhythm they had found for themselves all those months earlier returned to them within a couple of hours. The house – left in disarray when they had fled the island for help – had been given a thorough tidy by Signe on her own return, but there was still more to do. Before long, they were tidying the garden, checking the gas canister, making bread from the fresh starter carried in a jar from the mainland. As the smell of baking filled the house and the light began to shift, Clara realised how short the days were going to be at this time of year.

Time, for so long something that Clara had felt she was wading through, waiting for something to shift, now seemed to have the quicksilver quality of the light bouncing off the snow. There was so much she wanted to achieve now, and she realised she had to get on and do it. She had at last committed to art school, and would be starting with a portfolio full of work she had made during her time in Norway. Small paintings, intricate with details of plant structures, work she had lost herself in when she felt overwhelmed by everything she had been through in the last year. She had longed for that solace she had seen Nikita take in her work, and she had longed for the comfort the island brought to Maggie during her bleakest moods, and now she had found a way to access a space that felt like her version of each.

She already had a huge list of gardens, forests, trips she was planning as inspiration for further drawings once she had returned to the UK. She knew that she too would now carry this love of Måsholmen with her for ever – how could anyone who had spent time there not? But she also knew that it was time to head back, to make her peace with the life she had left behind, just as Maggie knew that she had to stay on the island a while longer. There would be future trips, for both of them. They were sisters now, truly, and for ever. But first, that final task.

Maggie silently lifted their coats from the wooden pegs by the door. They walked towards the beach as the sun was heading for the horizon. The sea seemed filled with fire as sunset set the sky ablaze. The sisters sat on the sand, the urn between them, and watched as dusk fell. Together.

# Acknowledgements

This novel would never have existed if it had not been for my editor, Ed Wood, having the confidence in my being able to write it. Thank you not just for this initial act of faith, but for your infinite patience in the face of lockdowns, isolations and homeschooling crises. Thank you also to Duncan Spilling for a jacket which captures the Norway I discovered as well as the one I imagined.

A huge part of this novel was written during periods of isolation, which meant that the various friends and colleagues who kept me going over the phone or online meant more than ever. Enormous thanks to Damian Barr, Clare Bennett, Melissa Marshall, Eleanor Morgan, Lucy Moses, Jessica Ruston, Polly Samson, Nikesh Shukla, Mary Kate Trevaskis, Emma Unsworth and Emily Williams-Seymour for everything, from doorstep drops of fresh eggs to two-hour-long text conversations into the dead of night. And of course to my lockdown crew, D and L, who allowed me so much space and time to write, at a time when the world felt so scary.

Perhaps most importantly of all, thank you to the independent coffee shops of Brighton and Hove, who provided comfort and caffeine during the bleakest of times. Thank you to Lou and the team at Flour Pot, all of the smiling faces at Pelicano, the makers of frankly indecent sandwiches at Fika on Norton Road, and the endlessly charming team at 17 Grams on Meeting House Lane. You all kept me going when I needed it most, even if I looked as if I was just shivering and miserable on your terrace!